ONCE UPON IN CRIME

a MYSTIC INVESTIGATORS omnibus

PATRICK THOMAS & DIANE RAETZ

PADWOLF
PUBLISHING

PADWOLF PUBLISHING INC.
WWW.PADWOLF.COM
www.facebook.com/Padwolf

WWW.PATTHOMAS.NET
www.facebook.com/PatrickThomasAuthor

WWW.MYSTICINVESTIGATORS.COM

ONCE UPON A CRIME
A MYSTIC INVESTIGATORS omnibus
© 2018 Patrick Thomas and Diane Raetz

ONCE MORE UPON A TIME
© 2011, 2018 Patrick Thomas and Diane Raetz

PARTNERS IN CRIME
© 2018 Patrick Thomas and Diane Raetz

Cover Art © Patrick Thomas

Cover design by Roy Mauritsen

SO MUCH FOR BREADCRUMBS originally appeared in an abridged form in Cosmic SF #2

ISBN 13 digit 978-1-890096-87-8, 10 digit 1-890096-87-3
Printed in the USA. First Printing

"You need to make more of the antidote," I said, hoping they'd listen to me. "I've got reason to believe that your plague has already been released."

"Impossible."

"Yeah—I don't think so."

The older man said, "Yeah, well I think so. The Green Plague is one hundred times more contagious than the Black Death and kills within an hour of exposure." He held up his phone, "Trust me—if it's been released we'd all know."

I felt stupid saying, "Trust me. Besides you're talking to an invisible woman so maybe you should start rethinking your idea of impossible. It's been released. Today. In LA. Templar-Mason needs your help to…"

An electrical strike came at me from nowhere and missed me by inches. Winsome, lightning bolts streaming out of his hands, came running into the laboratory.

"Run," I screamed at the scientists as I dropped to the ground and rolled.

Another bolt hit the lab bench, scorching everything. Thank the Gods it was asbestos—otherwise, it would have been destroyed in the first strike.

I crawled frantically across the floor, trying to find my still invisible spell kit. Without it, I was a gonner.

A third bolt sent the scientists scurrying under a lab bench. It'd held up to a couple of direct electrical hits. Gods willing it would continue to protect them.

I raised my charm bracelet and yelled, "Arrow." The silver charm disappeared, bolts flew, Winsome yelped and then disappeared. Damn—he was using an invisibility spell too.

CONTENTS

ONCE MORE UPON A TIME
A Fable Investigations book

PATRNERS IN CRIME
A Mystic Investigators collection

ONCE MORE UPON A TIME

a
MYSTIC INVESTIGATORS
book

PATRICK THOMAS & DIANE RAETZ

This one's for
the nieces
Chelsey, Kelsey and the prodical Nicky
-PT

Writing is frequently a frustrating process.
My thanks to my friend Matt for listening and
his advice when I got stuck.
-DR

SO MUCH FOR BREADCRUMBS

Phones never seem to ring at a good time. I'd been staring at code on my computer screen for long enough that I was willing to swear it was staring back at me. I wasn't happy; something was wrong with the program and I couldn't put my finger on it. But my nose itched, and for me that is a sure sign that something is wrong. I wanted to hit the computer—it was Friday at three o'clock and the system was due weeks ago. No way around it—I was stuck working yet another weekend.

I needed to test the system. I closed the door to my office and got out an aluminum baseball bat. I don't play baseball, but it was a weapon I could keep in the closet. Prof doesn't let us keep the good stuff in our desks unless we're on assignment. The Dexter program didn't count.

Since I had a sneaking suspicion what was wrong, I put on a snare pendant. The thing takes two weeks to prepare and I was down to my last one. Programming—at least the kind I did—is not for the fainthearted.

I disconnected from the network and hooked up the computer to a dedicated line we used for testing firewalls. No one else in the building would be at risk. Probably.

The next step was to activate the ward in my office. It was a silver circle built into the floor. I used the pin from a silver brooch I always wore to prick my finger. It was small, classic enough to be worn daily and the needle was sharp. A witch never knows when she needs blood.

A drop of blood brought the magic in the silver to life and my office was on lock down. Several of my colleagues, receiving the automatic alert on their computer, decided it was a good idea to start the weekend early and headed for the exits.

I didn't blame them. I wished I could go with them.

I clicked on a folder labeled sites to avoid at all costs and hit the first one listed. It was a site whose name I normally wouldn't dare speak aloud for fear of accidentally accessing the page and opening up a whole can of wyrms that I didn't even want to think about. And here I was, voluntarily walking into danger. Stupid techno-magic.

A second later the entire screen glowed like it had caught fire and the glass molded itself into a creature that was vaguely humanoid, except with too many arms and no legs. Oh, and it had tentacles. Lots and lots of tentacles. So maybe it wasn't humanoid at all.

The sprite came at me. And that's when the phone rang.

At this point most people would run, the sprite would give chase and kill them. Most agents would cast a spell hoping to fry or trap the demon. That had been my plan. But I'd spent so much of my teenage years sitting by the phone hoping that the guy-de-jour would call that I was physically incapable of letting the call go to voicemail. Therefore I lunged out of the way of the attacking sprite and grabbed for the phone. "Anderson," I panted, slightly out of breath.

"Jillian, I need you in my office, stat," Prof's voice was slightly accented. Not a good sign. Accents in any of the six languages the boss spoke meant that he was scared or angry. Since the sprite— which had formed its body out of my computer monitor and my glass desk—had already done about five thousand in damages, I was betting on angry. I should have let the phone just ring.

"Little busy right now," I panted swinging the baseball bat around my face like an overgrown mosquito net. While this knocked away one of the tentacles, it didn't do much damage to the Thing From Cyberspace.

"Now Jillian."

"Prof, I…" The sprite grabbed one of the steel legs off the desk and threw it directly at me. "Ouch!" I hadn't ducked out of the way fast enough. "Could you hold on a minute?"

Without waiting for a response I dropped the phone on the floor and grabbed the bat with both hands, and took stock of the situation.

Fortunately for me, like most sprites, this one was lazy and stupid. Sprites can make their corporal bodies out of anything available; their non-corporal bodies living easily in the web. This particular one was trapped in a Templar-Mason prison server. Metal and wood were both readily available in my office. I was lucky this one had chosen to form out of glass.

The glass sprite came at my face. I wound up and swung, smashing the thing to smithereens. If it had chosen metal, the fight would have been much harder.

With its body shattered, it was vulnerable. I squeezed my finger to get another drop of blood, this one on the snare. It flared to life and I pointed the light at the spectral image of the sprite. It screamed and clawed at the air as it was sucked into the pendant.

The light show ended when the monster was safely contained. My office was a mess, but at least I knew what was wrong with my program. The firewalls weren't modulating properly.

I was panting a little as I picked up the phone again, "Yeah boss."

It wasn't hard to hear his sigh, "Clean up whatever it is that you just destroyed and come see me."

"Prof, I didn't do any major damage."

"Then you're able to meet with me now."

"The program is not ready. And all the begging in the world won't make me release it if it still has bugs in it." Think a sprite or a regular computer virus is bad? A regular virus will just go after your system. A magic based one will go after the users and a memory dump in a person is a lot harder to fix than one on a network. Hard to back up a person. And a baseball bat would be useless.

"I think I figured out the problem though." Since I wasn't anywhere near the best in the company when it came to techno-magic, it had taken me a lot of time and a stupid stunt to figure out what the issue was. I had a sneaking suspicion that's why Prof assigned me to this job. My skills in this one area were sub-par. Never mind that I excelled in so many others, because an agent of Templar-Mason had to be the best in everything. Those of us who are members of T-M families are trained from childhood.

I'd been studying since before I could actually read and working since I was a kid. Grandma headed up a T-M missing persons division in Philadelphia—and I started scrying for her as a way of buying myself my first Ralph handbag—I think I was ten at the time. Now that I made full agent, I felt that I was entitled to some goof off time in the study department. Prof disagreed and since he knew there was no way I'd devote my free time to learning tech spells, he gave me techno-magic assignments instead.

According to him I was talented, but still a novice compared to some of our agents. From the tone of his voice, he didn't appreciate my means of testing the program. I had a funny feeling that Morganna—his second in command—would be having a chat with me. Soon. I hoped I was wrong. Morganna's chats usually took place in the gym, and I had enough bruises from the encounter with the sprite. I didn't need more from a martial arts class gone wrong.

"No, Jillian." Prof didn't bother to disguise the annoyance in his voice. "It's a new client. They are in my office. I suspect that their problem will require some of your… expertise." The pause and his tone of voice told me he wasn't talking about my computer skills.

"Oh, I'll be right in." I slid my feet into the three inched heeled Jimmy Choos I'd kicked off to ground myself during the spell. "Is it bad?" I had to admit that, contrary to my words, there was more excitement than concern or fear in my voice. It was the same excitement you hear in a news reporter's voice when something bad was happening. They don't want it to happen, but since it is, they want to be involved. It helps get that adrenaline fix.

"I suspect it's very bad," he replied grimly. The phone was not exactly slammed down, but it came close. I shut down my silver ward circle.

I shrugged my Kate Spade black suit jacket over the black silk shirt I was wearing and instinctively smoothed down the matching skirt. I took one moment to admire my shoes. One lavender, one black. I loved doing a non-matching shoe; it added a touch of rebel to my otherwise relentlessly professional image.

In the Prof's office were two people I recognized from the tabloids instantly; Robert Wade and his latest wife. Wade was an extremely attractive corporate genius, who owned, among other things, uranium mines in South Africa, forests full of hard wood trees in Germany and Canada and most importantly, the most productive oil refinery in the United States. Plus, he was one of the few people who had direct access to Mexican oil and the ability to ship it out of the country. All of which made him among the ten or fifteen most powerful men in the western world. Presidents, Prime Ministers and kings listened when he spoke. But, the overwhelming impression I got was not power, it was sadness.

Candy Wade, trophy wife number three, was a would-be fashionista who continually lived on the tabloid "Worst Dressed Lists." Staring at the rhinestone detailing on her hot pink mini dress, which made her look, shall we say, less than slim, I had total sympathy for Mr. Blackwell. Whoever was her stylist should be fired, immediately. She was trying for Flash, instead, she got Trash. Worse, she looked like slightly tubby trash. Ick.

I figured, unless she got pregnant and produced the Wade heir number three, she was going to hold her position as wife number four for less than another year. Gossip had it that wife number one was a love match; it had lasted ten years and two children, before she died tragically in a car accident. Mr. Wade had been trying to replace her for the last twelve years. As I stared at the current wife's over processed blond hair and the make up of an 'over thirty' who was trying to look 'under twenty' I figured he was looking in all the wrong places. Part of me wondered if he was trying to punish himself or something because she was just all wrong. And unlike her husband, I could get nothing off of the current Mrs. Wade at all. It wasn't my natural empathy that failed. It was as if the woman had no emotions at all.

Prof on the other hand was dressed for a day on the pier. His 'Old Fishermen Don't Die, They Just Wade Away' tee shirt I thought was particularly inappropriate given our new clients. But, I suspected Mr. Wade wasn't fooled by the Prof's balding head, pot belly, short stature and fishing garb. Prof, a regional director in the oldest and most secretive security firm in the world, was no one's fool.

I came forward and shook their hands. "What can I do for you?"

Prof answered for them. "Heidi and Gregory are missing." There was no need to ask who Heidi and Gregory were. The Wade teenage children spent almost as much time in the tabloid press as Mrs. Wade did, at least until recently. I realized I hadn't seen a picture of them in a magazine for weeks.

"How long?" I asked skipping the whole sympathy thing for the moment.

"Three days," Mr. Wade replied, keeping his voice even with an obvious effort.

My brows wrinkled. "Kidnapping?" It wouldn't be the first case in Templar-Mason's history, but normally I wasn't brought in for those cases. We had numerous ex-FBI and Interpol agents who were very well trained in that type of crime.

Mr. Wade gave an indecisive shrug. "There hasn't been a ransom note, or any demands."

I took a seat at the mahogany table in the office. "Is it possible that the children are away with friends?" I asked as gently as possible. I didn't want to accuse them of being bad parents, but as Heidi was a birthday away from being legal and Greg was only fifteen and both had been photographed skiing in Switzerland, yachting in Fiji and shopping in LA solo. I wouldn't even dare mention the paparazzi depictions of Heidi infamous partying and Greg's daredevil stunts. I figured there was a chance they'd just decided to go on vacation for a few days. Besides, in this business it's best to eliminate the obvious answers first.

"Oh for heaven's sake," Mrs. Wade pouted. "What a ridiculous suggestion." Her voice was whiny and her manner bored. There was no pretence of a loving step-mother offered. I downgraded her chance of lasting a year to six months tops.

I made a mental note to start a search for any legal activity that might signal that Mr. Wade was preparing for divorce, more out of curiosity than for any other reason. I was sure that the Wade Industry lawyer had put together a cast iron prenuptial, so Mrs. Wade probably wasn't at the top of the suspect list when it came to the children. No motive. Still, no reason to take her off it either.

"I can assure you that the kids didn't leave voluntarily. They have to have been kidnapped..." Robert Wade's voice cracked as he finished, "or worse."

Prof stepped in. "I've started a file on the case. Access name Wade1. In the mean time we'll run through the sequence of events. Mr. Wade, Mrs. Wade, please correct me if I miss anything, okay?"

The couple nodded and Prof continued, "Approximately three months ago Heidi and Gregory disappeared for two days."

"But they came back?" an obvious and foolish question. I bit my lip, wishing I hadn't asked it.

"Yes. They disappeared from a concert," Mr. Wade started, not allowing the Prof to answer.

"A rave to be more accurate," Mrs. Wade interjected. "Which they should have never been at. Totally passé." That was her concern? Lovely.

"They claimed to remember the concert—" There was a warning in Mr. Wade's voice that I heard when he said the word concert. He didn't want to think of his kids as doing something as outrageous as a rave. I wondered if Candy was dumb or arrogant for pushing it. I was willing to bet on arrogant. No one dumb could land the international bachelor catch of … well, ever, even for a short time. "—starting. They both agreed that they remember nothing after the second song. Their memories were complete blanks." He took a deep breath and added, "I employed some of the best non-violent interrogation specialists in the world. I assure you that if the children had seen or heard anything, we would have been able to come up with the information."

"Drugs?" I asked keeping my voice neutral.

"My children don't do drugs."

"Not all drugs are administered voluntarily." I thought of the date rape drugs that are so common at clubs around the world. "They could have been given something in a drink or perhaps injected?"

"There were medical examinations conducted after the children returned home. There were no traces of drugs."

I shared a look with the Professor. I was beginning to understand why I was chosen for the case. I was one of the strongest seers in the New York office—and the only one with a pop culture obsession. The more you know about your target the easier it is to find. I had about an 85% rate of getting a trace on a target when I had a personal belonging and knew something about them. My numbers dropped down to about fifty percent when I was dealing with a lot of unknowns.

That single glance also let me know that Prof would let me ask all the questions. Then we'd discuss the case afterwards. Probably not what he'd planned, but it was pretty obvious that Mr. Wade wasn't allowing him to brief me the way Prof wanted. "Do your doctors have any of the blood or urine samples left? I'd like to have our laboratory rerun the tests." We'd be looking for the standard drugs, but we also have ways of testing for stuff that other labs didn't.

"Why? I assure you…"

I cut off the man. "Your children are missing," I said as gently as I could. "And obviously your security people can't find them. T-M is the best in the business at these kinds of things. Let us do our jobs, okay?" In the background I could see my boss nodding and smiling.

Wade nodded his head as well. "You're right. I know you are." I didn't fill in the blank for him. The one that went And I'm a control freak. But the unsaid words echoed in the room.

"How'd you find the children the last time?" My question brought us back to the case.

He sighed. "We didn't. Greg found the way home."

"Excuse me?" I asked.

"This is going to sound—" He raked his brain for a word before coming up with "—unusual."

"I've heard some pretty bizarre stories." Wade had no idea. His world didn't include the kinds of things I'd seen.

"The kids went to a concert in Miami Beach. They were with friends, all of whom were well known to me." I made the translation in my own head. They were all heirs from rich families. "None of their friends saw them disappear. One minute they were sitting next to each other; the next Heidi and Greg were gone."

I thought about what Candy Wade had said about the event being a rave. If she was correct, there were a couple of things wrong with his story. Granted, I didn't frequent events like that, but even I knew that there were no seats, and people tended to be jammed in together. Add to the mix that drugs, alcohol and herbal refreshments which tended to be present and it was doubtful any of their friends would have noticed an explosion, let alone a kidnapping. If it was more of a traditional concert with seats and tickets and such, a disappearance would have been harder to arrange. I'd check the file Prof had set up and see what the truth was. I did have a question though, "Bodyguards?"

"Saw nothing," was the answer. "One minute they were there… the next, gone."

"So how did Gregory get them back home?"

"When the children woke up, they claimed to be in a one room cottage in Montana, in the middle of the woods. All their possessions were gone, except for the clothing they were wearing. All of Heidi's jewelry, her pocketbook, keys and, of course, cell phone was gone." Robert's voice got hard. "Whoever had done this to my children didn't recognize Greg's watch."

"His watch?" I couldn't help echoing.

"It's one of those five zone time pieces that are so popular."

"Was it fenced?"

"No, the scum who took my children didn't recognize the value so they didn't take it."

I was lost. How did a watch, even an expensive one help get the kids home? Before I could ask the question, Robert Wade continued his story. "It also had an internal GPS system inside of it. Greg used that to get them out of the woods and to a police station."

I shook my head at the obvious discrepancy in the story. "Wait a minute. If the watch had a GPS in it, shouldn't you have been able to locate it? I assume it had a tracking feature for just such an occasion. During the two days the kids were missing, I assume you were looking for them, right?"

The billionaire in front of me became stiff. There was no emotion in his voice when he said, "The GPS didn't produce a signal while the children were missing."

I nodded my head. Granted the things were supposed to work most places, but I'd heard stranger. "Did you go back to the cabin afterwards? The GPS should have kept the coordinates…"

"There was nothing there," he cut me off harshly.

"Nothing?"

"It was woods. No cabin. No clearing. Nothing."

"Were you in the right place? Maybe the GPS was wrong."

"No we were in the right place. The kids' footprints, leading out were easy enough to find."

"How'd they get there?"

"I have no idea. No footprints leading into the woods were

found. No sign of cars, trucks, motorcycles or even a horse. No indication that they were dropped from above. NOTHING!" He screamed the last word in frustration.

I stood and hugged the man. Maybe it wasn't terribly professional of me, but he needed it. Since Candy was filing her nails as he spoke, I could tell that he certainly wasn't getting that kind of support from his wife. "I understand," I muttered softly. "I believe you." It sounded like magic to me, which was a specialty of Templar-Mason's. Most of the world didn't believe it the stuff. We dealt with it regularly. Somehow it had found its way into this man's life. Our job was to make it go away.

His arms tightened for a moment before he pulled away. "Thank you," he said softly wiping tears away.

I turned away, knowing that a powerful man wouldn't like a moment of weakness being observed by anyone. My eye caught Candy Wade's and I knew we'd be having words because the look she gave me was full of anger, and if I wasn't mistaken, hatred.

"I assume you increased security after the incident?" I asked as coolly as I could.

"Doubled." I thought there might be gratitude in his eyes as he spoke. Probably for me saying I believed him. I imagine he'd gotten a lot of disbelief in the past few months from those around him.

The Prof interjected for the first time in what seemed like an hour, "We have all the security reports for the past six months in the file. You can read it when you're done."

I nodded in response to Prof's words and turned back to Mr. Wade. "So how did they disappear this time?"

"From the house."

"From the house?" I seemed to enjoy repeating things he said. The best time to kidnap someone was when they were out and about, shopping or partying or something.

"From their beds. They'd gone to sleep. I was home and I kissed them goodnight myself. They'd been staying in a lot more than normal, since the first kidnapping. For security purposes of course."

"Makes sense," I agreed.

"The next morning when they didn't come down for breakfast, no one was worried. Teenagers you know. But, when there was no sign of them by lunchtime the housekeeper went up to check on them."

"And?"

"The beds were slept in, but both Heidi and Greg were missing. No clothing was taken. No money or jewelry was missing." I didn't want to know what it cost him to keep his voice even.

"Security cameras?" Part of me wanted to say something sympathetic, but I didn't know what. So I stayed professional.

"Nothing. No sign of inappropriate entry, or of the children leaving. There were no cameras in their bedrooms, of course, but there was no sign of them in the hallway video."

"A person who knows where the cameras are could avoid them," I guessed but I know my voice sounded doubtful. On television, people were always skulking around avoiding cameras, but in reality, a good system was designed so that you couldn't do things like that. Maybe a conceal spell to fool the cameras, but I wouldn't want to count on it.

"Not bloody likely," Wade cursed. "Not with the system I had put in. Bank vaults have less footage."

I glanced at the Prof who nodded in agreement. Great, I thought, two kids who disappeared impossibly from their bedrooms. No wonder I was called in on it.

"Bodyguards?" was my next question.

"Outside their rooms. Same as every night since they disappeared. They saw nothing."

"I'll want to interview the guards. And I want blood tests on them as well."

Mr. Wade started to say something, and then visibly stopped himself. I smiled in approval. Prof was the one who said, "We'll get that set up."

Instead of directly questioning my methods, Mr. Wade

asked, "What do you expect to find with the guards?" Oh, powerful men. They just can't help themselves.

I smiled to myself, "I'm sure your people did a good job interrogating them. But I just want to make sure…"

"Of course," he quickly agreed. He hesitated for a moment and then added, "A friend of mine in the FBI recommended that I come to Templar-Mason. They are working on it too, but they don't have jurisdiction outside of the United States. He said that just in case it was an inside job, or the kids were taken out of country, there aren't jurisdictional issues…so far there isn't a ransom demand so we don't…" the professional manner faltered as the lost father poked his head through.

"And we agree completely," Prof broke in with a professional smile. He stood the two people up and ushered them to the door. "As soon as Jillian and I have an opportunity to review the rest of the case file, we'll establish a team. In the meantime, I'll have one of our agents escort you to your hotel. Please have her stay with you at all times. There's no saying that," his glance took in both of the Wades, "one of you won't be the next target."

Mrs. Wade gasped and her hand moved in a fleeting motion across her stomach. It took only a moment, but both the Prof and I caught it. I'd put money on her being pregnant. Which moved the woman up from annoying to top of the suspect list in less than one second flat. Now she had a crystal clear motive for getting rid of the children. Prof put his arm around the woman in a compassionate manner and moved the couple to the door. "Don't worry about a thing, dear lady," he all but drawled, in a much more courtly manner than I usually see from him, but I'm just a lowly agent, not a paying client. It seemed to work because she smiled warmly at him. "Morganna, one of our best agents, will interface with your security team," he was saying as they walked out.

I rolled my eyes making sure that the Prof couldn't see me. Morganna was the ideal that ninety percent of Templar-Mason agents aspired to. She was a tough as nails witch with an icy personality, a body honed and tempered by training with the SEALS, a mind trained at Oxford and, as far as I could tell, no life outside of Templar-Mason. She was his right hand woman; not just an agent but his manager of all back office activities. She liked to work behind the scenes—a king maker if you will, not the king. The fact that Prof was bringing Morganna onto the scene meant that he smelt danger.

I smiled to myself as I saw that Mrs. Wade had left her pink satin clutch on the leather chair. No doubt it was done on purpose. It'd give her an opportunity to come back and speak to us on her own. But in the meantime, I had a moment or two to rummage through it. No real surprises; a cell phone, make up, a hairbrush, keys, and a small wallet with two platinum credit cards and a drivers license still in her maiden name. Trusting that the Professor would keep them busy long enough, I jotted down the name and ID number on the license and palmed the cell phone. There was too much potential information on the cell phone to give it back without examining it. I'd call her in an hour or two and tell her that I found it dropped on the floor.

I'd just put the clutch back when Candy Wade marched into the room. "I want you to leave my husband alone." I had to give her credit for getting straight to the point. There was no beating around the bush with this woman unless maybe it involved a baseball bat. "Your phony sympathetic, poor you routine won't work. He's mine. Got it? Not available. Do I need to spell it out any clearer?"

"If you think you can get the letters in the right order, you're welcome to try." Let's say I don't always respond well to criticism. "Sound it out if you have trouble."

"A smart mouth won't carry the day. My husband's had a lot of women throw themselves at him, but I'm the one he decided to catch."

"A better argument for Prof's catch and release program I've never heard," I said. Candy was getting repetitive and she seemed easily riled. Maybe I could make her angry enough to give me something else. I put one Jimmy Choo clad foot forward to show her that I considered myself a player and yawned as if I was bored. "Seems to me that you're just a number; Mrs. Wade-the-fourth. Since he replaces his wives more often than his cars, I figure he's about ready to turn you in for a new model once the lease is up. And looking at you, I'd say you have a look of high mileage on you. I give you six months on the outside before he goes shopping again." I gave her a contemptuous once over, lingering on her harsh yellow hair and slightly protruding stomach before heading down to her sequenced sandals. "Maybe I can convince him to trade up sooner and go for a luxury model this time."

That did the trick nicely. After calling me every name in the book and a couple even I'd never heard before, her hands dropped down over her stomach and she screamed, "Not after the news I have to tell him. He'll be tied to me forever."

"Pregnant?" I asked, still sounding bored. Inwardly I wanted to shout BINGO. "That was clever. It'll buy you at least another year. And some decent child support." I let my eyes dwell on her shoes again. "You might even be able to afford something better than Payless." They were probably expensive, but the three-inch pink satin platform shoes were tacky enough to pass as cheap.

"Payless!" Her shrill scream echoed around the room. "My child will be the Wade heir. I'll be able to have all the top designers creating just for me."

I wanted to ask why she wasn't having that done now. After all, she supposedly had access to the Wade fortune. But there were far more important points to make. "Don't you mean one of the Wade heirs? After all, isn't the reason you came to us was to find the other two children and bring them back alive?"

Alarm bells went off in her head and after an instant of panic, Candy calmed down. "Yes, of course, one of the Wade heirs is what I meant."

I smiled like I believed her. "Tell me about your stepchildren." I wanted to keep her off balance, so I played the game like it was her court. "After all, Robert is probably a doting father. Blind to their flaws. I'm sure you've got a clearer view of the kids." I made my tone coaxing. "It'd make my job easier to know the truth about them."

She actually smiled at me. It was a calculating smile, but it was lovely. For a moment I could almost see how she'd attracted her billionaire. "They are teenagers and therefore, by definition, brats." I nodded my head as if in agreement, and she continued. "I'm much too young to be their stepmother—something that Robert's always agreed with." It's nice to know billionaires humor people too. "I always tried to be their friend instead."

"And as their friend?" I cajoled her.

"I can tell you that they aren't the angels Robert thinks they are. Greg is a computer criminal. The police started investigating him for hacking at twelve."

"What'd he do?"

"He broke into the DMV and gave himself a driver's license."

I couldn't help laughing. One of the richest kids in America and he had the same dreams as any other teenager in the world. A car.

The woman moved on to a more serious topic. "The so called concert was a rave. Gregory has been going to bars since he was fourteen. Can you believe that! Fourteen. I mean sure, sneak a drink from your parents' bar—we've all done that. But heavy duty clubbing? Some of those places are little more than orgies. Even I wouldn't go there." There was an outrage in her voice that told me she wasn't lying. The kid probably was a handful and a half.

"And Heidi?"

"That child is even worse. Can you believe she was pregnant this summer? I mean at sixteen years old. You'd think any teenage girl these days would use a condom. I mean, hello, AIDS."

My brain went ka-ching. Another reason for her to want to get rid of Robert's children. After all, Heidi's baby would be another heir. "What'd you do?"

"Talked her into an abortion of course," she said it as though it was obvious. She tried for a winning smile. "And it wasn't easy to get her to agree, let me tell you. I just wanted you to know that the kids could be anywhere. And very easily gone of their own free will. After they disappeared the first time, Robert kept them on a very short leash and they weren't used to it. Worse, they hated it. I could totally see them slipping out on their own. You should consider that during your investigation. They were probably drugged out of their minds on some crap or another last time they disappeared. It makes a hell of a lot more sense than their silly story about a magically disappearing cabin." She sniffed contemptuously, "I could have come up with a better cover story when I was ten."

I nodded my head in agreement; not bothering to point out that the very improbability of the story meant it was more likely to be true. I had too much to think about anyway. If Candy's version of the kids' activities was correct, the suspect list could be endless. Not that she was off the list, just that there were tons of others that could be added.

Prof came in with Morganna and Mr. Wade interrupting our conversation. A few minutes later, they were out of the office and the Professor and I were alone. I filled him in on everything Candy had said. The Prof agreed with me that it was imperative to find out whether the woman was telling the truth about her stepchildren's lifestyle, since it would help us determine motive.

"She's a solid suspect. I'll get the call history out of the phone; see if there are any suspicious numbers on it. Then I'll coat it with clary sage and see if I can get a vision off of it. At midnight I'll try a scrying spell on the kids. Morganna can get me a couple of personal items. Maybe if we're lucky we can have them home by morning. It'll probably take longer to figure out who is responsible, but the kids have to be the primary concern. I feel bad about anyone having to spend time with her. Talk about a wicked stepmother."

"Tell me about it," he agreed. Then he repeated the word,

"Stepmother" again. "Hmmn…"

"You don't think?" I said, my heart pounding and my blood pressure shooting up.

Prof, his face pale as death, responded with a single word, "Fable."

"Damn." It was the type of case that we all dreaded. Fables are real otherworldly entities that can influence people and events to try to live out their stories again. Despite hundreds of years of opposing them, there were plenty of things about them we didn't know. Still, we fought them wherever we encountered them. It was the reason the Knights Templar, now the Illuminati, founded the agency in the first place. I'd had a fraction of Prof's experience with them and I knew enough to be scared.

"I'm not sure, but we've got a couple of the elements in play."

"The wicked stepmother," I agreed, "A classic part of literally hundreds of fairy tales and fables. But what else have we got?"

"Worldwide impact," Prof stated calmly. "Wade Industries is as important, in its own way, as any kingdom of old."

"An industrial empire," I agreed, "And the heirs are at risk. Also classic." I headed over to a bookshelf in Prof's office and found one of the greatest treasures our company had, a first edition copy of Grimm's Fairy Tales. My office had a more modern printing, but Prof had managed to get one of the four original remaining books. I lusted after it with all my heart. Of course, he felt the same way about my first edition of the complete works of Hans Christian Anderson. And mine was signed by my great-great-grandfather. He, like the Brothers, worked for T-M. "But, if you're right, which one are we dealing with?"

"You know the drill," he ordered. "Put together a list of fables that deal with missing heirs. Maybe we can get a better handle on it. In the meantime, I'll call Morganna and tell her to get us the children's blood, ASAP. You'll need it as a base for some of the spells you're going to have to cast."

I nodded my head in agreement, but at the same time I put down the book of fairy tales. "I'd better play with the cell phone first. I want to have it ready before Mrs. Wade realizes that she 'lost' it."

Prof nodded agreement, but his hand shot out over my wrist as I tried to walk out of his office. "Work the fable aspect," he warned. He was as panicky as I'd ever seen him. Which wasn't much, but his hand trembled on mine, his skin was pale, and his eyes were huge. "They get more powerful the longer they go unchecked."

"And this one has gone on for months already," I said glumly.

I was out the door when I heard him say, "We almost weren't able to reverse my first. And if we hadn't…"

I went back in and took his hand in my own. Prof had been one of the seven "dwarves" who'd saved an incarnation of Snow White. He looked really good for a man of a hundred and twenty. Being touched by serious magic can do that to a person and Prof had been more than a little touched. As a matter of fact, it had been the Professor who'd figured out how to put the princess in cryogenic sleep after the wicked queen/stepmother had poisoned the girl. The story had run surprisingly true to the classic tale; In pre World War I Europe there had been a lot of small kingdoms, post WWI was shaped by the fable. "Snow White is one of the most powerful of all fables. The story went on for several years, and in the end, you were still able to get the curse reversed," I reminded him. "This one, if it is a fable, shouldn't be nearly as bad."

"True," he agreed bleakly, "But in the meantime, with the false queen ruling the country, a war started that never should have, and millions died as a result."

I didn't know what to say. He still blames himself for WWI. In the end, I promised Prof I'd do my best, and I went back to my office. My first priority was the phone. I swiped another computer and stepped over the rubble to set it up. I downloaded the data into the computer, every contact and the call log. I shot the info over to one of the computer techs and sent an e-mail to the janitorial staff. Normally, I'd be expected to pick up my own mess, but this gave me a free pass out of cleaning—except for the sweep I made inside of the protection circle. That was mine and I trusted no one else inside the circle.

In half an hour or less, I should have anything of value from the phone neatly analyzed. I asked another junior associate that hadn't made it out of the building to run through every known fable and send me a file listing possible fairy tales we could be dealing with in the order of likelihood. There were literally hundreds.

I had a small collection of specially prepared herbs and crystals in a locked drawer in my desk. I pricked my finger again to activate the silver circle and inside it, I prepared the phone with an ointment made of clary sage and sandlewood. Then I put the phone on a large piece of quartz.

I took my shoes off and placed them carefully on the edge of the circle. I flinched as I sat down cross-legged in front of the phone. I couldn't help it, Kate Spade suits deserve more. I sent a quick prayer to whomever might be listening—I knew it was someone, but I didn't know who—and opened myself up for a vision. If permitted, the phone would tell me what it knew.

"A package will arrive in the mail for you," I heard a male voice say. *"You know what to do with it."*

Candy's voice answered, "But what about… I can't afford to be caught."

"It's perfectly safe. No one will suspect you."

"I'm not so sure. There's plenty of money for all three children." It sounded like Candy was having second thoughts.

In response, the male's voice became menacing, "You're already in too far or would you like your husband, or the police, to find out what you've already done?"

"No," Candy capitulated, "What am I looking for?"

"Gingerbread vitamins. Make sure that the heirs take one each. The rest will be taken care of one way or another."

The vision, or more accurately the hearing, disappeared. I

came out of my trance and looked around the office. Somehow the room seemed dimmer. Darker. A chill passed through me. Or perhaps it was fear. The spell had left me with a certainty in my gut. It wasn't just a person we were dealing with. The man's voice had been tainted by outside forces. The Prof was right – it was a fable. It was our—and more directly my—responsibility to make sure that it reached "The End" before it finished. I was scared and I'm embarrassed to admit I liked it. It was the adrenaline junkie in me.

I called the Professor's office, but he wasn't answering. So I paged him over the office intercom. By the time he walked in my office, I'd put my mismatched shoes back on and my jacket was hung neatly over the back of my chair. The professional image was firmly in place. But my voice was too high and a little thready as I said, "Hansel and Gretel. That's the fable." I found some confidence in my Jimmy Choos—what every well-dressed, professional witch should have adorning her feet. I could do this. Forget about saving the world—there was no way I was going to let anything, even a Fable, hurt my wardrobe. I ran down the story for Prof.

His face grew grim, although he patted my hand. "A job well done." Then he growled into the intercom, "Get me the analysis of the damn cell phone, now."

A nervous voice replied. "I'm still waiting for transaction records from the phone company. I'll send it over as soon as possible."

Prof and I said simultaneously, "Get the records for the home phones too." Prof added, "Wade should be happy to agree, so we'll have no problems with getting permission."

Minutes later we got hold of Morganna. "Get a team over to the house. Make it look as though they are searching for possible clues. But what I'm specifically looking for is anything Gingerbread. Absolutely anything. Gingerbread Industries, healthcare, whatever. Even check the clothing for a Gingerbread label."

Without needing an update, she was in synch with us. "Hansel and Gretel then—it's a biggie. I'll go personally."

Prof added, "Go through both the husband and wife's possessions." I shot a look at Prof, but he shook his head, indicating later. "We'll get Mrs. Wade out of the house so that she can't try to stop you."

We were completing the briefing and just about to hang up when Morganna added, "Oh Jillian—on Monday we start Varma Adi. Be ready."

She hung up as I winced. Varma Adi is an Indian form of martial arts that deals with pressure points. It's violent, deadly and I've seen other agents unable to walk out of the ring after an hour session, "My office?"

Prof's eyes twinkled but all he said was, "You need to be a fully trained weapon."

I shuddered again and made a mental note to book a massage appointment for Monday evening. If I had any hope of walking on Tuesday I was going to need it. Deadly serious I turned to the boss and asked, "Mr. Wade? Do you suspect him?"

He shook his head. "Not really. No. But," he went over to my bookshelf and took down my significantly more recent copy of Grimm's Fairy Tales, flipped it to the correct page and read aloud, "'Oh you fool,' said she. 'Then we will all starve; you have better get the coffins ready' and she left him in no peace until he consented."

"Then you do suspect the father." I had to admit I was shocked. I couldn't see Robert Wade doing such a thing.

Prof shook his head. "We can't ignore the possibility, but no, I don't really see it. I'm more afraid that Wade is the next target. If she really is eliminating the heirs, then why not take him out too? That guarantees her unborn child control of the family assets."

I nodded my head. That felt a lot more likely. The next call was to Mrs. Wade, telling her that we'd found her cell phone. Since it was in a diamond encrusted carry case, and had some famous movie stars phone numbers in it, her desire to get it back wasn't surprising. I asked her to come back into the office to get it. I hinted that I had some more questions to ask about her stepchildren's bad behavior.

"She'll be here soon," I told Prof.

We got the list of people who'd spoken to Mrs. Wade during the last four months. There was a large number of what would be defined as normal contacts for her; family members, famous people, known charities, personal trainers and two stylists. None of the numbers listed seemed unusual to either me or the Professor. Unfortunately. "On television, it's always the tennis coach," I said trying to make a joke of it as we stared at the list. "Maybe we should start with the personal trainer?"

Prof shook his head. "I'll have Morganna get another team to work on it. You concentrate on the magical angle. Regular security can work on the rest." He paused and then said hopefully, "The good thing about the Hansel and Gretel fable is that the victims weren't killed immediately."

"They rescued themselves," I reminded the Prof.

"You can pretty much count on the fact that in more than one incarnation, the kids died," Prof said grimly. "But one of the key elements of the fable is that the children are kept alive for a reason. Let's work on the assumption that the same will hold true here."

"I'd like to use some of the kids' blood in the location spell," I said.

Prof nodded. "Do it."

"One thing is bothering me. Whatever is doing this has significant power."

"I'd say that the non-working GPS and the disappearing cottage more or less confirms it."

"Then why'd they let the kids go in the first place?" I asked. "I mean if they could hide them this well…"

"The superficial answer is that they underestimated the kids."

"And the non-superficial answer?"

"In Hansel and Gretel, the kids found their way home once

without trouble. I think that it is a key element of the story, so even the Fable couldn't stop it."

"Makes sense," I agreed.

The next few hours were basic police work. On the good side, the Wades returned to the office and I interviewed them again. We didn't get anything new, but Mrs. Wade didn't seem suspicious at all when I gave her back the cell phone. The blood was delivered and we found trace amounts of things that a normal crime lab wouldn't be likely to find or understand. Agrimony and anise, both herbs used for sleeping, were in the sample. More disturbingly, we detected hellborne, an herb that can grant invisibility, but has enough stimulant in it to cause serious heart damage. Since the mystic detector beaker glowed a very malevolent orange we had proof of two things. One, magic was definitely in play. And two, the bad guys weren't terribly concerned about doing permanent harm to the Wade children.

Morganna's team found the bottle of Gingerbread Personal Health and Well Being vitamins in Mrs. Wade's locker at the private club. Unfortunately, there was no address or contact information on the bottle. There was a bar code, so in time we should be able to find where the manufacturer shipped them from. We split the pills up; some were sent down to the lab for analysis. I took the rest to use in the spells I needed to cast.

Midnight found me in the middle of the woods at a resort Templar-Mason owned, wearing traditional witch's robes handed down to me from my grandmother, no makeup and bare feet. I was about as far away from the professional woman I tried to be during the daytime as anyone could imagine. And I was going to need a pedicure in the worst way after this case. Luckily, in my last contract, I had negotiated for it to be an acceptable charge to my expense account. T-M cuts the full agents some slack and I had no problem taking advantage of that. After all, they had been taking advantage of me since I could walk.

I'd cast a pentacle, the traditional star surrounded by a circle. In the center of it was a small copper cauldron steaming, not bubbling, with a potion that I'd brewed. It included rue, dandelion, lavender, hemp, three drops each of Heidi's and Gregory's blood and just a pinch of the Gingerbread vitamin. At midnight I swallowed the potion, which tasted every bit as disgusting as it sounded.

My eyes rolled back, I made a choking sound and for one long moment, I wondered if I'd managed to poison myself. I felt a surge of power from somewhere else as I collapsed to the ground, unconscious.

I awoke in a cinderblock room with a concrete floor. It was damp and dark, but balmy. Not cold like you think of most dungeons. My first thought was that I was in a prison of some kind. My second that my spell had definitely not acted the way I'd planned. It was supposed to show me where the missing children were, not bring me to wherever I was. But now I had a clue as to how they'd kidnapped their victims. The Fable or its pawns had figured out how to develop a translocation spell. In layman's terms teleportation. I understood the theory, but had never met a person, or even a coven, strong enough to pull one off. The magical energy needed was mind-boggling. Obviously, the Fable was supplying the mystic juice that my spell had accidentally taped into it. The vitamin had probably been charmed to react with the physiology of anyone who took it and let the spell find them. When I swallowed the potion with it and their blood, I became its victim too.

The room I was in wasn't locked. I wasn't expected; which was absolutely a good thing. Time for some recon. If the kids were stashed nearby, maybe I could get them out. If they had been transported here and driven away; I was screwed.

I skulked around in the dark for a while to find out what I was dealing with. All I had were my robes and the snare pendent around my neck. I hadn't had the time to dispose of the sprite properly and I couldn't just leave it lying around – someone might accidentally set it free and die for their trouble.

In action adventure movies there is always an opportunity for the hero or heroine to steal a security guard uniform or a weapon, rescue the helpless victim and escape, usually in the nick of time. Instead, I found a warehouse full of Gingerbread brand cosmetics, vitamins, moisturizers, and supplements. The packaging alone told me that the product line was expensive. I wondered why I'd never heard of them. I mean the moisturizer I use is nearly a thousand dollars a bottle. It isn't as if I buy drug store brand merchandise. And there were just too many jars and bottles for it to be a front. We were talking millions of dollars worth of product.

Outside I found a barbwire fenced parking lot with half a dozen cars, all with Tennessee license plates. The gates were locked, armed guards at the booth, and I suspected that there was a current running through the fence. There was no way I was going to be able to get under or over the fence without setting off alarms and possibly facing electrocution. It fell into the last resort category.

I found a hallway that was guarded by two well-armed men. Since it was the only place inside the plant that I'd seen security people, I figured that there was a good chance that Heidi and Greg might be there. But, as I glanced down at myself I had to admit that there was a zero chance of my being able to brazen my way past the guards. In a designer black business suit, sure. In ceremonial white witch robes, not a chance.

I snuck back into the warehouse area, hoping to find something to help me. I was desperate with no weapon, normal clothing, cell phone, or idea where I was. I needed help from a higher authority, but it doesn't always answer when I need it.

I hit the jackpot when I found ten bottles of chicory baby powder. Chicory grants invisibility and inaudibility, but usually it has to have been harvested at midnight on the night of the summer solstice, with a golden knife in perfect silence. The odds of finding perfectly prepared ingredients were slim to none, but it was what I had. Besides, it wasn't as though these people didn't use magic. They might have prepared it properly. Maybe.

I walked a simple circle in the middle of the warehouse, praying the whole time that no one would come and check on the stock. I could tell from the way the room was getting lighter, that it was dawn or a little past. That meant people were going to start showing up for work shortly, hopefully later rather than sooner. My only break was it was Saturday and hopefully they only had a skeleton crew on.

I sprinkled the body powder all over myself chanting in Latin the entire time. I had no way of telling if the spell worked or not. I crossed my fingers for luck and walked down the hallway where the security guards were. I held my breath and forced myself not to let my concentration fail, as I slid by them.

One guard stood up, and I was sure I'd failed when I heard some truly wonderful words, "Frank. I'm going to get a cup of coffee. You want one?" While Frank tried to find his wallet, I invisibly slinked past.

I skulked down the hallway, trying to hide in any shadows and praying that the spell I'd cast would hold. I stopped to look into the small windows on every door. The first two were empty, but in the third room I saw a girl—no a woman—who looked amazingly like Heidi, but an older version in her mid-twenties. The look-alike was staring mindlessly at a commercial for younger skin. As I watched the commercial looped and started again. Although I had problems believing she was the girl I was looking for, I slipped into the room and whispered, "Heidi?"

There was no response. I cursed to myself, figuring that the invisibility spell was interfering with her hearing me. I wasn't sure whether I had Heidi or not, but I wasn't about to leave any prisoner behind.

I came closer and noticed that there was an electric cable that went from the television to a computer. A second cable went from the computer directly into the woman's arm; something like an IV. I had a very bad feeling I knew what that meant. I tapped on her shoulder and was completed unsurprised when the woman didn't respond at all. She was under a spell. Evil, techno magic. Damn.

The next room held Greg who was also bespelled. The boy was staring at a television screen of his own. This one held an athletic competition. And while he still looked like a fifteen-year old, he was emaciated. No way on earth could a person lose twenty or thirty pounds in three days. He was in much worse shape than Heidi. At least she had years to age before whatever was being done to her was finished. If I didn't get the boy out, he'd be dead in less than a week.

The Fable was draining his vitality and her youth, but for what purpose I was clueless. Both of them being famous meant they had more to offer this kind of spell because the fame multiplied their natural resources, in Heidi's case beauty. For Greg, it was the extreme sports. He had won several first place prizes, despite his young age. Fame acted as a natural amplifier, given the magic a much larger pool to drain. Maybe they had found a way to infuse what they were taking into beauty products. That would certainly explain the exorbitant prices.

I looked at the program on the screen. I'm hardly a techno-mage, but thanks to Prof assigning me the Dexter program, I had enough basic skills to create a repeating loop. All I had to do was convince the computer that the last image it received was still going on. It took me about ten minutes to chant in the code. I wasn't sure it would work, but since Greg was wasting away in front of me, I didn't have much of a choice. I launched the program and unplugged him. I stifled the, "What the…" with my hand, and pulled him under my robe. He realized I was naked quite quickly, even if he couldn't see me. I prayed that the "Woe Momma!" that he whistled was muffled by the invisibility spell. I had to slap his hand down when he tried to cop a feel. Twice. At least I knew he hadn't been drained of all his energy.

The longest five minutes of my life later, there was no obvious sign of an alarm having gone off. I managed to get the kid into the next room where his sister sat, still staring at the same commercial. "Geez, Heidi looks like crap."

"Yeah, they've been sapping her youth," I whispered back.

I explained what I was going to do and the kid's eyes lit up. "I can help," he said. "I'm a techno-geek." Before I could stop him, he was over by her computer and typing away. "The endless loop is a good idea. I'm keeping that, but add a little random movement. Eyes blinking, body twitches things like that."

I nodded. Since I'd found myself someone light years ahead of me in terms of computer mastery, I let him do the metaphorical heavy lifting. "Know anything about fences and security systems?" I asked. "We still need to bust out of here."

"You broke in here without a plan to get back? Way to go super genius."

For one fleeting moment, I had sympathy for Candy Wade. The kid was a brat. Still, my answer should blow him away. "I was trying to cast a location spell to find you, when I accidentally tapped into the transport spell and was gated in here by mistake."

He nodded his head as though my words made perfect sense. "Like someone on the SyFy channel. Cool. Can you spell us out of here?"

I pointed to the computer. "Not if you can hack us out of here. It's much safer."

The kid sighed. "I want to see a spell before today is over," he warned. "Otherwise, I'm going to be very disappointed." That wasn't my problem. Most people learned about disappointment long before Greg's age. I guess money does as much harm as good, but now wasn't the time to try to de-brat the punk. His loop worked, so I disconnected Heidi. "You take care of sis, and I'll work on getting us out."

Heidi was, not surprisingly, hysterical, although whether it was because she'd been kidnapped, had aged nearly ten years virtually overnight or because of my invisibility, it was hard to tell. I did my best to calm Heidi down and tried to cast an invisibility spell over or for them. Unfortunately—in the way of magic—I wouldn't know if the spell worked until an outsider came by. The spell couldn't work on me; I was its caster and since I was using the same spell on both Greg and Heidi they'd be able to see each other anyway.

"Finished," he announced. "At eight o'clock the gates will automatically open for exactly two minutes. I fooled the system into thinking that an authorized car will be entering at that time. We should be able to walk out free and clear."

The kid was right—the gates opened. But damn it, the spell didn't work. I didn't know if it was the Fable, the kids not having latent magical abilities or shear bad luck, but the guards had no problem seeing the kids. "What the…" The pair of guards pointed their guns at the Wades and I heard the hammer cock.

"Run," I yelled, putting myself between them and the guns. I could maybe sneak up and take the guns unseen, but if they fired, being functionally invisible wouldn't stop a bullet.

As if listening to my thoughts, the uniformed guards each fired warning shots while shouting at the kids to "Stop or the next bullet goes right through your heart."

The kids were trained by an expert. Instead of doing something incredibly stupid-like running away-they both dropped to the ground and rolled, minimizing the kill shot. Stupid was left to me. I ran at the guards, ready to rumble.

Thanks to ten horrific hours a week of Morganna's self defense training for the last five years, I was pretty good at Krav Maga. The two quick strikes to the guard's shoulders were perfectly placed to disarm them.

Apparently, I wasn't the only one trained in street fighting. As I went for a disabling groin shot, kicks and punches came at me in a flurry of misaimed but very fast movements. I ducked, time and again, while getting in a few good licks here and there. Advantage me. There were two of them. I was invisible.

Just as I was congratulating myself that the kids and I would be able to get out in one piece, I took a lucky blow to the stomach that leveled me. I couldn't help the muffled scream that came out of me as I fell.

Less than a second later I had two men lying across me. Good looking incredibly fit men, but wrong time, wrong place. Call me old fashioned but I like my men one at a time. And they should buy me flowers, dinner, a drink… know my name before jumping me.

It was a bad angle but I tried punching the security guard in the stomach. He responded by rolling across me, trapping one hand. I kept the other one free by biting the guy's ear. He anticipated the head butt that was coming next and countered by leaning on my neck.

Meanwhile, guard number two had rolled off of me and grabbed his gun. In about one second I'd be dead and the guards would be free to go after the Wade kids.

It was dangerous, stupid and all I had left. I ripped the snare pendant from around my neck and activated it from the blood that was dripping from a cut above my left eye. Then I threw it at the computer in the guard shack, praying it'd work.

The light beam went straight toward the computer screen, the sprite riding the protons and merging itself with the computer. Without a mystical firewall blocking its access, its entrance to the real world took nanoseconds to begin. It turns out it had learned from its mistake, using the entire computer and part of the booth to form its latest body.

The guard on top of me knocked my head against the ground. I went still.

He assumed that I was unconscious and flew at the sprite. A hand made out of wooden boards slapped him down. The other guard turned his attention from the Wades to the still growing sprite. It had absorbed much of the shack and molded it into the same shape as it had before. Two arms were wood, one was glass and the fourth was wire and other assorted metals. The lower body tentacles were a little bit of everything.

The guard fired at it with all the effect of a peashooter aimed at an elephant. Fire could stop or at least slow it down, but I wasn't about to tell him. I wanted the sprite to wreck havoc—at least for a little while. Besides, there was enough magic around the Gingerbread compound that they had to have some mystic security in place. Let them deal with it.

I sprinted to catch up with the Wades, waving an unenchanted piece of wood, so that they could see me. They crawled out of the bushes they'd hidden in during my fight.

"You're lucky you did a spell," said Gregory, his skinny body moving at a good clip.

"No, you're lucky," I said.

He laughed and slapped me, his aim—regardless of my invisibility spell— was perfect—right on the butt. I grabbed his wrist, bent it back and threw him in a drainage gully.

"Touch me again and I'll turn you into a frog," I said.

His pupils were huge as he climbed out and back onto the road. "You can do that?"

Actually, not without a source of power and a lot of preparation, but he didn't need to know that so I grinned and said a confident, "Yup."

"Cool."

I glanced back, making sure that the guards hadn't gotten free to follow us. The guards were still fighting the sprite, but I saw something that made me grab the kids by their hands and scream "run." Superimposed over the plant was a candied gingerbread house. The door was open and I swear I saw an old-fashioned oven, with fire underneath. Even from a distance, the thing felt... hungry.

We ran for about a mile before stopping. Both kids were panting, out of breath and out of shape from the magic that had sapped their life force. It was time to make a plan. Sadly this time they knew enough to take his GPS watch. So much for breadcrumbs. Luckily we didn't need them. We were on a road that led somewhere. Plan A was to get me visible again and follow the road. Sooner or later-hopefully sooner-we'd find a phone and call for help. Plan B was to hide if something scary came by. I didn't have a Plan C.

"That thing," Greg asked as we were walking at a fast clip.

"A sprite," I interjected.

"You said it lives in the internet? Cool."

Oh crap. It didn't take a genius to figure out that the junior hacker by my side was going to search for one about a nanosecond after we got him home.

"Greg, don't go looking for trouble," I was deadly serious. "It's already found you and your sister. If you open up the door to magic it's going to…" I didn't get a chance to finish the lecture the kid wasn't bothering to listen to, because Greg screamed "Hide" and pushed Heidi—who was lagging several steps behind us—into the woods.

Two military issue jeeps were barreling down the road doing a hundred miles an hour, easy. For one second I hoped that we were saved. Then, with my second site, I saw the same image of a gingerbread house hanging over the cars. I jumped into the woods so fast I rolled into a small creek. My chicory washed off.

So much for invisibility.

A few miles down the road we found a—and I use this phrase very, very lightly—hotel/café called the Bane Moon Inn. It was a fleabag dump with weeds and broken furniture growing out of the pool, a moldy odor intertwined with the smell of the best barbeque I've ever smelt.

"Can we go in?" Heidi had been a trooper during the escape but it was clear that she was wiped and out of her element.

I shook my head, "I don't think it's safe for you." The jeeps had been heading this way. While I didn't think they had been going to fleabag hell, I wasn't sure. "Hide by the pool, and I'll go in. The kidnappers don't know what I look like so I'll be anonymous."

Heidi shook her head, "Not in that…" her nostrils flared as

she looked me up and down, "…costume you don't. You might as well be wearing a sign that says, 'look at me.'"

I glanced down at my wet witch's robes. The girl was right—no way I could pass for a lost tourist looking like I did.

"Cast a spell," Greg was all but hopping up and down at the idea, "that'll make you look dressed in a pair of jeans and a tee shirt."

"Can't," I admitted sheepishly.

"Why not?"

"No spell ingredients."

"Ah ha! So you couldn't have turned me into a frog."

"Not until I get back to the office." I glared at the kid, "I have to eat a live phidippus spider to start the spell—so don't make me turn you. I won't be a happy camper if I have to eat an insect."

Heidi made gagging noises. "Live insects—yuck."

I couldn't agree with her more.

I changed into Heidi's flannel pants and tee, leaving her to wear Gran's robes. True confession—I hated having the robes on someone else. Gran's magic—and now my own—were woven into the very fabric of the cloth.

I didn't like the Bane Moon. Not only was it a fleabag dump, I kept feeling like there was something I couldn't see—a force or a presence that flickered just out of view. Combine that with the vision of the candied gingerbread house hovering over the warehouse and I knew that someone from T-M was going to spend some significant time in Tennessee. I just hoped that it wasn't me.

I batted my mascara free eyelashes at Jimmy-the-desk-clerk and borrowed the phone. I was walking outside to tell the kids that we'd be picked up by the Tennessee police in ten minutes when I heard Heidi scream.

I ran outside to see Greg fighting off a guy twice his size with a deck chair. Heidi was attempting to bite another one as he dragged her towards a Gingerbread jeep. And I swear I saw a tentacle sneaking out of the swimming pool.

I grabbed a handful of dirt from the ground and ran at the

men screaming, "Prenda." If a body was buried on the grounds, its ghost would be called and under my control—maybe. Since I hadn't cast a circle or prepared the spell, it was a hit or miss. But as I told the Prof later, what other choice did I have?

I hoped for a dog or two—instead, I got five Confederate soldiers. "Attack," I screamed, pointing at the Gingerbread guards. They lurched ahead—muskets at the ready—towards me. Shit. The spell hadn't worked right.

My robes—on Heidi's body—were glowing like a beacon. "Help" she screamed.

I don't know if it was the robes, if Heidi had some latent magic, or just Southern courtesy drilled into the soldiers from a young age, but they turned to help her. Two shot ghostly bullets at the guards. Three speared the guards. And they fell to the ground in something I hoped might be unconsciousness—and feared might be death.

Their attack on the guards gave me time to grab another handful of dirt. I'd just chanted, "dissipare fantasmi," sending the ghosts back to their rest, when a large white woman came running out of the diner. "Dear God above!" she exclaimed, "What on earth happened here?"

"These kids are the Wade heirs," I said firmly. "And these men had kidnapped them. I'm a private detective hired by their father to try and find them." I gave a rueful grin, "You might say that I more than found them…"

The woman gave me a comprehensive look up and down, "You're too skinny to kill those men," she said getting right to the point.

"You have a better answer?" I shot back and the kids rambled something about magic and ghosts. We both ignored them.

She threw her hands up in the air and muttered something close enough to French that I suspected it might be Creole and then said, "What will be will be."

For about ten minutes it looked like I was going to jail for murdering two men, and honestly, I was shaking in my bare feet the whole time. The local jail cell was unlikely to have designer sheets and 20-inch mattresses. Plus Murder One carried the death penalty down here. Prof could probably get me off, but not before I'd spent some very uncomfortable time in jail. And the key word in that scenario was "probably." T-M is good, but not above the law.

What saved me was Robert Wade. While all the commotion was going on Greg borrowed Madge's cell phone and called his father. One call from Mr. Wade to the Governor, another call from the Governor to the Chief of Police and a radio message to the cops, who were in the process of reading me my Miranda rights, and the police couldn't release me fast enough, didn't want to know anything and declared the whole thing self-defense. We all ignored the waitress Madge's muttering about feeding the men to Mr. Snuggles—I felt like the cops on that one. I didn't want to know.

We were escorted to a small airstrip and Mr. Wade met us at the airport a couple of hours later. The look of relief on his face was indescribable. Both kids got a hug and Greg one of those "man to man" cuffs on the back of his head. I was surprised to get a hug too, and a whispered "thank you," in my ear. I was even more surprised that his voice in my ear created shivers down my spine. Falling for a billionaire was not on my to-do-list. I mean, sure he could provide me with endless shoes and handbags, but I'd seen Robert Wade at work. He wasn't likely to let his wife fight internet monsters and Fables in between dinner parties and charity events and I doubted I'd get an adrenaline high from a White House dinner. I mean, the dress I'd wear for that night would be incredible, and the shoes and the handbag, but… I pulled myself away from dreams and brought myself back to reality with a shake of the head. The guy was married—although I had every faith in the world that marriage was about to be terminated—my Gran raised me right. I didn't crush on married men. Ever.

On the ride back to New York, Heidi and I chatted about fashion, shoes, boots, and handbags while Greg babbled to his father about techno-magic and how he wanted his own personal sprite. The kid needed to apprentice with us immediately—before he loosed something on the internet that couldn't be stopped.

When I came into the office on Sunday morning Prof greeted me with a smile, and a rare, "Well Done," and proceeded to bring me up to speed. T-M satellite surveillance revealed that something had stopped the sprite, but not before much damage and havoc was wrought.

The rest of the team hadn't been resting on its laurels. When I disappeared Morganna confronted Mrs. Wade, and from what I understand, she hadn't been gentle. We don't exactly worry about people's rights when one of our own is in trouble. She'd sobbed out her part of the plot, Morganna said calmly, before the interrogation had gotten any more frightening than a broken chair and a magic light show. If I wasn't mistaken, Morganna seemed just a tad disappointed that she hadn't had a chance to break one of Candy's fingers or magically add twenty pounds to her hips and thighs. But it was hard to tell.

During the same confession, Candy told Wade about her pregnancy and tried to hold onto him through her child. He demanded a paternity test. It seems that his vasectomy was an enormous surprise to her.

She was being held on conspiracy to commit kidnapping. Somehow I don't think that the Wade family lawyers were going to act in her defense.

"We have to go back," I said turning the conversation back the events in Tennessee.

Prof's face darkened. "You might have caused the fable to retreat, but we have to be sure," he said in agreement.

"Maybe," I said doubtfully, thinking about the gingerbread house that I'd seen above the plant. "Arresting Candy takes the wicked step mother out of the equation. The kids have been rescued. We might have done enough to defeat the fable and force it back to the Neverafter—for a time at least." Without the kids or the wicked witch being killed, the Fable wasn't permanently banned. Unless Candy was the wicked witch—and I didn't think she was—the Fable would be back.

"You've still got work to do."

"Gingerbread Products?" I asked.

He nodded. "You're lead on the case."

I sighed and looked at my Gucci stiletto heeled shoes. A gift from a semi-separated billionaire to "thank me personally for saving his kids." He couldn't have chosen a better gift. I'd worn them because I thought I deserved the feeling of a job well done. "I'm going back to Tennessee?"

"Yup," he agreed.

"The cops are not going to take kindly to me in their territory," I argued. "And I don't look good in stripes." I doubted Ralph Lauren had come out with a prison uniform.

Prof shook his head. "Don't worry about the Tennessee cops, that's what we've got lawyers for." He pulled his fishing hat over one eye and pulled a rod out of the closet. "It'll take the associates a couple of days to get everything you need so you'll have time to finish up with the Dexter program first. I've got three calls in my voicemail looking for it to be released."

"Where are you going?" I asked suspiciously.

"Fishing," he replied walking out the door.

"Great. I find the kids, rescue them, fight a Fable to a standstill and I get to work through the few hours of weekend I have left. That's real fair," I said.

Prof shrugged. "Never said life would be fair. And you knew how this story would end. Let's just hope you ended the other one."

HAIR APPARENT

Prof and I got into a knock down drag out fight. I lost. So a week later I found myself in Tennessee with my tail between my legs. Not literally, fortunately. Prof was mad, but not mad enough to give me a real tail. That would be an abuse of magic he couldn't condone. I had my designer wardrobe packed side by side with a can of Raid. I was prepared for the inevitable bugs that were going to be sharing a room with me for the foreseeable future at the Bane Moon Inn.

The fight came about based on my choice—or lack thereof—of accommodations in East Black Hole, Tennessee. I had no choice about going back, but I wanted five star accommodations and room service, not the Bane Moon Inn, home to broken furniture, weird odors, ghosts and possibly a tentacled creature. Prof felt we needed to know more about the source of power behind the hotel. I wasn't so sure we wanted or needed to know anything else about that place. The power in that hotel had left goose bumps on my arms and chills in my spine. Somethings we might be better off not disturbing.

I wanted to have someone else from Templar-Mason go to Tennessee and finish the case. Barring that option, I wanted to stay at the Hyatt. I was willing to go head to head with the Fable. It was evil and someone had to fight it. I'd accomplished my mission the last time—sort of. Since the Fable still existed, there was still a battle to be fought. I was okay with that.

I was having problems with the fact that I'd killed two men at the Bane Moon Inn. It was self-defense, but I figured that the local police wanted to see me about as little as I wanted to see them. Jails scare me and not in the scared straight way. Plus—I'd never tell the Prof this—but I felt guilty. When I raised the ghosts to save Heidi and Greg I'd expected them to scare the guards. Not bayonet them. Seeing the spot where their dead bodies once lay was not going to be easy. In the few days I'd been home I'd managed to have an average of two nightmares a night as it was.

My past bit my present in the butt. I'd been vocal about my hatred of anything other than five star hotels. I firmly believe that luxury is a privilege that should best be enjoyed on a company expense account. There is nothing like being able to expense a lobster dinner to make it taste even better. The boss thought I wanted the Hyatt because it was a better class hotel than the Bane Moon, and he was right—to a point.

The point he refused to listen to was that there was something BAD at the Bane Moon. Something that cast a shadow over my skin, goose bump raising, stomach turning BAD. Bad enough that I thought Morganna should check it out. The Prof's right hand woman could kick my butt—magically and otherwise. Her chances of survival were much greater than mine.

Prof's eyes went blank, his voice got a distant echo to it that indicated he wasn't entirely in control, and the magic that lived inside of him insisted that I was "central to the story" and needed to be there. Since Fables use people to act out their story—for ill and on rare occasion good—I was a seer enough to know what the Prof meant. It meant I was needed in Tennessee and all the kicking and screaming in the world wouldn't make a difference. As a matter of fact, if I tried to avoid my destiny I'd probably lessen our chances of coming out the winner.

But I still didn't want to stay at the Bane Moon. Everything else aside, I just didn't feel safe there. It was one thing to skulk around in the light of day, another to be in a hotel room at night where ghosts walked. I knew the ghosts—I'd raised them, and they didn't like me. When I'm asleep my ability to defend myself is greatly lessened.

Prof didn't want to hear it. The witching hour wasn't a myth and many bad things happen at night, so I'd be more likely to find the secrets of the Bane Moon Inn in the darkness onsite instead of fifteen miles and one county away. Prof also pointed out that since I'd be skulking around Gingerbread Industries during the day, the only time I had left to investigate was at night. Which meant that I was supposed to do two jobs at one time and not sleep at all. I so needed a raise, or a company sponsored trip to a retreat someplace.

I stopped short and stared at the place where the two dead guardsmen had lain. My stomach felt like it had taken on a life of its own and was making me nauseous and trying to get out of me at the same time. My last few days had been seeped with soul searching. Was I glad that the bad guys were dead? I wasn't unhappy, maybe even a little on the happy side. Was I happy that I was the cause? No. Did I know that sometime in my career I'd kill a person? In theory, yes. It was part of my training since childhood. Was I ready for it? No. My last major assignment—in Rwanda—I'd been the seer. Tactical had gone in, I was in a tent two miles away 'watching' the action with a radio warning the fighters about attacks yet to occur.

I was distracted from my thoughts by Jimmy-the-desk-clerk coming out to pick up a package. "Hi," he said with a smile and high school quarterback good looks. "You're back."

"Hi," I smiled at him, relieved that Madge didn't appear to be around. I had no idea what I would say to Madge when I finally saw her. 'Sorry I killed a couple of guys out by your pool, and oh by the way I need a refill on my coffee' didn't cut it in my own head. I could only imagine how it would sound to her.

Jimmy got me a key, carried my bag, and steered me into my room, chatting the whole time about how the Huskies were doing. I took a wild guess that the Huskies were a football team, but for all I knew, he was chatting about the community college debate team. He opened up my door, exposing the burnt orange and yellow polyester bedspreads, the lumpy mattress and the dark green shag rug that clearly hadn't been changed since sometime in the seventies. My skin crawled at the idea of my navy and tan Jimmy Choos being exposed to whatever was living in that rug. More so than my feet. My feet washed easily.

"Um, thanks," I said, summoning up a smile from someplace. My heel snagged in the carpet and I flailed wildly.

Jimmy caught me and settled me onto my feet, "Doyouwanttogotothegametomorrownight?" he asked all as one word.

He seemed to be a nice normal guy. A nice normal guy who worked at a weird hotel that made my skin crawl. I hadn't met a normal guy since college. Normals did not work at Templar-Mason, and I missed them. Sometimes. Therefore my, "I can't. I'm working," was more reluctant than I would like to admit.

He looked at me with disbelief, "Tomorrow is Saturday night!"

I shrugged. "Tell my bosses that."

Jimmy left in a huff and I plopped down on the bed, not entirely sure what I wanted to do first. Well, that's not true. What I wanted to do was to get on a plane, fly to the barrier islands of North Carolina, check into a spa, get a massage and fantasize about having designers make clothing, shoes, and handbags just for me. But that wasn't going to happen anytime soon, even if I wasn't working.

Skulking around the Gingerbread plant was a necessity. The question was if it was wiser to go during the day with the place filled with employees or on the weekend? Or at night, which would get me out of Bane Moon duty. Looking around my less than acceptable accommodations, I decided that a Saturday morning was a perfect time to check out Gingerbread Products. The sooner I could get out of the back of beyond the happier I'd be.

That left the mysteries of the Bane Moon Inn. That's actually what had delayed my return to this half a star paranormal truck stop. After conning Greg into completing the Dexter Program—I told him it was a training exercise and the kid had it done in two days with only a couple hours of explanation on mystic programming; damn the brat—I'd had every possible search done on the Bane Moon and people who worked there. The Inn was located on overlapping lay lines, but that's all I had. Crossroads—lay line intersections—are usually neutral. Something bad had—or currently was—happening here.

I admitted to myself that the Prof would expect me to go to the lobby or restaurant and socialize—look for clues as it were. I also knew that wasn't going to happen. I was tired and the only thing I wanted to do was go to bed.

I changed into a La Perla teddy while wishing that I had brought along an old Oxford University tee shirt to sleep in instead. Not for comfort. Simple economics. At three hundred dollars, the La Perla deserved better care than the room could provide. My Alma Mater tee shirt could, and had, survived almost anything. When I was an apprentice witch in the secret Templar-Mason program at Oxford, I'd lived in the university shirts, since anything else tended to get destroyed when I screwed up a spell or potion; something that had happened far too frequently. When I'd finally gone a week without destroying any clothing my graduation gift to myself was a designer silk suit. It was the first official day of my life as a fashionista. I never looked back, but a few tee shirts were still living in my bureau at home. I wanted them with me. Bedbugs in La Perla were more than I could bear to think about.

Protecting the room was a given for me to have any chance of sleeping. Hawthorne is effective against ghosts and evil spirits, the fresher the better. But bringing a tree onto a plane tends to create questions; therefore I went with dried Hawthorne packed in an oregano container. I mixed in garlic flakes—everyone thinks garlic is for vampires, but it actually works really well on the walking dead—and sprinkled the mixture on the window sill and across the threshold. Then, with the competing scents of garlic, wood, and musk blanketing the room, I attempted to go to sleep. I resolutely ignored the "Jillian" I was sure I heard outside of my window and buried my head in the pillow. I didn't want to see the dead. Any of them.

I was three quarters asleep when I heard, "I need red from you. Red is next season's blond and I want to be ahead of the curve." The pained cry I heard in response jerked me upright.

"What the?" There was no answer. I got up, looked out the windows, put my ear up against the adjoining walls, but nada, not even the neighbor's TVs. Maybe I was hearing things.

But then why did I imagine red as the next blond? Any good fashion maven knows that there were certain immutable truths about being in vogue. No matter what color magazine editors push, there is no new black. Black is always in style. And the world belongs to blonds. California blonds in sporty little pink shorts to cool British blonds with their hair in a timeless French twist and the perfect black dress, blond is the color to be. I ran my hands through the cascade of honey, platinum, and gold that made up my hair. It took three hours and four hundred dollars every six weeks to hide the mousy brown I'd been born with, and it was worth every cent. So why had I dreamed red? The last thought I had before falling back asleep was that maybe I better reread this month's Vogue. Maybe there was something in it about auburn. Not that I wanted to change my hair or anything, but if I wanted to stay in the fashion game, I needed to know these things. And adding strawberry highlights to the mixture wasn't out of the question.

Saturday turned out to be a virtually useless day comprised of skulking around the plant. Security was upgraded. I couldn't get closer than binocular range without being spotted, although I tried. I did manage to confirm that the Fable still hovered over the Gingerbread Plant. Falling into the stream had destroyed the stash of chicory baby powder I'd stolen from the warehouse, and my odds of walking up to the front gate and charging a bottle was nil. Besides, at the level of magic in those products, odds are they'd set up something to detect that spell if I tried it again. Creating my own ingredients—in field conditions—was somewhere lower than non-existent. I had no idea how I was going to get into the Gingerbread factory now. Damn it.

I was so disheartened and tired I nearly walked by the diner, but a smoky barbeque scent wafted through the open door and my stomach growled in response. I still didn't want to see Madge, and I certainly didn't want to hear what she might have to say, but there wasn't any food in my room. I bit my lip, squared my shoulders and went in.

I was the only one in the restaurant and as I suspected Madge was waiting the tables. "Yankee girl," she gave me a disgusted look. "Still too skinny I see. What can I get ya? And don't you go trying to order no rabbit food."

"Well, it's only been a week," I offered with a rueful grin. I wasn't about to volunteer the fact that I worked hard to stay as thin as I was. Madge apparently didn't approve of me as it was.

I also wasn't going to bring up the dead security guards if she wasn't. "I should have a salad," I said slowly. She wasn't going to be happy with me, but my pants were tailored to my twenty-two inch waist. Gaining even as much as three pounds would affect the fit.

"Right, barbeque ribs coming up," Madge said with a grin I didn't quite trust. "A skinny little girl like you don't need a salad as an entrée. You need something to fill you up." She slapped her less than narrow hips, "Me on the other hand, I should spend a coupla weeks on the rabbit chow, but food is what makes life worth living. That and men."

I was about to protest her choice, but my stomach switched from growling to a gurgling that sounded an awful lot like begging to me. Madge even heard it. I smiled ruefully. "My diet hates the idea, but the rest of me…"

"You'll love it, Yankee Girl." As far as Madge was concerned, my name was Yankee Girl. It could be worse.

A few minutes later Madge dumped an enormous plate of ribs on my table. To my diet starved eyes it looked like enough food to feed at least three people; four if they were women trying to stay thin.

"Now you eat up now, Yankee Girl. And don't forget to save room for dessert." I would have told her that there was a snowballs' chance in hell of me having room for dessert, but my mouth was already full of sauce-covered pork.

She paused and her eyes narrowed like she was going to say something I might not want to hear. Then she said, "You don't go causing any problems at my inn. You hear?"

I gulped down the pork and choked out, "I'll try." I couldn't do better than that. I was on a mission. I hoped it wouldn't lead to anymore deaths, but the Fable was there—and they rarely left hungry.

"You do that." I clearly wasn't in good standing with her. What a surprise.

A man wandered out of the kitchen. The nametag said Al. The white floppy hat said chef. The brown paper bag said delivery. "It's for his ugliness. You want to run it up, or should I?"

My ears pricked up in curiosity. Who, I wondered was his ugliness?

Madge hit Abe on the arm. "That's not nice, sweet cheeks. Poor Raphael, God didn't gift him with looks. You know that he's got a good personality, most of the time at least and…" Madge was floundering for something nice to say about the mystery man.

"Huh?" I chanced the question while fighting for an expression of mild curiosity.

Her need for gossip warred with her distrust for me. Gossip won. "The poor man. There's so much wrong with him it's hard to know what to say."

The guy probably didn't have anything to do with Gingerbread Industries. They were dedicated to selling beauty, not ugliness. Then again, they had siphoned off and stolen ten years of Heidi's youth and thirty pounds of Greg's muscle. Who knows what they were capable of?

"Like what?" I asked.

"He stands about five foot two, but there's something about him that makes it look as if he's shrunk. You know, like when a person's got muscular dystrophy or osteoporosis or something. And it looks as if maybe he might be a hunchback. It's hard to tell under all that hair. He's got more hair than Cousin It, but weirder."

"How?"

"Well, it's all these different colors, but not in any kind of normal way."

"You mean he's dyed it green or purple? I hate punk," I volunteered. It's an affront to fashion. People should try to make themselves look better. Punk makes everyone look worse. Just thinking about a blue and purple tipped Mohawk is enough to give me shudders. My incantations trainer was a tall, thin natural blond who'd dyed her hair green and purple. I had nightmares the whole time I was in her class. To this day, I blame them on the hair.

Madge shook her head. "No, it's not that. It's more like his hair starts as brown. Then it becomes blond, then red then pitch black. And so forth. And he has the worst acne in the world."

I shivered. "Poor guy. It sounds awful."

Al wandered over. "That's the really sad thing. I make fun of the guy, but he can be very nice."

Madge chimed in. "And sometimes he's incredibly vacant. He seems like he just isn't there."

"Isn't there?" I parroted.

"It's like he is totally gone," Madge said. "He'll be talking to you and then nothing."

"Catatonic you mean? That sounds like he has a mental illness. He should get help." I wondered what a person with a sickness like his was doing at a hotel instead of at a hospital.

"He's been here for a year or so. He doesn't bother anybody and keeps pretty much to himself. I don't think he's left that room for the past nine months or so. Once in a while he has a visitor come by."

"Maybe a doctor?" I suggested hopefully.

"Maybe," Madge replied doubtfully. "But he doesn't look much like a doctor. Too well dressed. Distinguished looking. Like a reporter on television."

"He seems more like a business man. He talks like a businessman too," Abe said, "Always referring to things like production and next season's trends and such."

I felt like shouting "YES!" Gingerbread Industries management would talk of trends and production and what not. They might be making their mark at the Bane Moon. My expression must have changed from mild interest to conniving because Madge glared at me, "Raphael is a sweet boy and a guest of this here fine establishment. Don't you go giving him any problems. You hear?"

I nodded my head, trying to look like I was being truthful as I said, "I won't give him any problems." I mean if he was a victim of Gingerbread Industries, helping wasn't going to hurt him. Probably.

Madge gave me an up-and-down glare. She sniffed once and then turned away. I must have passed her inspection because she didn't say anything else about Raphael. Instead, she disappeared into the kitchen and returned a minute latter with a platter of raw meat. "I'm going to go feed Mr. Snuggles," she announced sounding defiant.

"Oh for Gods' sake!" Abe tried to take the platter out of Madge's hands and got nowhere in his struggles. "This is a grade A rib roast. Can you please not dump tonight's dinner in an empty swimming pool?"

"That swimming pool is not empty," Madge snapped back at him. "Mr. Snuggles is a distinguished guest."

"Distinguished guest!" Abe snarled, "More like a half a dozen over fed cats. And as far as I'm concerned the damn cats can eat gizzards and left over bones."

"Mr. Snuggles is an alien disguised as a ten-foot lizard as you well know!"

"It's cats."

My ribs were pretty much polished off and that was my excuse to exit. I stood as the two of them fought over the platter of meat. Fables I was trained to deal with. Catatonic strangers I'd either help or ignore as the case might be. Aliens disguised as ten-foot lizards or a dozen stray cats—not my division, and I intended to keep it that way.

Besides, if I stayed any longer, I'd be tempted to eat dessert and then none of my clothing would fit. The true secret to thinness, as any woman could tell you, is buying expensive clothing. I can't afford to replace them, so I have to stay thin. Period.

As I was paying Abe at the counter, he whispered to me, "Don't you worry none about what Madge's saying. Fact is she's downright crazy about that pool. Nothing in it except some weeds and garbage and stuff. You just go ahead and enjoy your stay here in the Smoky Mountains. There is an antique fair in town this weekend."

I nodded my head in agreement. Changing the subject from Mr. Snuggles to the motel's resident I said, "You should recommend to Raphael's visitor that if he goes catatonic on a regular basis, he really needs treatment. There are some good medicines…"

Al patted me on the arm. "I will. Don't you go worrying your pretty head about the Bane Moon's comings and goings." His eyes were pleading and he was acting almost like a protective father, almost like there was something he was too afraid to say out loud. "Okay?"

"Sure."

That night when I was nodding off to sleep I heard a voice saying, "…awards season is coming. Every person walking down those red carpets are going to want our products. After all, in Hollywood, you can't be too young, too thin or too pretty. And no one helps the truly rich reach those goals better than us."

A shriek of despair made me shoot upright. This time there was no doubt in my mind what I'd heard. I put together in my mind the comment about "red being next year's blond," and "awards season…"

"Thank you universe," I said aloud sincerely. I had no idea who was watching out for me, but clearly, someone was. I'd bet anything I owned, even my Gucci sandals, that somehow I'd wound up in a room next to operatives from Gingerbread Industries. My mission for tomorrow had changed. I wasn't going to be skulking around the plant. I was going to be having breakfast at the diner downstairs and pumping Madge for information at the same time. I was going to have to spend a lot of time in the gym when I got back to civilization, but if eating in the diner was going to speed up my departure time from hell, then it'd be worth it. Besides, the barbequed spareribs were the best I'd ever tasted. Maybe the alien in the pool had some secret sauce.

The next morning I was sort of disappointed, and sort of not, when, instead of Madge, a very young and beautiful girl was waitressing. Madge was a good source of information, but she was suspicious of me. This girl—I didn't know what she'd been told.

My heart sunk when I looked her up and down. She was an absolutely gorgeous natural blond. Somehow, even in my pink cashmere sweater, skinny jeans and brand new Kate Spade pink cowboy boots I felt frumpy next to this girl in her cheap polyester green waitress uniform. Sometime I hate true beauties. They make life so hard for the rest of us.

"You don't have anything low fat on the menu, do you?" I asked hopefully. "Maybe some yogurt or an egg white omelet?"

"Right," she agreed. "Belgium waffles coming right up." Before I could ask how we went from low fat to Belgium waffles she grinned and announced, "Madge told me that if a skinny Yankee with really great clothing was to come in here this morning I'm to fatten her up. She said that you looked too thin and stressed out, and needed some old fashioned southern hospitality to make you feel better."

I pulled out my compact out. "I don't look stressed out," I replied indignantly. "There's not a bag or a wrinkle in my face."

"The customer is always right," she said, agreeing without saying I was wrong. Her nametag read Darcy.

"Except about what she actually orders," I said.

"Exactly," she agreed. "Those are some really cute boots." Her eyes squinted and crossed for a second. "Sorry to disagree but there's something about you that says stressed. Not sure what it is, but it's there." I sat up straighter. If I had to take a guess, I'd think that the girl just read my aura. In the list of talents, it wasn't by any means the rarest, but to find it in a truck stop; I'd say it was very unusual. But then again everything about the Bane Moon was weird.

If I was going to be cast as the tense Northern, maybe I could make it work for me. "It might be a lack of sleep. The last two nights I swear I heard screaming coming from the room next to mine."

Her face paled. "You aren't in room nine are you?"

"No, why?" I asked momentarily diverted. "What's in room nine?"

"Don't know. But something is wrong there. What room are you in?"

Great. Prof would expect me to check out room nine. And I would—later. Gingerbread was my biggest worry which is why I let her change the topic. With her hidden talents she might be picking up on something there, maybe a spirit, but I had my priorities. Solve the case and banish the Fable. Then I'd worry about Bane Moon's multitude of secrets. Gingerbread had to be stopped. The people involved had resurrected the Hansel and Gretel Fable. I had to make sure it was gone. "Room twenty-one," I replied.

"You're next to Rafael," Darcy told me.

"The guy with the crazy hair," I asked. "Madge told me about him."

"I feel sorry for him," the girl confessed. "He never leaves the hotel. I mean ever. Not once since he moved here. And now he doesn't even leave his room."

"Agoraphobia?"

"I don't know," Darcy admitted. "But there is something about him that is very wrong. He only ever has one visitor—that awful Mr. Winsome." Normally I'd take her words as opinion, but if the girl was gifted her instincts were augmented by more than personal feelings.

"Why is Mr. Winsome awful?" I asked.

Darcy shivered. "He's cold. And oily, you know all smooth and mannerly but inside…"

"Inside?"

"You're going to think I'm nuts," the girl stated.

"Honey, I've been around the world and back again, and I've seen some things that really disturb me. Might as well give me a try."

Darcy's eyes told me this was something she'd wanted to talk about for a while. Her words came out in a rush. "It's like there's nothing home inside of him. No, that isn't right. It's like there is something inside of him; something amoral. Evil even."

She was uneasy talking about it. Maybe the girl had seen the fable looking out through Mr. Winsome's eyes.

"And the way he treats poor Rapunzel…"

"What did you say?" My hand shot out and gripped hers.

Darcy looked at me puzzled. "I said the way he treats Rafael is a crime. The poor man is always worse after one of his visits. Shaken and half catatonic."

"No, you called him Rapunzel."

"Oh that," she laughed nervously. "I nicknamed him Rapunzel one day because of his long hair and never leaving the motel, like he's holed up in a tower."

"What did he say?"

"That he was waiting for a princess to rescue him."

A witch better fit the description I thought to myself. Because if I wasn't mistaken, I might have just stumbled onto Fable number two, which meant we were in a world of trouble. I'd never heard of two Fables intersecting in one place. I'd put a call in to Prof and have him check Templar-Mason's files.

I must have become too quiet. Darcy shifted uneasily and was watching me staring nervously into space. "Um… I'll just put in that order for Belgium waffles then. Okay?"

"Sure," I answered, not really hearing her. "Sounds good."

She returned with an enormous plate of bacon, sausage, hash browns, two fried eggs, waffles, and whipped cream all covered in syrup, butter, and some strawberries. There wasn't a single item on the plate that had nutritional value equal to or greater than the calorie content. Forget about not being able to wear my skinny jeans, I'd be a candidate for a heart attack if I ate everything on the plate.

"You need anything else?" Darcy asked filling the coffee cup in front of me.

I shook my head slowly. "No, I'm good." I debated asking her if she had any interest in pursuing training for her talent. Templar-Mason has a good apprenticeship program, but one thing at a time. With no training and a Fable loose, she'd only get in the way and be a distraction if she thought her talent was real.

An hour, and my calorie allotment for the week later, I went to room nine and knocked. No one answered. The door was locked. I looked around making sure that no one was around and then put my hand up against the door and released my power. There were spirits on the other side, including the guardsmen I'd killed. "Jillian" they called at me.

"Lasciare il riposo morto," I chanted, urging the dead to go back to sleep.

They laughed, more grounded in the living world than any ghosts I'd ever seen.

I drew a containment ward on the door. Prof was going to have to send a team down to the Bane Moon later. As I walked away I whispered, "Sorry."

I skulked around the laundry room looking for a piece of Rafael's hair. I'd stuck a piece of sardonyx under my tongue to make it harder for someone to notice I was there. Sardonyx wasn't nearly as good as properly harvested chicory or hellebore for invisibility spells, but I was out of chicory and spell worthy hellebore was a bit hard to come by. I'd have to risk being caught skulking by the staff at the Bane Moon. They might be weird, but I didn't sense any evil on them. Fables were beyond evil. They didn't care who or what got hurt or destroyed as long they prolonged their stay on Earth.

I got lucky. I found a pillowcase with not one, but two long multicolored strands of hair that were exactly the way Madge had described to me. I took the pillowcase and both strands. I kept one strand. The other, and the pillowcase, I'd overnight to the Professor. The labs back at Templar-Mason should be able to provide me with a hell of a lot more information than I had now.

I went back to my room and got out my cell phone. My boss was fishing on company land. He hates to be disturbed when he's fishing and has a tendency to deal out punishment that would make a stay at the Bane Moon paradise by comparison. I had the receptionist put me through. She remarked on my bravery.

"Professor," my voice cracked in a combination of excitement and fear caused by excess adrenaline—my favorite addiction next to clothing and shoes. "I think we've got another Fable here."

"What?!" his yell echoed in my ears.

I held the phone away from me for a second as I rubbed my ear hoping to restore some hearing. "I've got a guy here with multicolored hair down to his feet that a Mr. Winsome, of Gingerbread Industries, doesn't let leave the motel. This flea-bag rat trap has a waitress who seems to be a sensitive and she told me that there seems to be, and I quote, 'Something inside of him that doesn't belong.' And then she told me that she'd nicknamed the guy Rapunzel."

I let that echo in the air. After a long moment, the boss said, "I've never heard of Fables working together. Ever. They can't play nice enough to pull it off—it's been theorized that the conflicting forces could start a war the likes of which we wouldn't want to see."

True enough. Two working against each other contributed to WWII. Together it could be far worse.

"Well, I think that's the situation we've got here," my voice squealed in excitement. Ah, the adrenaline rush. There's nothing else like it in the world. Well, except sales season at Barney's.

"I'll get the bible and review what it says about Rapunzel," the Prof said referring to the first edition copy of Grimm's fairy tales he kept in his office. I know he has the entire book memorized, but sometimes our first editions seem to go and change themselves. You read quick, think you read something new, but it's gone when you go back to look again. "And I'll put a team together to see if they can run down similarities,"

"And past means of defeating the second Fable," I demanded.

"That goes without saying."

"I'm sending a pillowcase that the victim has slept on. Unwashed. And a single hair strand. See what the boys and girls in lab coats can come up with, okay?"

"You've done well," the Prof told me.

My voice was softer than I wanted to admit to… a sure sign that I felt out of my depth. "Do you have any ideas? Because the way I remember Rapunzel the prince snuck into her tower and got the Princess pregnant. The witch caught them and blinded the prince. The princess wandered around for a year, had twins and then stumbled onto her lover who was living homeless on the edge of a desert. Her tears healed him and they lived happily ever after. No offense Prof, not only do I not want to sleep with this guy I've never met, but I don't want to have twins right now, or go blind, and that seems to be the path to a Happily Ever After. So I'm hoping for a better way, if you can think of one."

My boss' voice was grim. "You'll do what you have to, to stop this evil." It lightened slightly as he said, "But I doubt such sacrifices are necessary. I'll see what we come up with in our files. In the meantime, I do suggest that you initiate contact with the poor fella. There's no way around it, you're going to have to talk to him." With that, the Prof hung up the phone leaving me on my own.

Great, just great. What was I to do? Stand outside his bedroom and climb up his hair? I didn't think so. Besides the fact that I'm at best an adequate rock climber, it would probably hurt like Hell and hardly endear me to him when I could just use the stairs. Some surveillance of his room was in order.

The previous two nights, I'd heard screaming from the room next door right around midnight. Good old witching hour. My goal was to hear any conversation that might be taking place before the screaming, so I decided to set up my spell at ten. I had candles that burned for about eight hours. I figured that would allow a safe margin, and ensure that I didn't miss any chitchat.

I changed into my robes and then set up a consecrated circle in the middle of the green shag rug. Normally I'd use salt to walk a circle, but on that rug… no way. If the rug had been properly steam cleaned since it was installed sometime in the seventies, I'd eat my hat; the classic Chanel nineteen forty-one hat that had been worn by Ingrid Bergman. I'd won it at a Christy's auction for fifteen hundred dollars and it was my pride and joy.

The amount of salt that was no doubt already in the rug, left over from endless take out meals, could easy interfere with the spell I wanted to cast. My favorite spell ingredient was out.

So, instead, I cast a far more laborious circle made out of properly prepared quartz. On the inner side, I made a mini altar with a candle to represent fire, incense for air, a clean bowl of water with the hair I'd found in it, and good, old-fashioned dirt for the earth.

Elements of Earth and Air
Elements of Water and Fire
Your power to me please spare
For the situation upon us is dire

Guardian of the South

Water is thy element
Allow clear site
Within this bowl for viewing

Guardian of the West
Air is thy element
Bring the images I desire
To this place and time

Guardian of the North
Fire is thy element
As long as the candles burn
My spell I do invoke

Guardian of the East
Earth is thy element
A pinch of dirt to ground me here
And keep all harm away

This is my will
So mote it be

As I spoke I could feel a hint of moisture in the air, the curtains fluttering in a breath of wind, the candles flickering slightly and a slight shaking of the ground only I could feel. Prof had talked about something like that happening to him, but I'd never had such a response to a spell. I shivered, convinced more than ever, that I had wandered into something that shouldn't be.

I emptied my mind of everything and sat cross-legged in the center of the circle, the scrying bowl in my hands. Half whimsically I whispered, "Rapunzel, Rapunzel let down your long hair."

In every version of the Fable I'd ever heard of, the victim is a beautiful young woman with long golden hair. This Rapunzel was one of the most repulsive looking men I'd ever seen. His hair was longer than him, with absolutely no shape. It was matted, greasy and absolutely consumed him. Under the multicolored hair was a short, thin, almost emaciated guy with bad skin. It was as though growing the hair had sapped all vitality from him. I could see the Fable that rode him; a beautiful woman with golden hair that swept the floor and a cruel look. I shook my head, and even though I was afraid I had to smile. Even in the other-world, blonds ruled.

Then something happened I didn't expect. The man looked up, and his sunken, despairing eyes met my own. In all the fables Rapunzel has a beautiful voice and it is her singing that attracts the prince. This man's voice might attract a tone-deaf frog, but never a princess. "Help me," he croaked.

Even if I hadn't vowed to fight Fables wherever I found them, I still would have made the promise that I did. "I will." I wouldn't willingly leave anyone in thrall to a dark tale. Not if I could help it.

Then I put my finger up over my mouth in the universal signal for quiet. He nodded once, indicating that he understood me. Together, silently we waited.

At ten minutes to midnight, I heard a man's voice say with an echo of power that didn't belong to a human voice, "Rapunzel, Rapunzel let down your long hair." The emaciated creature that resembled nothing more than Cousin It stumbled over to the window, opened it and dropped the long length of hair out the window. To me, it was clear that his actions were not willing, but rather forced by the Fable that rode him.

A man, dressed in the finest tailored suit I'd ever seen climbed through the window. My first thought probably should have been to try and determine who or what the man was—or for that matter what rode him. Instead, I wasted a long moment trying to determine what designer made that suit. Finally, I decided that he must use a private English tailor; good enough that the future King of England should definitely give him his patronage. I then wondered why he would climb in through the window if the staff at the Bane Moon Inn knew about him. Admitting I had no answer to that one, I finally looked for the magic.

I'd expected was to see a fable riding this man as well. But there was none. This man stank of magic—black and dark as bile—but was ridden by nothing unworldly. In an instant, I knew what had taken place. This good looking, fifty-something distinguished man with great clothing had somehow summoned, not one, but at least two Fables to do his bidding. Probably for money. I shook my head in disbelief. Did he have an idea of what he'd raised on earth? Demons were tame by comparison.

The conversation between the two men didn't reveal anymore secrets. The red hair was growing in nicely, and the—I won't call him a witch. Sorcerers dealt with black magic and most of them would balk at being associated with this villain, but it was the best word I had—sorcerer was happy. He expected to get a good skin crème this season as well. Everything was surreally business like; a cosmetics executive inspecting a new batch of product. Which in an extremely weird way, the visit I was observing was exactly that. It seemed that while he draining part of Heidi's and Greg's essences, with Rafael Winsome seemed to be using him as a petri dish to grow the magic in. As far as I could see he didn't cast any new spells and Rapunzel didn't cry out in pain this time. I watched him go and then broke my spell.

"Prof—" By the time I made the phone call it was nearly one in the morning. There was unholy amusement lurking in my voice at the thought of waking the boss man up in the middle of the night. So I was disappointed that he sounded wide-awake.

"Yes Jillian," was the calm reply.

"I've got something," I told him about the spell I'd cast and the confirmation that the Fable in effect was Rapunzel. "But, it literally doesn't seem to fit right," I told him. "Every version of the Fable I've ever read has Rapunzel being a beautiful woman with an amazing singing voice and stunning hair. This guy is more like the Beast from Beauty and the Beast. His hair is matted, his skin is bad and his voice croaks."

"Three interlocking fables?" the boss asked sharply.

I shook my head even though he couldn't see it over the phone. "Maybe, but I don't think so though. At least I didn't see anything that indicated a third Fable. It could be that Rapunzel looks so bad because the power of the Fable seems to be gestating and growing inside him, then probably drained out into the Gingerbread cosmetics line," I offered.

"You don't think so," Prof wasn't questioning. He was telling.

"Actually I do think so. That's what happened to Heidi and Greg after all, although it was pulling from there attributes amped up by their fame. In this case, they are using him as an incubator."

"There's your pregnant princess aspect."

I breathed a sigh of relief. Yeah, I felt bad, but at least I wasn't going to have to get pregnant to beat the Fable. Next, I told the boss about the Mr. Winsome I'd seen in my scrying and my conviction that somehow Winsome had raised both Fables. "I think the Fable doesn't fit perfectly because it was summoned. It didn't come on its own. Rafael wasn't the story's chosen victim. I think Winsome is able to direct and control the Fable for personal gain."

The other side of the phone went dead.

"Prof? You still there?"

My answer was a string of curses that would have made the soon to be former Mrs. Wade blush.

"This changes everything we know about Fables."

"It could be a godsend. If we could learn how he controls them, we could teach all Templar-Mason agents. We could finally win the war against the Fables."

"Controlling a Fable isn't absolute power, but it isn't far off. It's too dangerous for anyone to possess, even us. If this Winsome can summon, warp and control Fables to his own end and all he's doing with that power is trying to get rich, he is the single most dangerous person on the planet."

"Crap."

"In the worse cases, the rider can be killed to end a Fable," said Prof.

Yeah, he was right, but it was a bad way to end it. "Rafael is an innocent."

"I let an innocent live once instead of doing the smart thing. Millions died. Trust me, one innocent on your conscience is better than millions. Although in this case, I think even that won't do the trick. You need to terminate Winsome."

"You want me to kill him."

"Yes. You have a problem with that?"

Sadly, not much. Part of my training was in how to take a life if necessary. By raising two Fables he's literally put the entire world in jeopardy. A Fable unchecked meant many more would die. Genghis Kahn, Vlad the Impaler, The Spanish Inquisition, and the Valentine's Day massacre spring to mind. Hilter and Stalin were part of separate Fables running parallel to each other. Each Fable engineered the deaths of millions and when they clashed the death tolls only rose. And there, of course, is Prof's personal shame. He had ended up playing the role of a dwarf in the Snow White Fable. He missed the happy ending and couldn't bring himself to kill the woman he loved even though she loved another. WWI was a direct result of just that one Fable playing out to a dark end.

The most recent massive failure to end a Fable was in Rwanda. We stopped it, but far too late to help its victims.

In the face of that knowledge of history, killing one man—Winsome—who willingly risked causing that kind of death and destruction, wasn't that hard a decision to make—at least in theory. Killing an innocent victim was far harder. The two men who I'd accidentally killed haunted me as it was—and they were far from innocent. Raphael was an innocent and his blood was not going to be on my hands.

"I'll stop it without having to commit the murder of an innocent," I vowed. Then I thought of something. "The Rapunzel legend is normally defeated by cutting off the enchanted hair. Right?"

"Yes. I'll have a full analysis completed and emailed to you in the next two hours. If the opportunity presents itself to end Winsome, you know what to do."

My stomach started doing flips and turns. I wasn't a cold-blooded killer. Could I do it? I guess I would have to find out. It was far easier to change the subject than dwell on it. "Send me that analysis as soon as it comes in."

"Right." With that, my boss hung up the phone.

Unable to sleep, I set up my computer, glad for the satellite connection that our techies had installed in it. Ten times faster than a cellular card and the Bane Moon didn't exactly offer free WiFi. A check of my e-mail revealed what Morganna's team had tracked down info on Gingerbread Industries. At present, it was a privately held concern with no major business loans. Not much else except for some passing references in glamour magazines and a corporate headquarters listed in a D&B report. They didn't advertise their product or even have a web page, although they have reserved a web address. How did clients find them? I e-mailed her Winsome's name, hoping she might turn up something else. My web search combining his name and Gingerbread Industries came up with nada.

Morganna included a scan of the magazine articles.

"Beauty is an eighty billion dollar industry in the United States alone. More than half of that is spent on anti-aging products. Gingerbread moisturizer, made from all natural organic materials, is the only product on the market today that is guaranteed to reverse aging. It doesn't just make a woman look younger. It actually reverses the ravages of time and restores the collagen in the skin to make it more youthful." Winsome was quoted in a cosmetics trade journal. It sounded like every moisturizer ad I'd seen on television this year, but given the magic this man had raised, I was willing to bet that he spoke the absolute and literal truth. The article also indicated that Winsome's business catered only to the Hollywood and social elite and like many of them, he went only by a single name. If you weren't known, you weren't getting the product. That didn't surprise me. With the amount of magic that was tied up in each bottle and jar, he couldn't afford to sell to just anyone.

He couldn't possibly produce enough product. But even I gagged when I heard how much the moisturizer went for. I'd never heard of anyone spending one hundred and fifty thousand dollars on an ounce of cosmetic. What, I wondered, did the A list think was in it? Did they care?

Prof's e-mail came while I was looking through the rest of the articles. We were right. The hair had to be cut. In one of our earliest records of the Rapunzel Fable, the golden hair had sapped the fertility out of the crops, creating a blight until the hair was gone. In another case, the girl's hair had grown in as pure gold and the Rapunzel had been a victim of greed—until she was shaved bald by one of our earliest operatives. Apparently, the fact that they were working under the mistaken assumption that it was the Midas Fable almost lost the game for them, but she recovered quickly. But in every single confirmed case, Rapunzel was a woman. There was some speculation on Samson, but that's all it was. I was bothered by the anomalies of having a male Rapunzel now, which only made my theory stronger. Did the summoning and outside directing change the rules enough that the normal means of beating the story wouldn't work? Better safe than sorry. Time to go make Rafael bald and send the Fable back into the dark of the Neverafter. Then I'd worry about Winsome.

Not that it'd be that easy. Fables can manipulate people and events better than the CIA and KGB did in their heyday.

I didn't bother with scissors. A normal pair probably wouldn't cut through that level of enchantment. So I took my athame—the knife I use for magical spells—and knocked on Rafael's door. "Open up. I'm here to deliver on my promise," I called through the door.

"I can't open the door. Only Winsome can," came the croaking response even as he jiggled the doorknob. I wondered how Madge and Abe kept the man fed if he couldn't answer the door.

Neither would appreciate being woken up.

"Okay." The door and the walls were paper thin. I knew that. But neither yielded to my attempts to break in. I figured that the room was warded and tried every reversal spell I could think of. Nothing worked, not even kicking it or using my credit card.

"My… Mr. Winsome comes in through the window," Rafael suggested.

I felt like an idiot. The window made perfect sense. The room was his tower. They probably handed him the food through the front one. It was reinforced to only open enough to slide a plate through. The way in was the one on the rear of the building. I felt foolish climbing up the outside of a cheap motel, but my years in Templar-Mason served me in good stead. Being in good shape is a must in this job, and at least once a year we had to pass a military like fitness test. Climbing a ten-foot wall is part of that test. I bitched and moaned about it, we all did, but I never once flunked. Never aced it or got near the best score, but never flunked it. The side of the building was a challenge, but I was grateful I was in my witch's robes, and not a designer suit. A nice pair of yoga pants would have been even better.

I shouldn't have been surprised that the window wouldn't open either. Again I still wasn't thinking right. Even Fables are bound by rules. They can only affect the world through manipulating their story, but they have to allow others to do the same.

I clambered back down to the ground and started playing smart. "Rapunzel, Rapunzel let down your long hair." As soon as I said the words, the window opened and the skein of hair dropped to the ground. When I touched it, I was all but pulled up and thrown into the room. And repulsed by the condition the hair was in. The man needed major conditioning. I'm not even sure a crème rinse would help much.

Rafael looked up with hope in his eyes. "Can you rescue me?"

"I'm going to try." I picked up a piece of the matted hair and my skin crawled. I'm not sure I ever touched any hair that disgusting in my life. "When did you wash this last?" I asked wrinkling up my nose. The room smelt from the filthy tresses.

"This morning," he admitted. "But it never gets clean."

"It must be part of the spell." I took my athame and tried to cut the hair, but it wouldn't go through even one strand. How the hell had he gotten two strands on the pillow case? Maybe a few fall out naturally so new ones can take their place. "Damn it."

"What's wrong?" his voice wavered as he spoke. Fear will do that.

"I have to cut the hair off to save you but it won't cut."

He didn't ask why I thought cutting his hair would help. He just pleaded, "Please, just get me out of here. Every time he comes, he hurts me." His words were as simple as a child's. But it was a desperate adult who looked out of his brown eyes.

"I'm going to help you," I said with as much certainty as I could muster. I knew it wasn't going to work, but I tried to push Rafael out the window. The room wouldn't let him leave. "How do you get out of the room to go to the diner?"

"Winsome takes me. The door only opens when he's here. I'd try to run away, but he said he would kill everyone here, even Darcy and Madge. I can't let that happen." He squared his shoulders and took a deep breath. "You aren't going to be able to help me, are you?"

If I was caught in that room, the Fable would make sure I suffered the fate of the prince in the story. Namely, I was going to be maimed in some way and sent someplace where Templar-Mason would never be able to find me. Not on my agenda if I could help it, but I couldn't leave the man without help. It wasn't in me. "I'm going to help you. I just don't how." Then I had a thought. "How did you wind up in Winsome's care?"

He shrugged. "My Dad was CEO of Gingerbread Industries. Winsome worked for my dad—his second in command and best friend. My Dad's will left Winsome as my guardian and the CEO of Gingerbread Industries. We used to make cookies and other baked goods."

That explained Winsome's control over poor Rafael. Magically speaking a guardianship, or parenthood, can give the magic user almost unlimited power over their charges; something that Fables loved to capitalize on.

"Winsome took us into the beauty product business."

Something about the story didn't fit. "Aren't you over eighteen?" Eighteen or twenty-one are usually the age of consent in the modern world. If Rafael wasn't close to thirty, then Winsome had been sucking age as well as looks, strength, vitality, voice, and good hair. He was certainly capable of doing something like that, and I needed all the details.

"Dad didn't trust my financial sense," Rafael told me with a wry grin that showed he'd survived with at least his sense of humor somewhat intact. "I was kind of a wild kid…parties, I'm ashamed to say drugs, toured the bar circuit in a band."

"Lead singer." It wasn't even a question.

Rafael nodded. "Listening to my voice now, it kills me not being able to sing." Refusing to give into his grief he bit his lip and got back to the original question. "The will doesn't give me any control of the company or my money until I'm thirty. Two years from now."

I sighed but didn't say anything. Rafael was indeed Winsome's by the rules of magic. I might be able to break the Fable, but I'd still need to figure out how to free him from the binding terms of the will. If this wasn't the most egregious forms of magical abuse in recent history then I didn't know what was.

It was nearly dawn. "I'd better get out of here. Neither of us wants me to be caught in here."

There was no hiding the fear that Rafael felt at that idea. "No, we don't," he agreed.

Sure enough, the only way out of the room was by climbing down the rope of hair. I hate it when a Fable is that literal. Especially when it involves something as filthy as that hair. Yuck.

I spent the next few hours staring at the ceiling, hoping for inspiration. There were modern, mundane solutions like using a gun. As an agent at Templar-Mason, I had several issued to me.

I was a competent markswoman, but I had a couple of problems with a cold-blooded shooting. One—and I'm afraid this was the most important issue—I had no desire to spend even one night in jail. Or risk the death penalty for first-degree murder. No thank you. I'd already committed two murders here at the Bane Moon. I doubted that a third death, even with our contacts, would get chalked up as accidental or self-defense.

The second problem had to do with the Fable itself. I seemed to have been cast in the prince's role. I'm sure that the prince had a weapon on him when he confronted the witch and look how that had turned out.

I ended up surfing the web and going through Morganna's research, without a specific search in mind except finding the answer to my dilemma. I found it in the form of another quote from the frightening Mr. Winsome in yet another trade magazine. "It doesn't matter what kind of damage has been done to your hair. Gingerbread Industries shampoo and conditioner will restore your hair to its natural beauty in just one washing. Guaranteed."

I smiled in unholy glee. I knew how to break the Fable. I still didn't know what to do about Winsome, but I figured better to deal with one problem at a time. I considered trying the chicory invisibility spell again. I could have the ingredients sent to me—but now I knew how powerful Winsome was. There had to be some countermeasure in place.

So I came up with plan B.

I changed into a pair of pinstriped wool trousers, blue cashmere sweater, white leather trench coat and my all time favorite pair of Jimmy Choo stiletto heel boots. One black, one white. Then, knowing that I looked my absolute best, I called in a favor. I had helped rescue Heidi Wade and her brother from Gingerbread's clutches. Heidi was almost as infamous as Paris Hilton and while there was no way she'd be let into Gingerbread's showroom, she had friends who would. She hooked me up with Janyette, one of the hottest singers on the charts. She was the type Gingerbread catered to. Prof had her flown in on one of the T-M jets.

Their showroom was in a small building adjacent to the plant, and Janyette was given immediate access. I was introduced as a hot new producer and allowed to buy a bag full of products. I used a cover e-mail to sign up for their mailing list and had to use the company credit card. My personal cards didn't have a two hundred thousand dollar credit limit.

Forty minutes later I walked out with a bag. Prof was going to have a cow when he saw the bill, especially since we weren't billing anyone for my time or expenses. Fortunately, T-M covered all reasonable expenses when dealing with a Fable.

I spent the time waiting for Winsome to arrive and leave preparing spells, but I made damn sure I took the time to pack up my wardrobe and stash it in the trunk of my rental car. If I was successful, Rafael and I were going to get the hell out of Dodge—or in this case the Bane Moon—tonight. And there wasn't a chance that my vacation wardrobe was going to be left behind. They don't even make stiletto heeled black lace up Jimmy Choo boots anymore.

Prof expected me to discover the secret to the Bane Moon, so mid afternoon found me staring at the empty swimming pool. Weeds, old furniture, and a dank moldy odor were present. A ten-foot lizard/alien wasn't. I even muttered reveal and threw some graveyard dirt into the pool. Whatever Madge was feeding—I couldn't see it. As I walked away I resolutely ignored the place that the dead once walked.

I stood by and unsuccessfully tried to ignore Rafael's cries during Winsome's nightly visit. Once he was gone I stood outside the window, once again in my robes to which I had added gloves and chanted, "Rapunzel, Rapunzel let down your long hair." Moments later, I was again inside Rafael's motel room clutching in my arms a bag of products, herbs and the strand of Rafael's enchanted hair I'd found the previous day. "Did Winsome know you had a visitor?" Stupid question really. Winsome would have done something if he'd known.

When he shook his head, I thrust the bag at Rafael, "Here use these. Now."

He just looked at me. "You want me to wash my hair?"

"And use all the crèmes. We're going to use their own magic against them," I explained not terribly coherently. "Somehow they've been sucking vitality out of you and into their product line. They've done it to I don't know how many others." Heidi and her brother were just the only two I knew about. "Using Gingerbread's line should restore power back into you. Go on. Use it. All of it." The last sentence was said with a wince. Part of me wanted to use the toiletries myself and see what would happen. I had nice hair and skin and all, but we were talking about magically enchanted skin care products. No sane woman would voluntarily turn that down.

Twenty minutes later the man who stepped out of the bathroom was completely different than the one who went in. Hubba Hubba. "Winsome's going to notice this visit," Rafael warned me.

I took my athame out. "If I'm not mistaken he's on his way here now." I knew that there was nothing nice about the smile that accompanied those words. Winsome had not only summoned the Fable, but made himself part of the story to better control it. The Fable would be doing everything it could into manipulating him back here.

"Whoa. What are you doing with that knife?" Rafael was definitely scared of me, for no good reason. He wasn't my target.

"Same thing I tried last time. Braid your hair, quickly." I stood there my knife in hand ready in case Winsome got to the room faster than I expected.

"Done."

I stepped over and without a word, sliced the long, now golden hair, off as close to the scalp as I could manage. Rafael winced. I smiled comfortingly. "Bald is the new blond." I took the hair over to the window, which flew open as I approached it. I tied it to an old iron radiator and I slid the braid down to the ground. "Climb down, quick. And hide." As soon as he was down I hauled the hair up again. It still had work to do.

The fable wasn't broken. The hair might be able to be re-attached, the mystic equivalent of hair plugs. The prince still needed to confront the wicked witch; or in this case, the witch needed to take on the sorcerer. Using my athame I cut a pentacle into the shag green carpet. I placed the single enchanted hair in the center of it. Off to one side, I made a circle of protection out of cedar. Then I cast my own wards on the door and windows. I took a moment to ask the Universe for help. This would work or I was dead. My heart was beating fast, my hands sweating and I had a wild smile on my face. Ah-adrenaline. If I was going down Winsome and the Fable wouldn't get me without a battle.

"Rapunzel, Rapunzel let down your long hair," the voice that called up was furious.

I threw the braid down and held my athame in one hand. The other had a mixture of agrimony, birch, and mandrake.

"What the hell have you gotten into now, you little…" Winsome's voice trailed off as he beheld not Rafael, but an angry witch in his place.

I held the athame like a dagger and without thinking, Winsome backed away from me, right into the pentacle. Excellent. I dropped down into a crouch; as though I was going to attack, and before he realized what happened I sealed the figure closed — blood dripping down my hand from the cut I made to seal it.

"What the…" Winsome tried to step out of the ward, but it was my magic, not his that had prepared the room. He was caught.

I stood in the middle of the circle of protection that I'd prepared, held my athame so that it reflected his reflection back on him, and chanted:

"Witch's power burning bright tonight
Herbs concentrated by this blade
Charge the spell; engulf with might
Here and now the magic's made.

Magic mirror used to reverse
Evil done inside this room
This man has cast a curse
May it become his doom
This room enclosed must contain
The power of one who has abused
His magical right is viewed with blame
One he entrapped within his ruse

Powers that are, Powers that be
Gather round this spell I cast
Empower my workings three times three
Send it forth to see it last

So mote it be.

As I was speaking Winsome tried to cast a counter spell in Latin. I didn't recognize it, but I could see a small green devil forming. He wasn't above summoning anything that could help him. I could feel the two magics straining together. The Fable wanted to help him. It really did, mainly because it did not want to return to the Neverafter, but it was still bound by the rules. It had to work through Winsome. If I'd planned anything other than a magic mirror spell I probably would have died. But when the two workings met; they rebounded back at him. I was drained and exhausted from the spell, but unharmed in my own circle of protection. The green devil was nowhere to be seen.

As I watched the dapper, distinguished man changed. His skin wrinkled, he shrank and his voice became froglike. I had a dark thought that he might try to summon the frog prince Fable. Because with the warts and pimples that formed as I looked at him, he looked like nothing so much as an angry toad and I couldn't help thinking of my role as the rescuing princess in one story might lead to him forcing me to kiss him or worse in another.

I had one of my guns tucked in a thigh holster. I pulled it out and pointed it between his eyes. My finger was on the trigger. My mind knew what he had done, what he might do again, but right now he was caught and helpless. As much as I knew it needed to be done, I just couldn't shoot him in cold blood. And if we could contain him, there was so much we could learn.

With luck, my circle would hold until I got backup. Then they could terminate or contain him—their choice. I tucked the athame in the belt of my robe, untied and wrapped the braid of hair around my neck. Then I clambered out of the window, using handholds on the building itself to climb down. My fingers were hurting and I broke two nails, but I made it down in one piece.

Rafael came out from inside a dumpster to greet me, "What happened?"

"I trapped him upstairs. At least for the moment." I took a deep breath; I was still high from all the action.

Suddenly there was the whirl overhead of a helicopter.

"What's that?" asked Rafael.

"My backup." Of course, they would have been more useful earlier, but they were here now.

Four men and two women in full armored response gear jumped off the copter and hit the ground. Three had wands, three had automatic weapons. At Templar-Mason, we don't mess around.

"I have the subject trapped in a warded pentacle in Room Twenty-three. The Fable should be broken, so normal methods of entry should work. You need me to accompany?" I asked.

"No, ma'am. We have this covered," said Howard, the team leader. As a full agent, I technically was in command, but these guys were easily special forces good. In a firefight, they were better than me.

Four hit the stairs at a run, while two scaled the side of the building in a fraction of the time it took me to get down. I heard the door smash inward and then things got bad. There were several flashes of light and automatic weapons fire, then screaming.

I pulled my gun. "Rafael, in the copter now."

"What's happening?" he asked.

"SHTF." Shit hitting the fan. Rafael listened. "Get him airborne," I ordered the pilot. "A Fable was riding him. It may not be resolved. We need him gone."

"Yes, ma'am. I'll stay in radio range if you need me."

The wind from the rotors blew my robes as the helicopter ate sky. I climbed up the stairs, but never made it to the top, mainly because Winsome was coming down the stairs, his hand now a claw wrapped around Tyna's throat. She was the team's tactile witch and a tougher lady I'd never met. She was bloody, bleeding and both her forearms were broke and jutting at what looked like very painful angles. Her eyes were full of despair. She didn't expect to make it.

"Let her go," I ordered, my gun trained on his head.

The power in his laugh was eerily inhuman. "Why? We're having such fun, aren't we dear? I'm afraid the rest of our playmates are all broken and dead. They don't make them like they used to. Now, you miserable excuse for a witch, get the hell out of my way or I'll wear her skull as a hat."

"Human skulls are a serious fashion faus pax. For your own sake, don't do it," I said.

"You think I'm going to listen to the bitch that ruined my plans?"

"That's witch, thank you very much."

"Do you have any idea what you cost me?"

"No, but I'd love to see an itemized bill. It'll make me feel like I accomplished something."

"You'll pay, just not yet. I'll keep this little lady as a down payment." Winsome forced something down Tyna's throat. I fired at his skull. Perfect shot, right at his eye. Would have ended up going through his brainpan too if he hadn't somehow disappeared.

"Shit." I went into the room. Winsome hadn't been bluffing. The rest of the tactile team had been ripped apart. This was my fault. If I had followed orders and killed Winsome, Howard and three other men and one woman would not be butchered to the consistency of hamburger.

And this murderous psychopath had another of T-M's people. One of my people. I was going to get Tyna away from him.

I called the copter down and got in the moment it touched down.

"Ma'am? Where's the rest of the team?" asked the pilot.

"The hostile slaughtered all, but Tyna. She's currently his hostage."

"Should I call for backup or the local authorities?"

"No time. He teleported Tyna away."

"Do you know where?"

"I have a pretty good guess."

As we flew away I distinctly saw a tentacle climbing up the side of the inn. Madge was right—Mr. Snuggles did live in the pool, and if I wasn't mistaken, he was planning on eating what was left of our agents. Jimmy came running out of the hotel waving something that looked like a stun gun from a good science fiction move. Huh—maybe he wasn't a nice normal guy after all. If I made it back down to the Bane Moon again I might just say yes to that date he'd wanted to take me out on.

Five minutes later I was dressed in assault body armor and getting ready to repel down to the parking lot of Gingerbread factory. I guess the yearly physical and training really was a good idea.

Now magic is a good thing, but it has its limits. I needed either prepared ingredients and materials or a source of power to draw on. The copter had some prepared herbs which I appropriated, along with a pair of 45 automatics and several grenades. I also took a gallon jug of whiskey.

No, I wasn't planning on getting my drunk on. Instead, I mixed in some psychedelic mushrooms, some of my blood and channeled my power into it. I said a spell that was enough on the dicey side that I'd rather not repeat it, but it worked.

I filled a giant water rifle with some, then made what was left into a Molotov cocktail. I lit the fuse and dropped it on top of the factory's filtration vents as we flew over, as well as onto the new guard shack. I repelled down to the back of the building and the pilot flew to the front. We put Rafael to work lobbing smoke grenades around the front of the building while I tried to sneak in the back. And I prayed to the Gods that any innocent people working past one in the morning survived unharmed.

The door had a keypad but was also made out of glass. I shot twice, then used the barrel of the gun to knock the remaining shards of glass loose and walked in. A lone guard was waiting. I squirted him and dove for cover.

It didn't take long for my spell to take effect. The alcohol took away his coordination and the mushrooms made him see things we were all lucky weren't there. With luck, my little fire-bomb had sent enough through the building that the rest of the staff were in similar states. Just to add to the fun I pulled the fire alarm. Might as well get as many people out as possible.

I made my way through the hallways. I passed a woman running from a nightmare only she could see. I was barely a blip on her radar.

I came to a door labeled Authorized Personal Only. I could see the ward on the door. Anyone not wearing the right amulet who tried to open that door would be incinerated.

I pulled the pin on one of my grenades, the explosive kind, and tossed it near the sheet rock on the side of the door. Winsome hadn't warded the sheetrock. The explosive would have no problem blasting me a hole big enough to step through.

Winsome was standing there waiting for me.

"I told you I'd make you pay. You didn't have to go to all this trouble to make it so easy on me."

Tyna was tied to a chair in the middle of a pentacle. I shot Winsome full in the face with my water riffle.

I waited for the spell to take effect. I kept waiting. Winsome licked his lips.

"Tasty. Blue Foot Psilocybin if I'm not mistaken. Top notch choice on the mushrooms, but the whiskey? Cheap crap. You're in Tennessee witch. I think it's a crime to use anything but Jack Daniels."

"Give me Tyna and I'll buy you a bottle of Jack as we leave," I said.

"You'll leave. It'll just be in a body bag."

I shot from the waist like I'd been taught. Winsome moved before the bullet reached him. Before I could get off a second shot, something slammed into my back, sending me sprawling across the floor. A few crates of face cleanser broke my fall. I broke the crates. Somewhere along the way, I lost both of my guns. I had dropped one and Winsome was holding the other.

"A gun, witch? You come to fight Fables and you resort to common firearms? I'm disappointed. I think I'll use this one on you. Preference for which knee I shoot first?"

"Your left, then your right would be fine with me," I said, tossing a jar of cleanser at him.

Winsome chuckled and catch the jar effortlessly. "Let see if I can't beat that sense of humor right out of you, shall we?"

I still had three grenades, but the way he moved he'd catch it and turn it back on me. Sadly, I didn't have much else by way of weapons so I reached for another jar of face cleaner. This stuff went for a year's salary, so even facing death I couldn't help myself from reading the ingredients.

I looked up at Winsome and smiled.

"What do you have to be happy about witch?"

I opened two jars. "I could never afford this stuff. If I'm going to die anyway, I may as well have a go at it." I tore off the scab on my finger.

Winsome shock his head. "You want to look good for your funeral?"

"Doesn't every girl want to die young and leave a good looking corpse?" I said, sticking my bloody finger in each jar.

"You assume I'm going to leave enough for Templar-Mason to bury, let alone identify."

"You don't look happy. Keep that up and you'll get frown lines." I tossed him a jar. "You need this more than I do."

As before, he caught it. "You think insulting my appearance is going to get me angry enough to get sloppy enough to let you escape?"

"Can't blame a girl for trying," I said. Now pretty and lengthy spells are best to help control magic. However, for something that you don't want to control, short and desperate can work too. "Boom."

The jar exploded in his hand, the cream covering him and acting like magic napalm. Winsome screamed in pain, running around like an inhuman torch. I tossed the second jar into the case of the rest of the face cleansers, picked up my mega soaker and sprayed the concoction. It hadn't worked on Winsome but it made short work of his pentacle. With the line broken, I was able to help Tyna up.

"Can you walk?"

The witch limped a step then put her arm around my shoulder. "I will. How the hell did you do that?"

"One of the main ingredients was angelica root," I said. I already knew they prepared the beauty products so they made superb spell ingredients.

Tyna got a glint in her eyes. "Which is used for fire and burning spells as well as youth potions. Brilliant."

"Thanks." Tyna was one of T-M's top witches. It was a major compliment.

In a gait reminiscent of a three-legged race, we ran for the exits.

A scream that sounded like it came from the pits of hell itself roared behind us.

"Witch, you are dead!"

I didn't even turn, just ran faster. "No, you are. Boom."

The second jar exploded, taking the rest of the hundreds of face cleansers with it. The room behind us exploded in a fireball. The shockwave knocked us to the ground and smoke filled the hall.

I was lost. I helped Tyna up.

"Which way is out?" she asked.

"I don't know," I said, desperately searching for an illuminated exit sign.

"I do," said a man from the smoke. For an instant, I thought it was Winsome. It was Rafael.

"I told you to stay in the copter," I yelled.

"You want to argue? Or you can come with me if you want to live." He was grinning from ear to ear. "I always wanted to say that. Follow me."

We did, I even grabbed the hallucinating woman and the guard I had had sprayed on the way in. In moments we were breathing beautiful sweet air. The helicopter touched down fifty feet in front of us. In seconds we were airborne, minus the Gingerbread employees of course. A minute later, the entire factory erupted into a tremendous fireball. I watched as the hungry gingerbread house stove collapsed into the fireball. Yes!

"What did you do?" asked the pilot.

"She creamed them," said Tyna, smiling through her pain.

Adrenaline gone, the next day I spent beating myself up. If I'd only shot Winsome when I'd had the chance, the team wouldn't have died. Even my vintage 1959 French Chanel suit couldn't make me feel better.

My first words upon walking into the debriefing meeting I had with the Professor was, "I'm so sorry." And then, "How is

Tyna?"

There was no lurking kindness in his eyes, "She'll survive." Unspoken was that the rest of the team didn't. "What happened, Jillian?"

I told him everything. When I got to the part where I'd trapped Winsome and hadn't killed him, the boss became furious. "In the last hundred years that I've been with Templar-Mason, I've never heard of an agent failing to take the kill shot when they had an enemy combatant in their sites. What the hell were you thinking?"

I looked miserably down at my feet. "I thought maybe we could contain him and find out what he knew. How he was raising the Fables." That sounded so much better than the truth. That I'd wimped out.

"You thought wrong, and in the process left the most dangerous sorcerer I've ever heard of alive."

"Yes." I paused a moment and then asked hopefully, "Maybe he died in the explosion."

Prof shook his head. "I had an agent on the preliminary investigation team. No bodies."

Part of me was glad no innocents had died. Part of me was devastated that Winsome had gotten away. I had no idea what to say. When the silence echoed for far too long I took a deep breath and tried to change the topic.

"At least we defeated the Fables," I offered.

"Did you?"

I thought about it for a moment. "Rapunzel, yes definitely." Raphael and I had shared a long ride back north. The golden haired woman was nowhere to been seen. "Hansel and Gretel," I made a weighing motion with my hands, "It collapsed into the remains of the plant. It's gone from Tennessee. If Gingerbread has another manufacturing facility it could be there, I guess."

"Great," Prof snorted. He rubbed his balding head, "What a screwed up mess you left behind. Just freaking great."

We finished up the debrief—T-M's contacts had already gotten the local authorities to declare the plant an industrial accident and OSHA was on its way to investigate. I couldn't imagine their findings were going to make any sense, but, that at least wasn't my problem.

Morganna stuck her head into the meeting. She looked as cold as ever when she said, "When you two are done, Jillian, come to the gym. You've got a Krav Maga session scheduled just about now."

I clenched my hands in my lap, but didn't say anything. If Morganna was as upset as Prof, she wouldn't hold back at all, and a beating was in my immediate future. I would be lucky if I was able to walk after that.

As Prof left the room he turned and said soberly, "Jillian I haven't decided what to do with you yet. Your lapse of judgment got friends of mine killed—and left a threat to international safety at large. I don't know if I can trust you in the field right now. I just don't."

As Prof left I realized I was almost looking forward to my session with Morganna. If she beat me senseless I wouldn't be able to think—and that sounded like a pretty damn good idea to me.

NO BUSINESS LIKE SNOW BUSINESS

I'd like to say that the months following my encounter with Winsome had been quiet, but that wouldn't actually be true. It was quiet in terms of finding Winsome, not so much in the home office. Prof had found a unique punishment for me—once I was able to walk after my beating from Morganna's hands and feet. I was in charge of finding Winsome. Then he cancelled all vacations until Winsome was located and he'd made sure that everyone in the office knew they were suffering through a hot vacationless New York summer because of me.

Normally, in the offices of Templar-Mason running an investigation was virtually a promotion. But not this time. On one hand, no company resource was to be spared to find him. That was the positive side.

The other hand… the less than fun side, was that I was not to leave the office—except for sleep, and I wasn't supposed to have a whole lot of that. The one exception being, I could go anywhere in the world that I thought Winsome might be. Immediately. But—the bastard I worked for had told our expense department that I was allowed to spend no more than one hundred dollars a night on a hotel. Period. Even in Boston. I'd had to stay in a motel in Southie to keep within the hundred-dollar limit. And commute by bus and The T! I still shuddered at the memory. Granted, I could have paid for a room in the city out of my own salary, but then how could I pay for my new Prada silver eel skin clutch?

For about the hundredth time, I contemplated giving my notice, damn the consequences. And for the hundredth time I realized that Templar-Mason was the only place in the entire world I could work. You tell me; where else can a clothes addicted, adrenaline junky witch find a six figure job? Especially since Templar-Mason is one of the few places on earth where people actually believe in magic. Getting a job as a non-magic using programmer is not on my agenda. I'm not in love with computers. And I don't get an adrenaline high from debugging a normal program. Where's the danger in that?

It was lunchtime and I'd snuck onto the internet to check the gossip and fashion pages. It had taken a tricky piece of programming to get around the lockout features that the boss had put on my sign-in to get onto the web page. But it was worth the work. I mean, how can a girl be a fashionista if she can't keep up with the latest styles? I was just staring at a picture of the immortal actress Georgette Blanche when the Prof said from over my shoulder, "I don't think you're going to find Winsome in *Hello!* Magazine."

Damn it. How did he catch me? I thought I'd gotten around the monitor on my computer. "Even slaves get a lunch break." I pointed to a plate of unflavored, previously canned tuna. "I didn't even waste time getting something edible."

"I should hope not," was my boss' curt response. There was no sparkle of warmth in his eyes as he added, "And I'm still curious. Is Winsome in *Hello!* because otherwise, you're wasting company time."

I shook my head slowly while playing for enough of a pause to come up with an answer, "No…"

"Then get the hell back to work," Prof said turning to leave my office.

"Do Hollywood stars look older to you?" I asked as he was half out the door.

"Stop wasting my time," the boss ordered me again, completely annoyed.

"No Prof, wait." I needed to redeem myself in his eyes. I was tired of the punished child treatment. "Shouldn't they start looking older?"

Prof turned around and sat on my couch. "Explain."

"Well." I said slowly, formulating in words a thought that had been lurking in the back of my mind for at least a week, "We put Gingerbread Health and Beauty out of business four months ago." Four long, non-shopping, crappy motel staying months ago. "Since they only sold to A-listers, and that by direct sale, some of the customers should either have run out of product or be on the verge of running out."

"Your problem is that they still look, according to the magazines, as good as ever?"

I nodded my head. "Not for nothing, but I buy lots of moisturizers, skin crèmes, and body buffers and I rarely stock up. I can't imagine all the A-listers have a year's worth of beauty supplies in their bathrooms. A few of the stars sure, but not all of them… if for no other reason, then at a hundred and fifty grand an ounce, they'd be afraid of the maid stealing some."

"Are you trying to tell me that you think Winsome is out there operating his beauty product line?" the boss asked sharply.

In response I gestured to the web page I was looking at, "Georgette Blanche has to be at least fifty. Tell me she looks a day over twenty-five."

He nodded his head slowly and there was a note of almost approval in his voice, "No—I have to agree with you. She looks like a child." I could see him comparing the photo to me. "You look older," he told me with brutal candor.

"I haven't been keeping up on my beauty routine as much lately," I snapped back. "What with the indentured servitude I apparently signed up for." I couldn't help it. My thirty-first birthday was three weeks earlier, and I'd planned my annual spa weekend, but the boss had canceled that too. You'd think seven days a week for four months would have earned me one lousy weekend off… but no. And don't think being told that a woman over twenty years older than me looked younger felt good. Then I got my mind back on business. "*OK!* Magazine had a story about two weeks ago calling fifty the new twenty. Trust me; there are plenty of stars that look this good. And none of them are showing up on the Fashion Police stories as looking older." I clicked a couple of times and up came a photo of Ivory Blanche from the Daily Mirror, "If you didn't know that Ivory was Georgette's child would you think that they could possibly be mother and daughter?"

Prof looked at the two of them. "No," he slowly replied. "Outside of both of them being unbelievably lovely, I wouldn't think they were related at all."

"But age wise?" I pushed.

"Sisters," he pronounced definitively. "Actually, I'm not sure that I'd even guess that Georgette was the elder."

I shook my head in return. "And she's the widow of a studio head, was named the Most Beautiful Woman in the World numerous times, appears on every best dressed list for the last twenty years, designed a clothing line, a perfume is named after her and she has more money than God. Meanwhile, Ivory…"

"Is the heir to the throne," the boss said wryly. "And if I'm not mistaken is considered the 'freshest face' in Hollywood. The new 'it' girl if I'm not mistaken. What they call a triple threat. Acts, writes, and directs."

"I'm impressed," I smiled. "I had no idea you were so interested in Hollywood." Then, for the sake of accuracy, and not—okay, maybe a little to needle him—I added, "By the way, a triple threat is singing, acting and writing. Directing isn't on the list."

"I stand corrected." Prof was deadly serious as he went back to my original comment, "If that's where the Fables are going to find fertile breeding grounds this generation, then Hollywood is my new obsession."

I nodded my head, with nothing left to say. There was a wry smile on the Prof's face as he changed the topic. "Your techno-magic skills are getting better if you managed to spend any time on *OK!* Or *Hello!* without me knowing."

I smirked. "I could say that I was looking for a sign of Winsome…"

"But in reality, you were checking out the Hollywood elite." I wasn't forgiven, but apparently my latest discovery had raised me up from being lower than dirt to possibility being equal to dirt.

"Checking out the latest in fashion," I corrected the boss. "The A-list is only a bonus."

The Prof stood up, rubbed his oversized belly in its "Work is That Annoying Time Between Fishing Trips" tee shirt, yawned and rambled towards the door. "I guess you have the lead you've been working towards. Maybe you'll get a weekend off sometime this year." He turned and looked sternly at me. "But not before you find Winsome."

I shook my head, half in dismay, half in amusement. As much as the Prof frequently gave off the deliberate impression of being an American redneck—with an occasional Austrian accent—he was a man more than willing to sacrifice anyone or anything in order to contain the misuse of magic. I waited until he was out of the door before I whispered, "I guess that means I can scan the gossip pages." It's always better to ask forgiveness than permission. But this way I'd theoretically done both. Wouldn't you know, he'd actually heard me, "Only in the line of duty," I was told. "If I catch you ordering even one designer suit on company time, I'll…" the Professor made a choking motion with his hand.

"Ja vole Mine Commandant," I snapped to attention. As he walked out the door, I collapsed against the desk with a sigh. I'd gotten away checking out my beloved web pages, but if anything, my scope of work had gotten larger, not smaller.

Figuring it was safe; I reset my "Alerts" to let me know about any major happenings in the world of fame and fashion. Then I got back to work.

I was on the phone for the hundredth time with Heidi Wade hoping that someone—anyone she knew had been able to come up with a lead on Gingerbread beauty care products. But she was coming up empty with the usual sources: personal trainers, gyms, high profile stylists, beauty consultants and "it" girls. Even Rafael was getting the run around and he technically owned the place. Or would in two years. Although he was in a protected location and was only permitted to inquire over the phone for his own protection. Either Gingerbread had gone out of business or all of their clients had been told that the Wades, their future CEO and/or Templar-Mason was person non-grata. I was betting on the latter.

My head was down on the desk and my hand had made my hair a tangled mess. "Any ideas at all," I begged the girl to have a brainstorm I hadn't come up with. After all—she was A-list all the way. I was just a want-to-be.

"Oh my Gawd," the girl screamed.

I held my Coach encased phone away from my ear and banged my head a few times in hopes of getting my hearing back. It didn't work particularly well, but the pain reenergized me. At least a little bit.

"What?" I tried to put some enthusiasm in my voice.

"Ivory Blanche is in the hospital," the girl gasped at me.

"What! What happened," I gasped back.

"No! No friggin way!"

I checked my alerts but as usual, the damn internet wasn't as fast as television coverage. What seemed like hours later, but was probably no more than a minute Heidi finally said, "You'll never believe this."

"Try me."

"Ivory Blanche was getting extensions when she had this horrific allergy attack. Hives in the back of her throat and asthma. They hit her with an Epi-pen but it did nothing."

"What do you mean it did nothing?" Epi-pens are pretty darn good at stopping most allergy attacks. "Does…"

"Well she's being listed as being in critical condition," Heidi interrupted me.

"Sounds like medical treatment isn't working," I agreed. I sent an all office E-mail asking anyone who had a radio or television to let me know what was happening with Ivory Blanche. "Does she have a history of serious allergies?" I couldn't remember hearing anything about allergies or asthma in the tabloids, and I kind of thought that I would have known something. The press loves to tell stories about how the perfect people are "flawed."

The first response, from one of the numerous people whose vacation got canceled, was an unprintable E-mail that suggested that I stick my head someplace very dark and smelly.

A moment later Prof came charging into my office. "What in God's name is going on," he asked his eyes wild.

I put my hand over the phone, "An allergy attack hospitalized Ivory Blanche." Prof looked like he was about to explode and possibly fire me when I added significantly, "At her hair dresser's. While she was getting extensions. Which requires combs being stuck into her head."

The Prof dropped heavily onto the leather sofa in my office, his face pale as death. "Snow White?"

"Or a repeat of Rapunzel. Then there is that fable where the girl's hair grows unchecked. It might have something to do with that. Or it could mean absolutely nothing at all."

The internet had finally caught up with the television and I was able to keep myself updated on the story so I politely got Heidi off the phone. "We have no proof that a Fable is involved," I told the Prof as soon as I was free.

"We have no proof that there isn't one," he replied sharply. "A healthy young star suffers a near fatal allergy attack while getting hair extensions. The tabloids couldn't come up with that story."

After all the Elvis love child stories, I thought it was very possible that the tabloids could indeed come up with a story like that. I probably wasn't the best candidate to be the voice of reason for Templar-Mason since I was pacing frantically around the room. But I have to say I tried. "We don't even know that her allergy attack was hair related. For all we know, she ate peanuts or something at a restaurant before getting her hair done."

Prof threw me a dirty look. "How about we make a bet. I'll

approve the Kate Spade boots you keep trying to expense if the allergy attack has nothing to do with a Fable." I thought it was justified. My rose pumps were destroyed in the Tennessee affair and my contract did allow for replacements. Prof disagreed.

"And if I lose?" Dreams of the hand-stitched footwear were dancing like sugarplums in my head.

"You owe me one."

I shook my head slowly. "I need a real stake." Especially cause I'm going to lose. I didn't say the words, but I thought it… really loudly. I should have been smart enough to reject the bet completely, but the feel of buttery leather flashed into my brain short circuiting my reason.

Prof smiled evilly. "You wear knock-offs for a month. Shoes, bags, suits, jeans, everything. Even underwear."

I thought about the La Perla bra and panty set I was wearing. Pure silk, hand cut and stitched, embroidered butterflies in say… strategic places, and pure decadence. Involuntarily I whimpered.

"So you're not willing to take the bet! You do think it's a Fable."

"I do think it's a Fable," I admitted. I was about to say, no bet, when out of my mouth came the words, "But I'm going to take it anyway." I whimpered again, knowing that I was going to hate the feel of spandex stretch jeans. But at seven hundred dollars a pair for soft buttery primrose leather, I was going to gamble. Besides, I didn't want it to be a Fable. If it was a Fable, Winsome had probably summoned it somehow and I was responsible. Well, not completely responsible—God knows that Winsome was responsible, but stopping him was my job. So I was really hoping that it wasn't a Fable.

"Since we both think it's probably a Fable, we'll start from there," Prof announced. As he was heading to his office to grab the "Bible", the first edition Grimm's Fairy Tales, he turned and smiled at me with a truly evil grin. "I can't wait to go shopping with you. I think Payless will be our first stop. Then maybe one of those club bulk stores." I shuddered and his smile grew wider.

Slowly I walked over to my desk and out of a locked drawer took the autographed copy of Anderson's Fairy Tales. My great-great-great grandfather had signed it some hundred and fifty years ago and sent it to my great-great grandmother at Templar-Mason for her personal use; which is why I had the book instead of one of the senior partners. I had to learn Danish to read it, and it was well worth the effort. Great-great-great grandfather Hans had dealt with more Fables than any other investigator. True the Grimms had a higher count, but that was between the two of them. Hans worked solo. Sometimes, in the stories, he told it was like he was talking to me—telling me how to handle the world gone mad.

Prof walked back in with the book. "I'll send an e-mail to Morganna. I want every story with fatal hair, combs, hair care, etc. analyzed and a list of possible Fables that could be involved in the Ivory incident."

I nodded but my attention was distracted by the 64 inch LCD television that was being rolled into my office. I threw a quizzical look at my boss while the technicians hooked it up. "Couldn't find anything larger? Maybe in one of the conference rooms?"

The Prof ignored my jibe completely. "Alison…" Prof's secretary, "…is monitoring the television for updates on Ivory's condition, but I thought that we should have access to anything important."

It was only a few minutes later that a breaking news bulletin came across the screen, Georgette Blanche to speak on her daughter's critical illness.

"That was fast," my boss commented.

Fables love to act through mothers, step-mothers, and eldest or youngest children. So we're far more skeptical when a mother is involved than a father. Both the Prof and I viewed the press conference with a cynical eye. Georgette Blanche approached the podium, directly in front of the Santa Clara hospital in LA, immaculately turned out in a black vintage Dior suit that looked, at least to me, a little too funereal for my taste. It was a beautiful outfit, but with her daughter in critical condition, it seemed a little tacky. A camel or gray suit would have been equally flattering and considerably more hopeful. A thought occurred to me just before Georgette started talking,

"Shouldn't a doctor be doing this conference?" asked Prof.

"And miss the opportunity to perform before her beloved public? Get real!"

"I am devastated to announce that my only daughter, Ivory Blanche is in critical condition after an allergy attack that occurred while she was having hair extensions put in for her role as Briar Rose in Sleeping Beauty." That was her name when the Grimms fought the Sleeping Beauty Fable. The original, at least as far as T-M knows, was Talia. Our agent Giambattista Basile fought it almost two centuries earlier than the Grimms. "It appears that her head was accidentally penetrated with a comb that was saturated in Crotein Q; an ingredient used to create soft, shapely hair."

I was at my desk surfing the web as fast as Georgette could speak. "She's right on that one Boss. Crotein Q is found in plenty of hair care products." He stared at the screen unmoving as if willing Georgette to give us the information we needed to cure Ivory. Or maybe he was fighting to see if there was a Fable surrounding Georgette. No modern technology had ever managed to capture one, but we all hoped.

Georgette paused to wipe away a tear that trickled perfectly down her cheek, "Unknown to us Ivory has a rare allergy to Protein Hydrolystales of which Crotein Q is one. Enough of it seems to have been absorbed by Ivory's blood that she isn't reacting to treatment and is at this time in intensive care." More tears spilled and were seemingly ignored by the beautiful actress speaking. "I'm asking for your prayers on this painful day. She's in God's hands now."

Reporters called out questions, which Georgette ignored. My mind was spinning; did Georgette just say that her daughter was not expected to recover?

"Sleeping Beauty," Prof questioned. "It can't be that easy, can it ?"

I shook my head. "There's nothing easy about Sleeping Beauty. The princess sleeps for a hundred years, sometimes taking her entire kingdom with her, while waiting for her prince to be born. In the meantime, the witch rules the land unchecked for a hundred years." The more famous the fable, the more damage it can cause. The War of Aragon was caused by the untimely death of Joan of England. Give me an obscure Russian Fable about a fox learning to fly anytime. The obscure tales do a lot less damage.

Prof shook his head. "No, I mean the fact that she's acting in Sleeping Beauty. Too much of a give away isn't it?"

"I'd say the fact that the girl was injured by something hair related is what eliminates Sleeping Beauty." I had the T-M Fable database open on my computer, along with versions of the story called, Briar Rose, Thorn Rose, The Sun, The Moon and Talia and The Glass Coffin. In all those versions the thing that puts the princess into a 'sleeping death' is spinning related… a piece of flax or the need of a spinning wheel. I just didn't see the connection.

The boss leaned over my shoulder and started a search on my computer. Moments later there were hits on hair weaving, hair spinning, extensions, synthetic hair, yak hair and hair blending. "Want to double our bet that one of those pages tells you how to use a spinning wheel to make fake hair?"

Two months in knockoffs. I might kill myself. Besides, the last article on the first page was entitled, Spinning hair for softness. "No bet." I sighed and added, "And Sleeping Beauty is an option." Then I shook my head and said, "Maybe we'd better figure out how to cure the girl and figure out what we're fighting later."

Prof smiled evilly. "You figure out what's needed to get Ivory up and acting again. I'll work on getting us access." The door slammed behind him and I sunk my head in my hands. How the hell was I going to create a spell that was able to combat an unidentified Fable that attacked in an unknown way? Hours of research later I had one solution; a solution that the woman in me recoiled at. Still needs must when the devil drives and all that.

Eighteen hours later I was in Los Angles wearing blue scrubs, a medical badge that declared my name to be "Jillian Anderson, Respiratory Physician and Allergist," with an affiliation to the Royal College of Medicine, London, England. It's harder to check foreign credentials and T-M has offices around the world. By the time any checks can be run, the credentials would be real enough to work. Apparently, I was a leading allergy specialist and professor with several world-class papers to my name. Temple Mason's staff must have worked overtime on that one.

Prof had found an in on the case through Happily Ever After, the production studio making the film. Ivory was worth a lot of money alive to them. Dead the movie was a goner and they had contractual rights over her medical care. Since "Ms. Georgette" wanted her daughter cared for by a private team of doctors that she was going to hire—hoorah for contract law. There was even a loophole in California law for visiting consulting doctors who weren't licensed.

I had no idea if we were getting paid for the job. If a Fable was loose, Prof wouldn't care. If a Fable wasn't loose… well, Templar-Mason is a huge company with a lot of overhead. Someone had to pay for the upkeep. To be honest I didn't care. I was close to Hollywood, Beverly Hills, Rodeo Drive and best yet—Prof was on the other side of the country. Even he didn't have the minions to keep me away from shopping that far away from him.

People were chattering at me as I walked purposefully down the hallway, medical bag clutched in one hand. Inside, the potion I'd conjured up for the job was just a placebo. I was placing my money and Prof's faith in me on one and only one thing—a razor I'd charmed to dispel magic. If a Fable was in play, the contamination was still somewhere on Ivory's head. I'd bet my life on it.

More to the point, I was betting her life on it.

I got into the room, scrubbed up, pulled on the mandatory latex gloves and took at look at my "patient." Unconscious, in a coma, and with a ventilator over her mouth Ivory Blanche was still unbelievably beautiful. Her black hair, spread across the white pillowcase, seemed almost to shine from within. It seemed a crime to pick up a scissor and take the first snip.

"What are you doing?" a scandalized voice asked.

"Cutting her hair," I avoided looking anyway except at the girl lying in the bed.

"But…" and "Her hair is priceless…" and "What the hell," made me realize that the room had as many movie people in it as it did medical staff. At least I hoped so. Because Hollywood was totally and completely screwed up if it was the medical staff upset at me cutting Ivory's hair.

Once I had her hair down to barely more than a crew cut, out came the placebo potion and a razor enchanted with a dispel magic charm. There was magic flickering around her—but no sign of a Fable. As I lathered up her hair and took a swipe, reveal her naked skull, I have to confess I was relieved… and just a touch disappointed. The adrenaline junkie in me had expected a harder battle. As I took the last swipe Ivory coughed into the breathing apparatus and muttered something that could have been, "Where am I?"

I was knocked out of the way as a team of experts went over to help the recovering "movie princess." Help included everything from removing the breathing tube to someone tenderly rubbing Ivory's hand and reassuring her that she'd grow back her hair in "no time" and that the studio would get Ivory the best wigs that money could buy. I think I even heard someone recommending that she endorse a wig designer during her recovery. My help was clearly not needed—so I left.

It was with a happy grin that I sent the following email over my phone:

To: TheProfessor
From: FashionMagic

Our Sleeping Beauty is asleep no more. The empress has no hair. Only a shimmer of magic in the air.

Please approve expense report for Kate Spade boots as promised. Returning on an 8:00 am flight out of LAX. See you tomorrow.

I grinned. Winsome was still out and about, but if Ivory wasn't a fable victim then I was free for about fifteen hours in LaLa Land and unless Prof was lurking about on set I had a date with Rodeo Drive. In addition to some quality shopping, I might even be able to schedule a facial or a body wrap. I'd sleep on the plane and refreshed, replenished and re-wardrobed I'd be ready to fight the forces of evil.

My plan didn't go as anticipated. I'd changed and was just pulling a cashmere trench over my sundress when my blasted mobile email beeped.

To: FashionMagic
From: TheProfessor

Morganna hacked GB's account. See attached. Get your butt out of the stores, girl and back to work. Prof

To: FairestOne
From: MagicMirror

Your order has been approved and your credit card has been billed. The below listed products will be shipped in the next twenty-four hours. We have added, as a special gift, sample hair extensions from our new product line—at no additional cost. A survey is attached. Please tell us what you think about these new, real hair products.

If you have any questions about your order, please contact customer service at 800-555-1234.

Thank you and have a nice day.

I scanned down the list and noticed that the customer service notice had come out a mere two days before Ivory's mystery allergy attack. But that wasn't the cause of the "damn it, damn it, damn it" that I was muttering as I called the Prof. "It's Snow White," I snarled as soon as he answered the phone.

"Explain," he barked.

"You tell me what other fable, fairytale, epic poem or nursery rhyme has a princess, a magic mirror and hair care problems?"

"None," he snarled. "Exactly none."

"That's what I thought," I snapped back. We were both losing it, and I knew why. Snow White was one of the most powerful fables in history and the amount of havoc it could wreck was almost unfathomable. The Prof had faced it once, and I'm sure that he had never thought that he'd be responsible for defeating Snow White again.

The only Fable that was stronger, to my knowledge, was Cinderella—and that one hadn't been released in hundreds of years. Snow White had caused World War I. The world was nuclear now—I didn't want to see what could happen if we didn't get this Fable bottled up—fast. And I knew I wasn't alone in that concern.

"What's my in?" I asked. "I mean there isn't any reason for Jillian Anderson, allergist, to hang out on the set and watch Miss Blanche, is there?"

"Give me an hour," the boss said. "I'll work something out with the studio people."

He was about to hang up when I said, "Oh damn."

"What now?" Fear and aggravation fought in his voice for dominance.

"I'm going to have to wear Payless for a month," I bitched.

Prof laughed. He laughed so hard that I didn't have to be in the room with him to see the tears trickle down his chubby cheeks, or his hands held over his belly. It wasn't all at me—I'd managed to release a summer's worth of tension in one unwitting statement. "Girl, I'm going to go with you shopping for all of your off brand clothing. I think I'll have you wear polyester granny underwear." He hung up.

With that, I threw up a little in my mouth. I knew exactly what he was talking about—the kind that left elastic band imprints in the flesh and came in cheap trashy colors. The gods must hate me. Why, oh why, had I made that bet?

I was tempted to pop out and find a place to get a manicure, but research was more important so I made myself comfortable in the cafeteria and sipped distastefully at a cup of coffee. Hospital cafeteria food was as bad as advertised. In a city famous for good nutrition and coffee, I couldn't begin to understand why no one in the kitchen thought of cleaning the coffee machine. I run vinegar through my machine weekly.

First, I ran the search under every parameter I could find. I was right. There was absolutely no other fairytale, fable or nursery rhyme that this could possibly be but Snow White. Of course, there was the faint, highly unlikely possibility that I wasn't in a fable at all—but I knew that fate wasn't that kind. Gingerbread Industries, magic mirror, a movie princess, hair care problems… it all added up. To be honest, the only thing I hadn't tripped over was the dwarves, and I had no doubt they'd appear shortly.

Secondly, I called the customer service number that was

listed in the email. The number "wasn't accepting calls at this time." At least not from me. If I had a chance to steal Georgette's phone I was going to. A good techno-mage could cast a spell that tied one phone to a number. Dialing Gingerbread's number from Georgette's phone could yield vastly different results.

I ran every search I could—As far as I, and all of Templar-Mason could tell, Gingerbread Industries no longer was doing business after I blew up their Tennessee factory. So, I asked myself, how could a business that catered only to the elite have no phone number and no address, and yet be capable of shipping millions of dollars worth of product? Where did they store it? How was it manufactured? How did I get some? I hadn't come up with an answer when, fifty-seven minutes after my initial conversation with Prof, a bald man—maybe fifty or so—dressed in tweed walked up to me. "Dr. Anderson?"

"Yes?" I answered cautiously.

"Can I speak to you for a minute?"

"Yes."

"A friend of yours told me that you've got an interest in film making."

This has to be something that Prof set up so I went along with it. "I've always been fascinated by Hollywood," I said fairly truthfully. My fascination is with Hollywood fashion, but I figured that wasn't relevant to the conversation.

"He said that you were working on a script for a new medical drama and needed to know more about how life on a set works."

"Absolutely," I lied.

"Well, Dr. Anderson—I have a proposition for you. Quite frankly, Miss Blanche's health is of utmost concern to the executive management of Happily Ever After. I don't understand exactly what it is that you did to bring her out of the coma," he paused as though hoping I was going to enlighten him. Instead, I gave him a serious look and nodded my head as though I was fascinated by what he said. "The prognosis for Miss Blanche's recovery was very grave."

This time I said, "I know."

"We don't want any relapses and so the board is prepared to offer you a position as a personal physician to Miss Ivory Blanche for the duration of the filming of Sleeping Beauty. The pay is one hundred thousand dollars a month and we expect to film for another eight weeks."

I was in so much shock I couldn't say anything. Doctors in LA got a hundred thousand a month to hang out on movie sets with the beautiful people? Damn—I was going to study medicine as soon as I got back to New York. Do you know how many shoes I could buy for a hundred thousand dollars a month!

Maybe it was because I hadn't said anything, but he cracked and seemed almost human instead of a careful businessman for a moment, "I know it's an imposition to ask you to leave your practice, but Ivory's health means a lot to not just us, but to a lot of people. And you would learn a lot about how movies are made. I'd make sure that one of the producers spent a lot of time with you."

I kept my fingers crossed that my cover identity was good enough that I wasn't going to wind up in jail for impersonating a doctor as I said, "It is an imposition, but I think I could probably make arrangements with one of my colleagues to cover my practice while I am gone. I need to make a few phone calls, Mr.?"

"Antone Steward," he said holding out his hand and my jaw almost dropped again. He was one of the most famous producers in Hollywood. Prof was definitely pulling out all the stops on this one.

He ushered me into a private office at the hospital, then to the desk and walked away—closing the door behind him. As soon as I was sure I was alone I called Prof again, "Two hundred thousand dollars?"

"Our fee," he said coolly.

. "Two hundred thousand dollars for eight weeks of my time. You are so paying for those Kate Spade boots," I muttered

"I beg your pardon," Prof's cool tone told me he didn't appreciate my shoe obsession at this moment in time.

I changed the topic, "You do realize that I know next to nothing about conventional medicine. I'm a witch—not a doctor. Not even a witch doctor. I know only a little bit more about healing magics than the cyber kind."

"So fake it," he ordered dismissively. "You shouldn't need to do much doctoring on the set anyway."

I half-heartedly argued for another minute or two, but I really couldn't put any energy into it. He was right—we needed to contain the Fable and if this was my "in" on the set, then so be it.

Before he hung up Prof said, "And Jillian. Don't fail me again."

Hollywood doctors don't just make a lot of money—they also live pretty darn good. The studio put me up in a 1500 square foot, two bedroom suite filled with silk, tapestry, crystals and down comforters covered in five thousand thread count sheets—at the same hotel that Ivory was staying in for the duration of the filming. I have no idea why—we were in LA and Ivory famously shared a two hundred acre estate with her mother in Malibu directly on the water. Still, I was beyond grateful that Ivory was staying in the hotel. If Georgette was the wicked queen, distance away from her mother was a must. The more access Georgette had, the more likely Ivory would die. Plus—after Prof's budget hotels—this was luxury I could appreciate.

I snuggled into a sinfully comfortable bed and opened up my laptop. We presumably had a queen, a talking mirror that would egg the queen on to kill Ivory, our princess. I needed to find the dwarves, the huntsman and the prince—before the next attack. At least I knew what the next attack was—somehow or another, Georgette would give Ivory an article of clothing that would asphyxiate her.

To: TheProfessor
From: FashionMagic

Prof:

Please ensure constant monitoring of the Fairest One's email, web pages, twitter accounts and all other means of communication. At some point, the magic mirror will provide her with an article of clothing for Ivory. I need to know the moment this happens.

Me.

The next day at "work" I was shown into the first aid trailer—a first aid trailer that was equipped better than my doctor's office. So well, in fact, that I hoped they either used the equipment from movie to movie, or donated it to free clinics in need of help. I had hope for the fact that this set did, in fact, donate the movie equipment since there was a donation box for the Salvation Army along with a personal appeal letter from Ivory at the entrance to each trailer. Curious I glanced into the box. It was half filled with canned goods. I did get a good chuckle to myself when I realized that there was at least a case of caviar in the box. I wondered what the hungry would do with fish eggs; I doubted toast points and Crème Fraiche were standard accompaniments at most food pantries.

"I'll leave you to get settled." Antone Steward had shown me to the trailer personally—something that surprised me. "Try to keep Ivory healthy." He hesitated for a moment and then said, "I've known Ivory her whole life. Her father was one of my best friends. It almost killed me when we thought she wasn't going to make it." He wiped his hand across his eyes and suddenly looked ten years older. "I don't want to lose her."

I answered the pain that was in his eyes the only way I knew how, "I'll try my best," I vowed.

It was a good thing that I started work on the set on a Friday and that Ivory wasn't due on set until Monday since what I knew about medicine was about the same as any college educated girl who didn't major in biology or chemistry and got her anatomy training the old fashioned way—from boys, not books. Which is to say I knew next to nothing about treating the injured or ill.

Thank goodness for the internet. Or so I thought. After spending two hours on medical websites I decided that I'd never pass as a doctor. I mean what the heck is a bronchiole and what's the difference between that and an alveoli and more importantly, why would I care? I mean does a doctor really sit there and say, "Yep—that sounds like your bronchiole are congested… take this pill for two weeks and if the infection hasn't cleared up…" Actually, come to think of it—that might be what my doctor said when I had bronchitis. Damn.

I was proactively mixing up a potion to heal an infection—essentially penicillin done the magical way since I wasn't allowed to prescribe in the United States or anywhere else for that matter—when a female voice called out to me, "Hey Doc."

I jumped. The woman, misunderstanding my surprise said, "Take it easy, Doc. I didn't mean to scare you."

I made some noise that was somewhere between 'that's okay' and 'I'm fine.'

The woman continued, "Ivory just wanted you to look at the costume she's going to wear for today's shooting. After 'the incident' word is, you're to inspect everything she's exposed to."

It was being called Doc that had me jumping out of my skin—not surprise because for the first time in two days someone actually walked into the trailer. It's not every day that a woman realizes she's been cast as a dwarf in a fairy tale after all. I should have expected it, and the same role as Prof had, but still…

The woman introduced herself. Her name was Nina and she was the costume supervisor for the production. She held out a hat and veil combination while wearing the greatest distressed jeans in the history of jeans. I was temporarily distracted from what she was saying by the way the holes in the jeans formed a teeny tiny Statue of Liberty. Wow—now that was art. "If you could just take a look at this hat first since I need to see if it fits over Ivory's wig, and then I'll show you to the costumes."

I took the truncated cone hat into my hands and forced magic into it. I probably looked weird standing stock-still and concentrating on said costume piece, but I'd accomplished what I had to. The hat was free of anyone else's spell. "It is fine," I said pretending to examine the construction of the hat.

That accomplished, I followed Nina silently into a fantasy world of costumes, jewelry and designer gowns that I would kill for. Every color of the rainbow seemed to glitter on the racks— each encrusted with enough feathers, rhinestones, and beading to make any Hollywood starlet swoon. And each costume seemed, to my concerned eyes, specifically designed to kill Ivory. Each and every one had a corset built right into it—perfect for suffocating a hapless princess.

I went through the motions of inspecting the costumes, but I knew in my heart that I needed to use magic. I needed to ward the costumes. And in order to that, I needed to be alone.

So, late that night, I snuck back onto the set. Well—I'm not sure how much sneaking was involved in driving up to the studio set, showing my ID card, and being waved in, but since I was wearing my hand stitched witches robes handed down to me by my grandmother when she retired from the trade, a silver charm bracelet that was made up of real charms and had a medical bag stuffed full of dragon's blood reed harvested during a solar eclipse, I didn't want anyone to see me. I mean, how would I explain that to the mundanes? I had spent my down time at the office making the spells on the charms in the bracelet. Normally, I wouldn't have had the time to invest in making so many, but since Winsome got away, I had nothing but. And I decided I needed magic I could draw on at an instance's notice.

I went into the trailer, flicked on the lights and cast a protection circle around me and the workbench. I'd need to break it later in order to ward the costumes, but I had work to do—and as always a protection circle was the safest way to go.

I heard a noise from behind one of the costume racks. "Who's there," I called out. Two blue bolts of light came flying at me. "Shield!" I yelled. The two bolts bounced off of my circle and crashed into racks of clothing—scorching the costumes and filling the room with smoke and the smell of burning feathers. The silver charm I'd bought from Bloomingdales in the form of a shield disappeared into oblivion, but saved my hide.

In front of me crouched a small, hunched over, loathsome figure. "Winsome," I snarled. Damn it. I wasn't prepared for a wizard's duel. I didn't have a wand on me. I glanced at the door. No way was I getting out of the trailer before Winsome got me.

"Help," I screamed at the top of my lungs. Maybe if I was lucky a security guard would hear the uproar and interrupt us.

Winsome clapped his hands together and the trailer shook; boxes fell, racks of clothing fell to the ground and I thought the seams of the trailers might be buckling.

"Stabilize," The charm of California I'd made into an anti-earthquake charm disappeared.

"Arrow,' the fleet of crossbow bolts my one attack charm created were waved effortlessly away by Winsome. Damn it. This man had more power than I could imagine. More power than anyone I've ever seen—even Prof. I didn't know if it was because he raised the Fables—or if he'd been able to raise the Fables because of his power, but he was so out of my league it wasn't funny.

He clapped his hands together again and a lightning bolt came streaking at me. "Shield," I gasped out—forgetting I'd already used the one on my bracelet. I could hear Winsome laughing as electricity arched through my body. Pain arched from my hair to my toes as the world went black around me.

"Doc! Doc!" I could hear a young man's voice off in the distance. To my befuddled mind, he sounded frantic. "Doc! Wake up."

"Don't wanna," I tried to mutter. My voice was so dry it came out as a croak. I ached everywhere from my head to my toes. My magic was at an all time low. I didn't want to wake up. I wanted to die.

In the background, I could hear someone say, "Thank God. She's alive."

Alive. Of course, I was alive. No one dead could hurt as much as I did.

"Doc, please. Open your eyes. We can't get to you and you've been hurt."

I was later told that out that it took about fifteen minutes to wake me up, once they'd stumbled upon me. It was morning— I'd been unconscious for hours. I could understand why everyone, from the security guard who had found me, to the on set paramedics who tried to rescue me were frantic. They weren't equipped to deal with unconscious people lying in a circle that barricaded them from aid. To be fair, probably seventy percent of the people who were able to deal with that situation worked for Templar-Mason. Most of the rest were bad guys.

My protection circle had held—it was the only reason why I was alive. Not only that, but it had burnt itself into the floor of the trailer. Since it was still intact, no one could enter the circle until I dismissed it; including my would be rescuers.

I didn't have the power left to truly dismiss the circle, but it was mine and I could crawl across it. Once out, I collapsed and let the professionals help me. There were a million questions and I answered all of them, "I don't know" or "I don't remember." Mundanes are just not ready to hear about wizards duels in the middle of a costume trailer. Hades—neither are wizards… not even me. And I was the witch in the fight.

They bundled me into an ambulance. As I was being carried off on a gurney I saw Ivory lurking behind the trailer looking scared. Maybe I should have said something to her then—but really, what could I say?

I borrowed a cell phone and texted Prof letting him know that I was enroute to the hospital after an encounter with Winsome. My cell was fried. One of the hundred questions I didn't answer was how on earth my robes had survived completely unscathed when my skin, my shoes, my underwear, hair, cell phone and half my bracelet was burnt. I didn't say anything, but I promised myself a call to grandma sometime soon. She was one hell of a witch—and I owed her big time.

Prof waddled into the hospital room wearing a shirt that said, "Just Keeping it Reel."

His greeting was abrupt but his eyes were worried as he said, "I told you to shoot the bastard when you had a chance."

I glanced warningly at the door. One of the great joys of being in a hospital besides 180 thread count sheets and robes that expose everything you want to keep covered, was the complete lack of privacy. There wasn't a doctor, intern, or nurse who knew what the meaning of a closed door was.

Prof waved his hand and power filled the room in a way that made me envious. Prof had more power in his little finger than I did in my whole body. That was my theory on why a man who was at least one hundred and twenty looked fifty. Well, that and his staring role as the head dwarf the last time Snow White came around. The same role it had chosen me for this time around. Magic touches people in strange and mysterious ways. "We won't be disturbed," he said needlessly. "Now tell me what happened."

I told him about the dresses and my theory that a corset would be used to suffocate Ivory, my plan to ward the costumes and stumbling onto Winsome in the costume trailer.

"I told you to shoot the bastard," the boss said, clearly frustrated.

"I didn't have a gun on me," I shot back. "I was going to ward the costumes, not engage in a wizards duel at midnight."

Prof shook his head. "Have I taught you nothing?"

"Virtually," I muttered under my breath, but I wasn't being fair. He hadn't taught me nothing. He'd taught me everything.

He ignored my comment. "Always go armed. Always. You aren't powerful enough to go head to head with Winsome and keep coming out in one piece."

He was right. Bullets didn't play by magic's rules. Copper encased lead coming at a person at 340 meters per second had a way of leveling the playing field in a hurry. If Winsome had been packing, I'd likely be dead. Still, "Even if I'd been armed I doubt I'd have had a chance to get the gun in my hand—much less shoot—before he got the lightning bolt off at me. And I'd need something that shoots about a hundred rounds a minute to actually hit someone that fast." I didn't mention that the assault team Winsome had destroyed was armed. Prof knew it and wanted me armed anyway.

"We'll never know," Prof said. He didn't say it out loud, but I knew that when I got back to New York there would be a different kind of hell to pay. Best case Prof would find another four hours in the day for me to practice at the gun range. Worse case—I'd be working out every day with the security team… and those guys had a training regimen that was modeled on the Navy SEALS—and then made harder.

"I'm not armed now," I confessed, although why I felt bad about it I couldn't say. I mean, even if I'd had a gun, someone would have taken it from me during the admissions process.

He pressed two guns into my hand. The .22 caliber handgun I recognized. The two inch long gun with a key ring attachment had me raising my eyebrow. "It's a SwissMiniGun—the smallest gun in the world. It's fully loaded and, for its size, it packs one hell of a wallop. Best of all you can carry it anywhere since most people think it's a toy. Your carry permits are in place for both guns—so don't worry—you're legal."

I checked the safety and slid the .22 under the cover. I never would have told the Prof this, but I felt better with a weapon.

We talked strategy. Filming was shut down while the police investigated the incident. Prof had already spoken to the correct authorities and the whole thing was going to be passed off as an electrical incident.

Morganna was on the set running security until I returned and Prof promised me that work wasn't going to resume on the movie until I was up and running again. He could buy me a couple of days—and according to him—I wasn't going to need more than that.

As he started to leave I grabbed his arm, "Can you stay?"

He shook his head sadly, "No, lass."

"Please?" I hated to admit it, but I was scared. Winsome was too powerful, the stakes were too high and I wanted Prof leading the charge. I was happy to assist, bring up the rear or high tail it back to New York and take over his duties; but Prof was the best. We needed him fighting Winsome.

"The Fable has chosen you… Doc," he said trying to grin and failing miserably. "There's no room for me in this story. It would only give it the advantage."

"Six other dwarves," I tried. "Can't we cast you as one of the other dwarves?" I thought for a moment and then added, "Maybe grumpy?"

"Nay lassy, the cast for this go round of the Fable has already been set. Your dwarves are out there—you just need to put together the team. If I tried to barge in now I'd do more harm than good—I feel it in my bones." Uncharacteristically he leaned down and kissed my forehead. "Sleep now and don't worry. I'll hold down the fort until you're better." With that, he was gone and the normal hustle and bustle of the hospital resumed around me.

My next visitors were Nina, Ivory's personal bodyguard Kevin and the Prop Mistress Cara. I was in the process of saying things like "hi," and "I'm going to be fine," when Nina burst out with, "Good God! What do they have you wearing?"

"A hospital robe?"

She shuddered. "Whatever it is—it's got to go." In about ten second's time with no ceremony and less regard for my bruises, she bundled me into the bathroom and out of the robe, "Doc— what on earth were you thinking?"

I thought she was referring to my nighttime expedition in the trailer and started to answer when she cut me off, "We never, ever let anyone see us looking less than out best."

"The hospital's been poking and prodding me since early morning. I've only been in a room for about two hours," I protested.

She kicked the hospital robe into the corner with a look of distain and pulled out an exquisitely stitched silk, frothy negligee set, "And you should have called me five minutes before they put you in an ambulance," she scolded me. "You're one of us now."

It took me longer than it should have to ask who "one of us" and "who everyone else was." I was distracted by the nightgown that I was pulling on with no concern for my bruises. Shallow— yes that's me. I was busy saying, "Holy cow. This is gorgeous."

"Thank you," she said with simple pride. "I made it."

"You are one talented lady."

For one moment Nina preened, and then she whipped out her phone, "Michael—you need to get down to Mercy and bring the full kit. You've got work to do."

I looked a question at Nina. "Ivory can pull off pale and fragile without help. You just look a wreck," she told me not unkindly, but with brutal honesty. "Michael is Ivory's personal makeup artist. He's the best in the business and he'll have you looking fabulous in no time."

Nina was definitely a kindred soul. As she kept me locked in the bathroom we talked fashion, her dreams of someday having a runway show, and men. By the time I asked the question that was bothering me, I suspected I already knew the answer, "Nina, who is one of us?"

"Excuse me?" she seemed lost—which makes sense given the fact that we'd been discussing the fact that the latest runway collections seemed to have been inspired by street art—but I needed some information and I wanted to ask before we were interrupted.

"You said that I was 'one of us.' Who is 'us'?"

"Ivory's entourage. Well, let's see. It started with Cara, Bev and I—we were Ivory's Beauties."

I interrupted her, "Um—I've never met Ivory when she was awake."

"You saved her life. That gives you automatic admission." She waved away my concerns with a dismissive hand gesture. "Anyway, then Michael, Kevin and Jeff joined and we were the Sexy Six."

I was going to ask what would happen if Ivory decided she didn't like me, but Nina just kept on talking, "And now with you, I guess we're…"

"The Magnificent Seven," Michael said as he walked through the door. I had shivers—and not just because he was beautiful. I had shivers because Nina had just found me my dwarves. But for the record—Michael was GORGEOUS. With a capital everything.

And completely uninterested. I don't know of he even saw me as a woman. He looked me up and down, seeing everything from the chip in my pedicure to the burn spots in my hair. "Right so—are we going with fragile, sickly or what?"

"Heroic," Nina stated firmly. "Wounded but heroic."

"Right then, I'll stay away from purples and blues. I think I'll base in peach tones."

He spoke the whole time about the color choices he was making, the brushes he was using, crèmes verses powers, etc. By the time he was done, I was convinced I could recreate his work in my sleep. Meanwhile, Nina decided that I would look bravest with my hair in a French braid.

I was escorted to bed—looking fragile and heroic—and tenderly placed into a bed that had been changed to include a down mattress topper, Egyptian sheets and king sized pillows. Prof had one kind of magic, but celebrity definitely carried its own.

"Say Doc, what happened?" Cara asked.

"Yeah," asked Nina. "I've been dying to ask too. What the hell happened? The costume trailer looks like a freaking war zone. I don't even want to think about the repairs I've got to do." She threw her head back theatrically and asked in a tragic voice, "How could you let the green D&G get burned? How?"

I debated how much to tell them. I mean, even if we were five of the seven dwarves, were they ready for the truth?

I hesitated too long because Kevin stuck his chin out pugnaciously, "Don't even think about lying girlie." I looked a question at him, and he shrugged saying, "I can see it in your eyes."

"You're right," I admitted. "I just don't know how much of my story you'll believe."

"I'm a big Sherlock Holmes fan," Michael interjected with what I already knew to be a rare grin.

Kevin volunteered, "I served in the army and I've done the impossible. It just takes a little bit longer."

"And I like Alice in Wonderland," Cara added.

"It was Through the Looking Glass," Nina hissed at Cara.

"Was not."

"Was too."

While the two of them descended into she said, she said debate I very quietly asked Kevin to call Bev and Jeff. If I was going to confess to six impossible things before dinner—breakfast being long since past—I should have the rest of the dwarf pack there. I was mixing metaphors in my own head, but who cared?

It turned out that Bev was a tall, powerful black woman who

was Ivory's personal trainer and Jeff was Ivory's personal assistant, "Chief cook and bottle washer. If you need a hippo relocated to Kenya I'm your boy."

I blinked, "Is there a lot of need for the relocation of hippopotamuses to Kenya in Hollywood?" I just had to know.

"More than you know, Doc. More than you know."

"Right then, um-good to know?"

"So why are we here? What's going on?"

I had a feeling that Kevin would call me on any sugarcoating I did, so I gave it to them fairly bluntly, "I work for a security firm called Templar-Mason and I'm here to keep an eye on Ivory. She's under attack from a group called Gingerbread Industries. I fought a man called Winsome in the costume trailer last night. I think he was trying to alter one of Ivory's costumes so it could kill her. Any questions?"

"I cry foul," Bev said in an accent that would make the Queen jealous. "That trailer was not damaged by any ordinary fight. I've taught Royal Marines to fight in enclosed spaces, and I've never seen a place as destroyed as that one."

"If I didn't know better," Kevin added, "I'd say that there was an earthquake—but just in the trailer."

"You wouldn't be wrong," I muttered to myself.

"What did you say?"

"Nothing."

"She said that you would be correct in assuming an earthquake took place in the costume trailer," Beverly unhelpfully informed Kevin. "And I am absolutely certain that Doctor Jillian Anderson will be happy to tell you how an earthquake could be localized to just a 40 yard trailer any moment now."

Bitch—I thought to myself. But it wasn't true. I'd muttered the words that she used to force the truth. She was just scarily acute.

"Well, okay…" I said slowly. "But this is the part that's going to make you feel like you fell down the rabbit hole."

"See, I told you the quote was from Alice," Cara whispered

to Nina.

Nina theatrically smacked her hand with her head, "Alice was in 'Through' as well."

Kevin, Bev, Michael, Jeff and I ignored them.

"I'm a witch. Ivory is being attacked by a Sorcerer who has raised the magic behind the Snow White Fable to kill Ivory."

They broke into laughter and I shrugged, "See I told you that you wouldn't believe me." I had a flashlight charm on my bracelet and I took it out of the drawer next to me.

"Turn out the lights please." Michael obliged.

"You mean you're serious?'

"Yup. Light." At my command, a ball of light came out from the bracelet and hovered in front of me. I directed it to float around each of my fellow dwarves.

"She's serious."

"Off," I said and the light returned to my bracelet. I sank down exhausted from that little display.

We got past the "OMG!" the "How Cool is That!" and most typical for this group, "You don't dress like a witch," and got down to business after Nina offered to make me a witch's hat. I passed.

Two exhausting hours, six irate nurses and one doctor's visit later I'd told them everything. It only took another hour to hammer out a plan. Prof would get me out of the hospital. Nina and I would inspect and ward every costume in the trailer while Kevin stood guard. Bev would keep Georgette away from Ivory, Jeff would keep Ivory on the set and away from stores, mail and anything I couldn't ward or inspect. Michael would make sure that Ivory didn't touch a beauty product that wasn't part of Michael's already existing cosmetics kit. Basically Ivory wasn't going to be able to take a breath without one of us analyzing the air.

It was a good plan—but I knew deep in my heart it wasn't going to be that easy.

The next evening I sat drinking at a bar with Ivory and the other six dwarves and knew I was missing something. For starters—there were the "Magnificent Seven." Guys and gals alike they were, on the whole, perfectly normal twenty-somethings looking for love. Or a good time. Or, as the night got later, a hook up. The Professor had been surrounded by some of the top mages in Europe. I got Woo Woo girls. And guys.

Then there was Ivory. I looked out at her, dancing on top of the bar, wearing a skimpy little red dress worth more than a car and a blond wig, and shook my head. I could hear our one and only conversation in my head. "Oh My Gawd!" she cried looking into the mirror as her regular posse, which now apparently included me, sat around the trailer watching her get dressed. "Oh My Gawd!"

"What's wrong Ivory?"

"I can't go out!" Tears streamed down the young beauty's face. I wondered if I was the only one cynical enough to wonder whether I was watching a first class acting job.

"You have to," Jeff bluntly told her. "You promised to open AFIRE for Mitchell Andrews months ago. And you know that no one can open up a new club like you can."

"But, but, I have no hair!" Ivory bawled.

Kevin put his arm around the tearful actress, "You are so beautiful that no one will even notice." As she buried her face in his shoulder he stroked a slow hand down her bald scalp, nestling her closer. I wondered if everyone else knew that Kevin harbored a crush on our heroine.

Fifteen minutes later, everyone in the room except me had chimed in on why Ivory should go to the opening of AFIRE. Everyone told Ivory how beautiful she was, how special she was, and while the girl seemed to revel in the attention—it seemed like she was looking for something else. Finally, feeling awkward, but unsure what else to do I added to the conversation, "You could be an inspiration to others who've been sick. There are tons of kids with cancer who have lost their hair and they could use a role model."

I'm not sure what I expected, but a simple, "ick" certainly wasn't it.

So, sitting in the VIP room, at a club opening that should have been one of the highlights of my life; I sat and brooded. Ivory was most definitely the chosen one. The story had progressed to the point where I could see the dark haired princess shadowing Ivory. And unlike Raphael, it fit her perfectly. And yet if didn't make sense to me. The heroine should be brave and bold—not shallow and selfish. The Fable should be important. The Snow White Fable changes history—literally. It wasn't just WWI. Phillip the Second of Spain married Mary I of England instead of his mistress because of Snow White—and a reign of terror started that killed thousands in "Bloody" Mary's Name. For the life of me, I couldn't imagine Ivory's death causing anything except two weeks of incessant tabloid coverage.

Research time. Snuggled back under my blankets in the hotel room of my dreams, I was busy running Google searches. There were three million, eight hundred and fifty-three hits on Ivory, over six million hits on Georgette and a mere one hundred and eighty thousand hits on Ivory's father, businessman turned producer turned studio head Dartagnan Lopez.

Three days later, Prof, Morganna and I had no idea how many other people were still digging through information about the Blanche family. I'd found out the most deliciously amazing things; Apparently, Georgette 'worshipped' Marilyn Monroe as a teenager and rumor had it had dated a member of the SLA. Hanoi Jane had nothing on Georgette when it came to protesting the Vietnam War. In fact, not only did she protest the war—she went so far as to donate money to the North Vietnamese.

It was all disturbingly juicy stuff. For example—Marilyn had gotten sucked into the Camelot myth and look what it got her. And the SLA was a fake liberation front dealing in death, destruction, and dismemberment. It said volumes about the lady's character, and made it crystal clear why a Fable would find it easy to work through "Ms. Georgette." But still, in all, I didn't have anything tangible. Anything that would explain why Ivory was a chosen one.

I was still scanning through the millions of stories written about the Blanche family when Nina came running into my office—frantically screaming. "Oh My God! Come Quick. Ivory isn't breathing. Hurry!"

Shit. Attack number two must have come from a source that I wasn't expecting. Morganna hadn't gotten a hit on the email and my wards hadn't gone off with the costumes.

I grabbed the medic's bag stuffed with a handful of assorted potions I'd brewed up. Heaven alone knew what I was going to face this time.

Kevin was performing mouth-to-mouth resuscitation on Ivory where she'd collapsed, just outside of the makeup trailer. Bev, next to him, reported the facts quickly. "She isn't breathing but she's got a pulse. It's a little erratic, but…" An AED sat over to one side, unused and apparently unneeded to shock the heart.

The unconscious actress was wearing a pretty laced up sundress. I was damned if I knew how the lacing on that dress could be choking Ivory, but if the Fable held true, that's exactly what had happened. I took one second to look for the magic I was sure was holding Ivory in its grip and as I expected Ivory was cloaked from head to toe in a spell of a sickening green shade.

"Get me a pair of scissors," I yelled as I attempted to unfasten the dress that Ivory was wearing. The laces were knotted tightly and wouldn't open.

"Come on baby, breathe for me," Kevin begged as he took a breath.

"She can't," I told the man. "Her dress is suffocating her."

He ignored me, "Come on baby. You can do it," he took another breath and continued mouth to mouth.

Nina came running back to me with a big pair of sewing shears.

"Perfect," I dumped a dispel magic potion onto the scissors and cut into the dress. It was like trying to cut into molasses. Every time I had a piece of the fabric cut it seemed to reknit itself together, even with Nina and Cara trying to hold the fabric apart.

I poured a second potion directly on the dress—it started smoking and Ivory skin began burning under the force of the magic.

"You're hurting her," Kevin gasped out between breaths.

Sweat poured down my body as I fought the clothing, "If I don't get this dress off of her, she'll die."

"She'll die if you set her on fire," he yelled back at me.

"That's it," Bev exclaimed. "I have an idea." She ran off leaving Nina, Cara and I to futilely fight the cursed dress.

A long minute later she came back with really old theater curtains, "They're asbestos. I would bet anything it is bloody magic resistant." She slid it under it the loose part of Ivory's dress. "Pour some of that potion stuff on this part of the dress," she urged me. I did as she suggested and the dress literally burned up, while the curtains protected Ivory.

Slowly, piece by piece, we dissolved the dress—until there was nothing left for the spell to hold onto. Light flared around all of us—and then Ivory was breathing on her own again.

"What happened?" the Ivory asked, waking to find herself naked in Kevin's arms—with all of us bunched around her.

"An accident," Kevin told Ivory gently—holding her for one last lingering moment before wrapping her up in the curtain. "You almost got burned, but we protected you.

It was an explanation. Not a good one in my opinion, but I was exhausted, covered in sweat and hoping that somehow the day's activities were going to manage to stay out of the tabloids. I did have two questions, "The dress you were wearing, where'd you get it?"

"It was my mom's," Ivory told me, standing and somehow

tying the curtain around her in such a way to make it look like a designer toga.

"Georgette's?" I asked.

"Yeah. Why?" She glanced around wildly, "And where is it?"

Kevin jumped in to answer that one, shaking his head slightly at me, "It caught on fire, Ivory. That was the accident you were just in."

"How?" she asked. Then she looked down, still confused over her recent extreme wardrobe malfunction. "I don't seem to be burned."

He answered the second question. "Bev wrapped you in asbestos curtains and saved you."

"Asbestos curtains," she sounded as incredulous and asked the question I'd been dying to ask as well. "Where the hell did Bev find asbestos curtains?"

"Cara keeps everything," Bev said affectionately. "She's the original pack rat." Kevin helped Ivory to her feet, and then, keeping his arm around her, led her to her dressing room.

Meanwhile, as I knelt exhausted in the dirt, Bev whispered to me, "I thought they might be handy when you briefed us the other day. If bullets are magic retardant then I thought asbestos might be as well."

"You did?" I looked at her in amazement.

"Well, it's resistant to just about everything else," she said with a smile. As I continued to look at her in disbelief she shrugged. "I was born in Asbestos, Canada and Da wasn't relocated to London until I was five. With all the health issues associated with asbestos, believe you me, I found out everything I could about the product. Fire, water, sound, heat—asbestos is resistant to all of that. So why not magic? I decided to pull the curtains out and put them some place I could get to them if I needed them."

"Well, that was brilliant thinking," I told her. "And something I absolutely wouldn't have thought of. You saved Ivory's life."

"All part of a day's work," Bev said with a smile.

I disagreed, but kept it to myself—most personal trainers

didn't fight magic on a daily basis. But I didn't bother saying that, instead, I said, "We should talk later and see what other nuggets of brilliance are living in your head."

"How the devil did you manage to miss the personal wardrobe," Prof's voice thundered through the phone that evening as I was reporting in.

"I don't know," I confessed miserably. "I was so focused on the cosmetics and costumes that I didn't even think about her casual clothing."

"You've got to do better than that girl! Fables wreck mayhem and destruction on the unwary. You've got to cover all contingencies."

Prof ranted and I did absolutely nothing to defend myself. He was right on so many levels it wasn't funny. I'd screwed up— royally. Bev and Kevin had saved Ivory's life—not me. Everything I'd counted on: wards, emails, even Georgette coming to the set, hadn't happened. I'd failed and the world was damn lucky that Ivory was still alive.

Bottom line was that I had one more chance. Somehow—in the coming days—Ivory would be attacked by an apple. Either Winsome or I would win. Right at the moment, my money was on Winsome. He was a better mage then I'd ever be—and Apparently, he was smarter than me as well.

Prof's rant finally started winding down and I interrupted him, "Did you find out anything about Ivory's past? Anything that might tell us why Ivory is so important? I mean, honestly Prof, I haven't spent much time with her—but she isn't anything special—if anything she's kind of empty headed."

"Nothing tangible," he admitted. "But I've still got people searching. But don't worry about Ivory being dim—there's something there, I'm sure of it. There always is." The voice of experience didn't calm me this time.

"Damn it," I exploded. "I need to know. It's this huge missing piece of the puzzle and without it I feel like I'm fencing in the dark with Winsome. He wants Ivory for a reason."

"You'd be better off figuring out a way to stop the next attack," Prof told me coldly. "You won't need the reason if you can keep Ivory from being poisoned. Make a list and think about the non-fruit kind of apples. Things like iPods and ipads, appletinis and jewelry made in the form of an apple. That's where you need to put your effort now." With that, my boss hung up the phone.

I was in my hotel room, making a list of products that we were somehow going to have to keep away from Ivory when I heard a knock on my door. "Come," I said not looking up from the list, assuming that it was one of the Magnificent Seven. Instead, it was a stunningly beautiful woman wearing a maid's uniform. I blinked twice. Yup—Ivory Blanche was in my hotel room dressed as domestic help.

She saw my confusion and shrugged. "It is easier sneak around a hotel as 'Ivory the Maid' then 'Ivory the Movie Star.' Nobody really looks at the help." She made herself at home on the end of my bed and looked me up and down a couple of times. "Nina likes you. She said you're a kindred soul."

"If that means I'd kill for a Christian Dior ball gown and a place to wear it, she's probably right," I said jokingly.

"Would you?" Ivory was deadly serious.

"No," I answered her honestly. "Don't get me wrong—I love clothing, but certainly not enough to kill. Or hurt someone. Or steal." I realized that the litany of things I wouldn't do for a designer gown was too long to go into so instead, I added, "If I want the dress that badly—I'd just buy it."

There was darkness in Ivory's eyes as she said, "I know people who would do anything—literally anything—to go to an A-list event in a designer gown. They're all over Hollywood and they'd run me over with a car out for a chance to be a line in a story in the National Enquirer."

"Sounds like a lousy way to live," I commented.

"It can be," she agreed. "It's all I know. Sometimes I dream of living in a little house in the country, or going to college, or having a normal boyfriend my agent didn't vet for me…." She faded out. I must have passed Ivory's test because she let me see the intelligence she'd thus far kept hidden. "I haven't been having random allergies and accidents, have I?"

"No."

"The electric accident you were in—the one in the costume trailer—that was supposed to be targeted at me, wasn't it?"

"Sort of fifty/fifty you and me. I interrupted a scheme to kill you—but Winsome has a lot of reasons to hate me." Mainly the mystic napalm I'd bet though.

"Why don't we notify the police?"

I shook my head and smiled kind of wistfully. Police help would be great. "Even if I could convince the police that you were being subjected to random attacks they wouldn't be able to help."

"Because what's happening isn't normal." At my look of surprise, Ivory said, "Nina told me that the world had gotten weirder than I was used to. So will you tell me what's going on? Who is this Winsome person and why on earth would he want to kill me?"

"You'll find it impossible to believe."

"No, I won't," she said with a little smile. "Bev, Michael, Nina and the rest of the gang all vouched for you." I thought her smile got just a little sweeter when she added, "Even Kevin eventually told me to listen to you."

"Even Kevin?"

She sounded a little wistful when she said, "Kevin's more than a little bit over protective. If he thinks I'm even the slightest bit hurt he goes all big brother on me."

So much for Kevin's unspoken feelings, I thought to myself. His love was doomed if Ivory put him in the brother category.

So I told her. Everything. It took about an hour and at the end of the story, she seemed stricken. "Mom wants me dead?" she cried, "You can't be right. Mom's always been there for me. Always."

"Fables work through mothers," I told her carefully omitting the fact that they need fertile ground to start with. "Think of this like a form of possession. Georgette might do something under the influence of a Fable that she'd never willingly do otherwise."

"Like in the Exorcist." Ivory nodded in understanding.

I nodded and added urgently, "You've got avoid anything to do with apples." I handed her the list I'd been working on while saying, "You've got to stay away from your mom. And you've got to be very, very careful—at least until I can figure out what's going on. Okay?"

She nodded, albeit reluctantly. "Okay. But work fast." As she left the room I saw something that chilled me. For the first time I saw the dark queen like a huge shadow hovering behind Ivory. The fable was getting stronger. And time was running out.

I hated doing it. I really hated doing it. My luxury hotel room would never be the same. But I needed a workspace that was safe, secure and mine. I never felt home in the first aid trailer—there I felt like a fraud. The hotel room, on the other hand, was my idea of nirvana. Thus the decision to trash a 1500 square foot slice of heaven.

The dwarves—plus Snow White—showed up to help. Ivory seemed scared and spooked—but then again who could blame her? She was the knowing target of a murder plot after all. She pitched in and—as much as Kevin would let her—helped shove and carry everything into the bedroom. I couldn't help but notice that anytime something was too high or too heavy, Kevin was there to lend a hand. It was funny how he didn't seem to have the same concerns when I was standing on the back of the couch trying to remove the curtain rod from the balcony doors and nearly fell. But then again the utterly gorgeous Michael—he of the black hair and pale green eyes—was there to catch me, so who was I to complain? He wasn't interested—and honestly, I wasn't there to find a guy—but hey, a girl could look, right?

Finally, we were done. The living room/dining room area, the kitchen and the bathroom echoingly empty. I banished everyone to Ivory's suite and promised to come upstairs myself—if and when—I finished and was free to sleep.

I worked harder that night than I ever had before. I cleansed and blessed the hotel room and created the biggest protective circle I'd ever made—which I burned directly into the floor. I replaced the shielding charm several times over on my bracelet and created every new charm I could think of and had the time and the power to cast. It was a grand total of five types, although Morganna taught me how to make a couple of multiples. I'm glad I had an unlimited cell plan. Morganna talked me through two charms I'd never even attempted before and taught me some tricks with the shield charm. I whipped up some basic potions that had served me well so far like healing, magic detection and dispel magic.

And then I abandoned magic long enough to take the Prof's advice into consideration and modify it. I fashioned the mini-gun into a necklace. It was a little gaudy for my taste, but no one would think that was I was concealing a weapon. Or not…is it a concealed weapon if it's worn publicly as jewelry?

I created a suicide bomb out of nail polish remover, hydrogen peroxide, and car battery acid. It was unstable as hell and I hoped that the glass thermos liners I poured the bombs into would hold. But the odds were high that I was going to encounter Winsome again and Prof was right. I didn't have the magic ability to fight him again and again and again. He'd win a wizards duel. But I hadn't gone to Oxford for nothing. My organic chemistry classes were long, painful and I'd gotten an A despite my deep hatred of titrations. In social history, we dissected the activities of the IRA and later the al-Qaeda attacks in painful detail. I knew that sometimes throwing in the unexpected could change the odds. I didn't want to use the bomb—if I did the odds were high I would die—but I needed to be prepared.

Finally, I worked on the potions I wanted to create least. They would put Ivory in a state of suspended animation for about 24 hours. If Winsome managed to get to Ivory—and after the dress incident I had no faith that I would have any advance notice— the potions would buy me a day. If the day wasn't enough… well, I collapsed on the floor exhausted and utterly drained. I didn't have anything in me to create another potion. I was done. Period.

I felt like I stole the three hours of sleep I managed to grab before it was morning. Ivory needed to go to the set and I needed to go in search of answers. Prof was wrong. I felt like I was fencing in the dark. Ivory was nice—but I still didn't know why the Snow White fabled wanted Ivory. I needed to know what doom Ivory's existence could prevent.

I hoped that Antone Steward could help me. I carried my spell kit, which was masquerading as the doctor's bag with me. Until we knew what was going on, I wasn't going to be unprepared for a minute. One mention of Ivory's name and I was escorted directly into his office. Two minutes of small talk and a three minute debrief of the previous day's events, one "well done" and I was free to ask my question, "When we first met, you said that 'Ivory was important to a lot of people.' What did you mean by that?"

"Well, the studio has a big investment…" he started to say.

"It's more than that," I interrupted. "And it's more than personal. There's more there. I'm sure of it. I can feel it" He started to put me off, probably completely confused by my incomprehensible begging but I persisted. "Please. I think someone is trying to kill Ivory and I need all the facts. I'm missing something—

something important."

All hell broke loose. My Blackberry chimed and an intercepted email flashed across the screen. "Fairest One of All!!!!!!!!!" was all it said.

"Oh Gods, No!" I screamed looking at it.

"What. What it is?" Antone was frantic. His phone, his cell started ringing and his secretary ran into the office pale and shaken.

"Ivory's collapsed again…"

I cut her off—not needing to be told what happened. "Where?"

"Just outside of her trailer. Kevin Leach is down too," the secretary screamed as Antone and I ran to the set.

We ran into the rest of Ivory's entourage and several members of the crew skidding to a halt around the downed couple. Kevin had collapsed—somehow holding Ivory to him. Neither was breathing, and Ivory had a piece of paper in her hand. I could see a half eaten apple as part of the logo. No question about it remained. This was the attack.

An older woman wearing office casual clothing—I didn't recognize her—had apparently tried to help and was collapsed across them. I looked with my magical site and could see that all three were encased in a sickening orange spell that seemed to have tentacles that were reaching out toward the rest of us.

"Shit—they're contagious as all bloody hell. Think plague, but worse people." As bystanders started drifting back I commandeered a crying Jeff. "Take anyone who isn't one of the Magnificent Seven or Antone over to my first aid trailer. I'm going to have to check them. Later." As they all stood there stupidly I screamed, "Move." They took off in a run and I prayed that they were listening to me. I needed to make sure that little tentacles of this magic spell didn't spread everywhere.

"Get me the asbestos curtains," I made it a general order; Bev took off like a flash.

"Nina, get your sewing kit. I'm going to need you to make

the fastest gloves you've ever made."

I was just finishing texting Prof –"Get help here fast. Ivory down. Apple attack successful"—when Bev dropped the curtains in my lap.

"What do you want me to do?" she asked.

"Nina's going to have to make a couple of pairs of gloves or mittens or something. If I touch Ivory without protection, the magic will kill me."

I don't know how she did it, but I swear Nina had a working pair of asbestos gloves made for me in less than two minutes. And at that, it was none too soon. Gingerly, desperate not to touch the girl with anything but the gloves, I poured just a drop of a dispel magic potion on the edge of her dress. It burst into flames, instantly.

"Gods above help me," I muttered a fevered prayer. Somehow I got a drop of the potion inside the girl without it touching her lips. No flames. Thank heaven, we had a chance. The spell hadn't penetrated all of the inner organs yet.

I managed to get about a quarter of the potion down each of the three victim's throats without any major mishaps—although Kevin's lips did get pretty badly burnt. But honestly, that was the least of his problems. I then split the suspended animation potion in roughly thirds and forced the drought down their throats. With the potion divided, so was the time. With luck, I had eight hours to pull off a miracle.

I tried to take the paper out of Ivory's hands—but it had a second trap on it, and burst into flames as soon as my asbestos clad hand touched the document. Damn it to hell.

I dumped the three victims onto the asbestos curtains and wrapped them up tightly—covering even their faces. For the eight hours in question they weren't going to be breathing, and the magic couldn't be allowed to spread. "I've got to get them someplace safe. Someplace no one will look for them."

Nina spoke for the group, "Are they dead? They didn't seem to be breathing." Tears were pouring unchecked down the faces of various members of the group.

"Not if I have anything to do with it," I vowed grimly. "I've got about eight hours to save their lives. Now, where can we put them?" I asked impatiently. "Someplace that no one can find them."

"We need to call an ambulance," Antone insisted, pulling out his Blackberry. "Get them on oxygen. Something."

I put my hand over his. "There isn't a hospital on the planet that can help these three. This is magic. My only chance is to find the man who cast the spell and break it at the source."

"Say what?"

"She's telling the truth," said Nina. "You saw the fires."

"I don't know," he sounded hesitant.

"I do."

There was a moment of silence as we each were lost in our thoughts. I don't know about the others, but I said a quick prayer for help. Cara interrupted our thoughts, "The prop house," she volunteered. "It's such a mess—" she wiped tears away and took hold of the curtain. "—that no one can find anything in there."

"Careful," I warned everyone. "Touch only the curtains. Under no circumstances can you touch even the slightest bit of any of the victims." I hated using that word, but it was the only one that was appropriate.

Antone, Bev, and I stood watching the others carry off the shrouded bodies. As soon as they were out of sight, Bev turned to me. "You're going after the man who did this. I want to come too." It wasn't a question. It was a demand.

"I am. You can't," I was blunt.

"But…"

"There are things for you to do here." Bev was rock solid. She'd be okay as long as she had work to do, "First things first. I need Georgette's cell phone. I don't care how you get it—I need that phone ASAP."

Antone wiped tears off of his cheeks, "It'll be on set somewhere. Or maybe in Ivory's trailer. Check there first."

"What?" we both asked together.

"The other woman. The third victim? That's Georgette."

"What?" I repeated stupidly. "How?"

"I don't know how. But that was Georgette."

"Are you sure?"

"I've known the woman for over twenty-five years. Trust me. I've seen her in every costume and makeup job you can imagine. That was Georgette. Why she was dressed up like a little old lady, I have no idea."

I did. The Fables are suckers for tradition. The queen dresses up like an old woman to deliver the apple in several versions. Snow White is supposed to fall, but Kevin got involved and threw the dynamics off and the queen fell into her own trap.

As Bev ran off towards Ivory's trailer I said, "We need to talk."

He was still staring in the direction of the prop house, loss in every line of his body, "Yes, we do."

Before I could follow Antone in the direction of his trailer my phone rang. I glanced down. In the last ten minutes or so, I'd received twenty-five text and email messages. I hadn't heard one of them come in. "Yes boss," I said picking up the call that was ringing angrily in my hand.

He didn't waste time yelling at me. "I've got three agents at security trying to get in and help you," he barked at me.

I didn't bother briefing the boss. There was too much to do. Instead, I said, "I'm hoping to have Georgette's phone in a couple of minutes. Get Morganna ready to do a full trace on the contents."

"She's en route from San Diego in a helicopter," he paused for a minute and then said, "ETA 40 minutes. Clear a landing spot."

"Yes, sir." He didn't say anything more so I asked, "Where are you, Prof?"

"On a private plane leaving from Portland, Washington. I'm at least three hours out."

"Shit. I don't think I have time." If I waited for Prof that would leave me only five hours.

"I told you before, girl. There isn't room for me in this Fable," he sounded sad. "This is your fight. I'm coming in to hold down the fort."

"Copy that," I didn't like it—but no one asked me.

In short order, I had the three agents working with everyone on the set; making sure that they weren't infected with the mad, evil magic that had encased Ivory and performing a mass hypnosis. I needed everyone on the set to believe that Ivory, Kevin and a production assistant had been overcome by a stomach virus and were resting— not lying lifeless. That way if I managed to break the spell there would be fewer problems to deal with later.

Bev was running security. Unless someone from Templar-Mason gave the order, no one was getting in or out of the set. A magic user would be able to get past her, but at least I wouldn't have to worry about the paparazzi running around taking pictures. Plus it kept Bev busy and not likely to stow away in the trunk of my car hoping to help on the kill and destroy mission.

I was sitting in Antone Steward's office with about thirty minutes to spare before Morganna touched down, staring at Georgette's phone, paging through the contact list, praying for it to give me a lead. No luck.

One venue down, I looked at the producer. Even though he was Prof's contact I wasn't sure how in the loop he was. So I asked, "Do you know what just happened?"

"Georgette, Ivory and Ivory's security guard appeared to be dead. You claim it's magic and that they're alive. You did something "magical"—" He made air quotes. "—to preserve their lives for about eight hours and then hid them in the prop house. I got that much at least. I'm not sure how much I believe—but I got the gist of it."

"Every word is true." I didn't give him time for questions. Instead of pacing around the room, I attempted to summarize everything that happened in one hundred words or less. "There's no time for the full story. The short version, as unbelievable as it sounds, is that there is a sorcerer named Winsome. He's been using magic in order to rearrange the world to suit himself. Generally, when he attacks someone, we wind up acting out a famous story like Hansel and Gretel. Or in this case Snow White." Antone started to say something but I put up my hand to stop him from objecting. "I know, it sounds crazy—but it's true. That's why you hired Templar-Mason, isn't it? Because some part of you knows that we're the only people on earth who have any chance of saving Ivory's life."

He nodded, reluctantly. "Actually your boss called me up and told me that you could save Ivory's life. I'd never heard of Templar-Mason until then."

Wow—the Prof was a better salesman than I thought. Not only did he get me into the hospital room and onto the set—he actually managed to get us paid in the process. I might have been impressed if I had the time. Instead, I asked, "What I desperately need to know from you is why Ivory? What is so special about her, or what does she have, that he'd want to kill her?"

"Obsessed fan?" Antone offered dryly.

I shook my head. "Not a chance. He's after something that belongs to Ivory and I've got to figure out what it is. All I know is that there's an apple involved. Snow White is always killed by an apple. Always." I paused for a moment and then a little more coherently said, "The logo of the paper Ivory was holding was of a woman's hand holding a half eaten apple. I think the paper was how Ivory was attacked. I'd bet my life that there was a poisonous spell on it. I've got to find the apple company in question."

He'd already been pale and visibly shaken by the day's events. Now he turned sheet white. "EVE," he whispered.

"Eve?" Okay Adam, Eve, and the forbidden fruit could be a link.

"EVE is a research lab that specializes in biomedical research. Its logo is that of a woman's hand holding a half eaten apple."

"Tasting the tree of knowledge?"

He nodded and continued, "I was very good friends with Dart—Ivory's father—for many years; we went to college together. As a matter of fact, I got into the business because of him. I was his lawyer and then later his junior partner. I helped him close the deal for EVE." He smiled a sad smile in remembrance. "In 1973 EVE became famous for their questionable research into biological warfare. They'd 'manufacture' a disease—like smallpox—in order to develop a cure. Many Vietnam War protestors feared that EVE was working for the government and making some of the diseases available—as well as the cures. Dart did some research and realized that there was more than a kernel of truth to the story. Protesting wasn't working So Dart tried a more effective approach. He bought the lab lock, stock, and barrel in 1973."

"How'd he get the owners to sell?"

Red rimmed eyes looked into mine, "He made them an offer they couldn't refuse."

I nodded my head in understanding. Dart—and Antone—had planned to take the company down—one way or another. So all I asked was, "And then?"

"Dart redirected the research into areas that he approved of. He didn't fire any of the employees—he felt that it was safer to keep an eye on them. He made sure that it was to their financial advantage to stay with the company developing vaccines and pharmaceuticals. If they left and took their questionable knowledge with them, they'd lose everything.

"And then Georgette came along. You can not begin to imagine Georgette when we first met her."

"I've seen the pictures and read the stories."

"They don't even begin to touch on it. She was more beautiful than anyone I've ever seen—before or since. Wild to a fault. Kind hearted but oh so easily swayed. One day she'd hold a banquet for the war hawks, the next day she was speaking at an anti-war rally. Her opinions changed like the wind, and she was absolutely committed to each and every opinion she had—until she changed her mind again.

"I remember that a guru she'd found Lord only knows where, told her that she needed to be with the people to understand the people better—and that night she tried to sleep on Hollywood Boulevard in furs, jewelry and a gown she's worn to a banquet earlier that evening. She got mugged instead." His voice told me a truth that I hadn't known. Antone Steward was in love with Georgette—and had been for a long time.

He sighed. "Dart loved Georgette the moment he met her. She was the worst possible choice for a man with political aspirations like him…"

I jumped. Somehow in all my research, I hadn't known that Dartagnan Lopez had planned on running for office.

"You didn't know? Before Dart met Georgie," I suspected that Antone Steward was the only person on earth who could call Georgette "Georgie" "He was planning a run for the Senate. But Georgette was such a political liability that he gave up those plans instantly. Nothing anyone could say would convince him that Georgie wasn't the right girl for him. Instead, he decided to remake the world by buying—well everything. Vast rainforests of land he intended to leave untouched forever. Coal mines with safety problems. Munitions plants that had a reputation of selling to the IRA. You name it, he bought it. EVE was the first of many purchases Dart made to create a better world."

Antone pulled himself out of memories of happier times and said, "Dart loved Georgette—but he knew that she was weak and couldn't be trusted with his more controversial purchases. So when he wrote his will he left Georgette money, land and a clothing line. Everything else was put into a trust for Ivory—with me as the executor. She inherits it on her twenty-fifth birthday. Two weeks from today."

"Who inherits EVE if Ivory dies before her twenty-fifth birthday?"

"Ivory's will leaves everything to Georgette. Ivory's never

seen Georgette as an activist. She's only seen her as her mom."

"Damn." I started thinking aloud, "I bet that EVE has a formula of some sort that Winsome wants. Meanwhile, Snow White will run unchecked probably releasing some germ warfare or poison into the environment that will kill hundreds of thousands."

"Excuse me?"

I'd lost Antone and I didn't care. Instead, I had a different question. "If Winsome wants EVE, why on earth did he let Georgette fall to the poison?"

"Occam's razor suggests that Winsome has some way of inheriting the lab from Georgette. Maybe a codicil to her will."

"It could be that simple," I agreed. "Or maybe Winsome didn't plan on Georgette falling to his magic." That thought gave me hope. If the Fable had gone wrong then maybe it wasn't about to wander the land free forever. Maybe I could stop it and create the happy ending that would retire the fable. Maybe.

"I need EVE's address." I only hoped that it was someplace I could get in a short period of time and that Winsome would be there. Otherwise, we were screwed. A paper with the address and mapped directions came out of the printer almost as fast as I could talk. EVE was in the Silicon Valley, some four hundred and fifty miles away. Even borrowing Morganna's helicopter that was three and a half hours away. In theory, a private plane would be about two hours faster. In reality, it would take just as long to get to a plane and get air clearance. Bloody hell—time was not my friend.

Morganna came running into the office and I tossed her Georgette's phone saying, "There's a way to get in touch with Winsome somewhere on this phone. Find him for me. I'm taking the helicopter and heading for Sunnyvale."

As I was running out the door Morganna pressed something into my hand. "You might need this."

I shoved it into my pocket and kept running. I'd look at it later. I could hear Antone saying in a bewildered, yet kind, voice, "She's going to a research facility that Ivory owns in Silicon Valley. She thinks she can break the spell there."

Helicopters are no place to cast a magical spell. Morganna had passed me a bottle that contained a single Gingerbread brand Personal Health and Wellbeing Vitamin and about a tablespoon of Gingerbread Brand Chicory Baby Powder, lifted from our own labs. With them, I should be able to cast an invisibility spell and teleport myself. I'd done it before—Winsome's company used powerful magical ingredients that added an unimaginable boost to my own power. But the noise of the helicopter, my earlier spell casting in the hotel, and not being grounded by earth left me incapable of casting any major spells. So I shoved them in my YSL cargo pants pocket, gripped the medicine bag tighter and stared at the phone, willing Morganna to call me with information all the while trying to come up with a master plan.

When I landed I had a text message waiting for me. "You're on the right track. Winsome somewhere in Silicon Valley. I can't get a better trace—he's warded the number. Will update soonest." The text was two hours old.

I texted back, "Arrange private plane to be on standby for my return." A plane would buy me at least two hours. Hours I knew I was going to need. I was already out of time. If I had to take a helicopter back LA I'd need to leave now to get back in time.

I was going to go with my instincts and assume that Winsome was somewhere at the EVE facility.

EVE Biomedical Research Incorporated was housed in a beautiful dome shaped building that glittered blue in the sun and was as secure as Buckingham Palace. Actually, it was probably considerably more secure. EVE wasn't in the tourist business after all.

I paced the parking lot. I'd called, texted and emailed Antone. His secretary's line went to voicemail and I'd left an urgent message for her too. He hadn't responded. I needed his help desperately. The EVE receptionist wasn't going to allow me into the laboratory unless I had an appointment. I didn't even know who I wanted to talk with. One thing was certain though—Antone had the clout to get me in. I mean, for the next two weeks he all but owned the place.

Fifteen minutes later, after not hearing from anyone, I called Morganna. "I need Antone Steward," I announced abruptly. "Can you get him for me?"

Her voice was strained. "No one can get him for you. He's dead."

"WHAT!" Had the fable gotten him too?

"He broke into the prop house—Gods alone know why— and began unwrapping Georgette. We didn't know until it was too late."

"Oh bloody hell." He was probably the Huntsman. Sadly, they end up both in love with the queen and dying more often than not. Somehow in the past, he probably protected Ivory, maybe without even knowing it.

"Yeah."

"Any chance…"

"No." The second that passed felt like a year. Then Morganna said, "I had the three other agents create a containment circle, but they say they can feel Winsome's spell flickering at the edges. They're all that's standing between massive contamination."

"Prof there yet?"

"His plane was diverted to San Diego."

Damn, wonder how the Fable managed that one. "Can anything else go wrong?" Morganna answered, "Yes. You could fail to get the cure."

Damn it. That was blunt enough. "Time's a ticking. Call me if you get a trace on Winsome. Or anything else happens that I need to know about."

Plan B was to use the Gingerbread chicory to create an invisibility spell, hope Winsome wasn't expecting me to do a repeat performance and then act like a heroine out of a Grade B action movie—right down to fighting crime in high heels. Seriously— the boss would have the right to double my month in Payless— just because sometime in the hour it took for me to leave LaLa Land I should have considered shoes. I mean seriously—what was I thinking?

The chicory worked. For how long I had no idea, but it worked. I hoped like the devil that our office had more stashed away, because evil as Winsome was, his ingredients worked like no one's business.

I stood outside in the parking lot, waiting for someone who had an access badge to get something from their car. Ten minutes later I'd snuck into the building close on the heels of a smoker wearing a lab coat who'd sucked down his nicotine with the desperation of an addict who had gone too long without his fix. I stayed close on his tail as he caught the elevator down—even the elevator was key carded.

Gathering intelligence is not easy—even when invisible and inaudible. In some ways, it might be harder. You can't open doors, use a computer or flip through papers easily. People are bound to notice a door opening with no one there. I couldn't even steal a lab coat and pretend to work at the lab; I didn't have any more chicory and there was no way I could recast the spell. So I was pretty much dependent on listening to people's conversations.

On Sublevel III I made a find that chilled me. One entire laboratory was filled with Gingerbread Peppermint Foot Bath. Unless some rich A-lister who happened to have a foot fetish, was working in the lab, I had to assume that Winsome had infiltrated EVE further than I'd thought. EVE might be Gingerbread's new R&D facility. I didn't know enough about think tanks to even guess how EVE chose the projects they were working on. But it didn't matter. Remembering how Winsome had treated Heidi and Greg Wade, and his godson Rafael I needed to be on the look out for some poor person having their life source sucked out of them.

I followed a false lead about using honey and pears in shampoo to the cafeteria thinking that perhaps the two women who were talking were unwitting—or witting—dupes of Winsome. I finally figured out that they weren't the people I was looking for when one of them pulled out a bottle of Herbal Essence and asked, "Now how can we upgrade this into a fifty dollar a bottle shampoo?" The people I was looking for were making a thousand dollar a bottle shampoos—and were supplementing the honey with magic, not pears.

I stood at the edge of the soda fountain dejected. I was almost out of time. I had no idea how to find Winsome, how to reverse the spell or how to save Ivory's life. If Snow White got to run rampant this time, it was my fault. Prof was right—I should have shot Winsome when I had the chance. To add insult to injury, I was thirsty and couldn't do a thing about it.

"I don't understand why we've been asked to resurrect Project Johnny Appleseed," a man's voice penetrated my gloom. He was a good looking man; probably in his late twenties. His hair was already graying and very fit. He had the look of a man who ran the marathon every year and was definitely not what I expected to see in a research lab. I tend to expect my researchers to be skinny and pale from lack of the sun. I was stereotyping, but years of watching Hollywood dramas did set a certain standard in my brain.

His companion, a longhaired aging hippy, looked much more like I expected. Both wore lab coats. My ears perked up and I drifted in to listen closer, "Not here. Come on." He jerked his head, and the two of them left for their lab—a rather old and unmodernized lab—Diet Coke in hand and me close on their heels.

"This is very upsetting," the hippy said. "I almost quit EVE the first time I was assigned to Appleseed. I mean, here I was, a Vietnam War protestor and I was assisting in the development of a plague that could be carried by food. You can't convince me that we weren't planning on spreading the plague through Red Cross rations. Thank God that we were bought out just in time."

"So why do you think we were ordered to resurrect the project?"

"Al Queda," the response came instantly. "We aren't winning this war on terror and I guess someone decided to change the way the war is being fought." The hippy's shoulders slumped. "I thought Mr. Steward was smarter than that. He's got to know that poisoning the food supply is going to kill thousands—maybe millions of innocent people."

"They won't deploy the operation until we've got a functioning antidote."

"Which we've…" the other man started only to be kicked by the hippy.

"Troydesy itsy." Fortunately, I spoke Pig Latin as well as the next girl and could translate instantly in my head the rest of the conversation. "The computers could be…" He nodded over to the turned off laptop. "You never know. Play for time. Mr. Lopez would never have permitted this research and hopefully his daughter won't either. We only need to delay for two weeks and then she takes over. Somehow I'll figure out how to talk to her."

Bloody, bloody, bloody, bloody hell. A visual scan of the lab didn't show a nicely labeled test tube that said, "Antidote."

"I hate to do this," the younger man picked up a beaker of a clear liquid and walked over to a rack with 8 test tubes in it. "These could save hundreds of lives…"

"Don't think like that," the hippy ordered. "That's how scientists have gotten sucked into biological and nuclear weapon development for years. We always believe that we're doing something good—only to create more evil."

"I guess."

I needed to create a diversion so that I could acquire a couple of test tubes of the cure. Even more than that I needed the formula for the cure. I had no doubt in my mind that this was the pestilence that Snow White was looking to inflict on the world and the Fable wasn't going to be waiting for Mr. Clean Cut and Mr. Hippy to release the cure. As a matter of fact, if Snow White got completely loose—these two would be early victims. I guaranteed it.

At the other end of the lab bench was an empty glass beaker. I knocked it onto the floor with a loud crash. They both jumped. "What the?"

While their backs were turned I stole a test tube. At least that was the plan. Unfortunately, Mr. Hippy turned around just in time to see the test tube floating in the air. "What the?"

Mr. Clean Cut came flying across the room and tackled invisible me. Sadly the test tube wasn't invisible and gave away my location perfectly.

"Oooomph," the breath was knocked out of me and I bumped the test tube tray as I fell to the ground The tray crashed to the ground behind me. It shattered in a shower of glass and serum. Instinctively I rolled, cradling the one dose of antidote I had towards my body. I now officially had the only antidote. Cripes.

I kicked out with my leg and planted a good hard kick to Mr. Clean Cut's face. I didn't want to hurt him. I just wanted to get free, so the spurting blood that ran down his nose made me cringe. It also completely justified the three inch heeled Betsy Johnson boots I was wearing. I never would have been as successful in sneakers.

"What the…" I'd regained my footing and planted my boot on this Adam's apple. The precious test tube I put into my bra. Eventually I'd get it into my spell kit—which I'd dropped in the course of the fight and was still invisible—but for the moment the padding and fit of the bra were the best protection I could offer the tube.

"Quiet," I cut him off sounding as menacing as I could. I was lucky I was invisible. A woman who is one hundred twenty pounds in cargo pants, boots, and a short blazer might be stylish on Rodeo Drive, but certainly not threatening in real life. "Was antidote in the test tube?"

"Yes," he gasped out.

Hippy was trying to sneak over behind me, but I ground my invisible foot deeper into Mr. Clean's throat. "I wouldn't," I ordered. The squeaking that came from the floor reinforced my words.

"You need to make more of the antidote," I said, hoping they'd listen to me. "I've got reason to believe that your plague has already been released."

"Impossible."

"Yeah—I don't think so."

The older man said, "Yeah, well I think so. The Green Plague is one hundred times more contagious than the Black Death and kills within an hour of exposure." He held up his phone, "Trust me—if it's been released we'd all know."

I felt stupid saying, "Trust me. Besides you're talking to an invisible woman so maybe you should start rethinking your idea of impossible. It's been released. Today. In LA. Templar-Mason needs your help to…"

An electrical strike came at me from nowhere and missed me by inches. Winsome, lightning bolts streaming out of his hands, came running into the laboratory.

"Run," I screamed at the scientists as I dropped to the ground and rolled.

Another bolt hit the lab bench, scorching everything. Thank the Gods it was asbestos—otherwise, it would have been destroyed in the first strike.

I crawled frantically across the floor, trying to find my still invisible spell kit. Without it, I was a gonner.

A third bolt sent the scientists scurrying under a lab bench. It'd held up to a couple of direct electrical hits. Gods willing it would continue to protect them.

I raised my charm bracelet and yelled, "Arrow." The silver charm disappeared, bolts flew, Winsome yelped and then disappeared. Damn—he was using an invisibility spell too.

The arrows distracted him enough that I was able to grab

my kit, which I literally crawled over. I threw salt in the air and yelled, "Circle."

Salt flew everywhere, glinting with the power of the spell. It wasn't a circle, but, hopefully would provide at least some protection.

It didn't. The next strike missed me by inches and had me huddling next to a file cabinet that looked like it escaped from the 1970s.

"Shield," I cried and climbed under the lab bench with the scientists.

The next strike bounced off the shield, but made the bench creak from the force of the magic. Morganna had helped me make it stronger, so it held. A second bolt drained it and it faded out of existence. The scientists next to me were shaking, "What the…" was about as coherent as they got.

I had a question of my own, "What is Winsome powering his lightning bolts with anyway?" I asked myself aloud. "No one is that powerful."

Another strike—another shield. Thank the Gods that I'd put multiple shields on the charm bracelet. Morganna had taught me a trick that allowed me to make six for the relative price of one and up the power in the process.

The hippy muttered, "Electricity. The lightning strikes are electricity."

"Huh?"

"E—MC2."

Damn—could it be that easy? "Look," I hissed. "If I can create a diversion and get you guys out of here, you've got to kill the power and evacuate the building. Tell them that there is a terrorist attack in your lab."

"Anything."

I drew the gun from my cargo pants. "Get ready to run."

I fired in the area that Winsome had last struck. Misters Hippy and Clean Cut ran like the devil himself was chasing them.

It hurt to move. I'd been fried, burnt, and slammed against

an asbestos lab bench. I had beakers containing God knows what rain down on my head. And as I looked down, I saw my body returning to the visual spectrum. Whatever was in the glassware had ended my invisibility spell. Now I was wet and covered in gook. Worse, for all I knew I'd also been infected with Gods knows what.

I fired the entire clip at Winsome, but he was ready with a shield spell that made mine look like it was made of balsa wood. Prof was wrong. Guns didn't work. And he was right. I didn't have enough magic to handle Winsome on my own.

He approached like some loathsome toad chortling like a mad man. He had no idea what he was about to unleash on earth. Worse—he didn't care. All he cared about was endless power. Another thunder strike had me rolling away, still trying to protect the antidote in my bra. Why I bothered, I didn't know. There was a snowball's chance in hell I was getting out of this lab alive.

I rolled on top of my medicine/spell bag and felt something hard inside of it. My bomb of terror. The last ditch, if I had no chance of escaping, homemade TNT. That was pretty much where I was at, so this was it. My personal doomsday.

I poured the solution onto the floor and felt in my pockets for a match or a lighter. Nothing. No biggie. In a moment Winsome would attack with lightening or fire or something else that would light the solution on fire and we'd be dead. Prof and Morganna would likely kill Ivory, Kevin, and Georgette—and burn down the prop house. I didn't know what would happen to the Fable if the principal players were dead; maybe it would mean banishment. Or maybe it would rule forever. But my best guess was that if everyone involved in the story was dead it'd at least have to head back to the Neverafter.

The next blast from Winsome was wind. He slammed me up against the wall, hard enough that he could have broken my back. Idiot. Didn't he know I needed fire? He raved something incoherent that I ignored while groping down my pants looking for a match, a lighter, a piece of flint. Damn it—why wasn't

I a smoker? A small round pill rolled out of a hole in one of my pockets. The Gingerbread vitamin.

I put the pill in my mouth with a sliver of hope. Then I taunted Winsome, "Running out of steam are you?"

Blazing hot, steamy air, blasted me. "Damn it, now I need a facial."

"You'll get your facial in hell," he screamed at me.

"No way. Not when I'm this close to Rodeo Drive."

I needed fire. I have no idea where I found the strength, where I found the power. But I was able to send the tiniest magic missile spell I'd ever cast directly at the explosive.

"But if I can't get in there, I'm willing to see you in hell," I muttered. Not original dialogue—but sometimes you've got to go with a classic. I swallowed the pill and prayed that I'd find myself anywhere but here as a fireball erupted.

The world went black and fell away. I fell with a thud onto— something. My head spun and for a moment or two, I think I passed out.

When I woke up I was lying on a pile of boxes. I'd apparently fallen from the sky onto a pallet of, of…I leaned over and read, Gingerbread Personal Health and Wellbeing Vitamins.

Oh crap. I was still in enemy territory. Worse, I had no idea where that was. On the plus side, I was alive. That had to be worth something, right? I had no idea what time it was. Everything was gone except my clothing. My bra was wet and—oh damn it— filled with fine, broken glass and what I assumed was the last remaining dose of antidote. Or not remaining as the case might be. My cell phone was smashed past repair. I didn't even know if there was any time left—not that I had the antidote necessary to save them, anyway.

I almost gave up and sat there waiting to be found—but I pulled myself up. Somehow—if I could get back to the set in time I could… I didn't know exactly what I would do… but it was my job to finish the Fable. I didn't have the right to get myself arrested or thrown in the dungeon or whatever the Gingerbread

Masters would do to me. Besides Winsome might not be dead and could try to follow me the same way I escaped.

I stuffed a pocket full of vitamins. I didn't have the energy left to craft a spell, but they were the closest thing to spell ingredients I had. Besides—one pill was enough to teleport me. If someone caught me sneaking around this Gingerbread warehouse I'd swallow another pill. Maybe it'd cast me elsewhere. Who knew? If I kept swallowing the vitamins maybe I could be teleported around the world and back again. Or at least anyplace that had a stash of Gingerbread vitamins—at least I assumed it was sympathetic magic that landed me here—where ever here is.

It was remarkably easy to sneak out of the warehouse. The place was in an uproar; people screaming into phones, screaming at each other and in general behaving like the end of their (corporate) world had come. I hoped that it was Winsome's death that had triggered the panic and I was grateful the chaos helped me skulk out of the warehouse virtually undetected. Or maybe that was an average day for them.

I was on the streets of a city, but I was damned if I knew what city. Tall concrete and glass buildings, a generically named twenty-third street; I could be in any major city in the world. No convenient newspapers and damn it—no pay phones. Not that they would have worked anyway. 99.9% of all payphones left in the world are broken. I went up to the first business suited man I saw, "Excuse me, can I…" he brushed past me as if I was still invisible. So did the second man and the first woman I tried to speak with. I looked down at myself. Yup—I was still there. The chicory hadn't somehow or another made me disappear again. The fourth man I approached handed me a dollar. Well—at least I had proof that someone could see me. The fifth woman walked past me then did a double take. She squinted at me and said in an extremely accusatory voice, "A homeless beggar in this season's Yves St. Laurant!"

"I'm not homeless," I looked down at myself, "I've just been through a war and back." She looked at me like I was crazy. "I was attacked and got away."

She talked over me as if she couldn't hear me, "I've heard about people like you. You beg during the day, make money hand over fist and live the high life at night. I should report you to the authorities…."

I interrupted her, "All I'm trying to do is make a phone call. Can I please borrow your phone…"

"If you think that I'm going to loan my phone out to a dirty, fraudulent…" As she spoke I could see her eyes go to my feet once, twice. She was looking at the three inch heeled Betsy Johnson boots and if I wasn't mistaken she wanted them. Badly.

I looked down at them myself. They were scuffed, burned, soaked and covered in muck—but a good shoemaker would be able to restore my Betsy's to their former luster at a fraction of the price of buying them new. The woman who was yelling at me wore serviceable boots. I'd guess Macy's, $59.95—retail. "I'll trade you—my boots for one phone call."

She squinted down at my shoes, "What size are they?"

"Size 9."

"My size."

This was not a surprise. I'd estimated her size before I made the offer. While she was debating I asked a question, "Where am I?'

The woman, understandably looked confused, "West 23rd Street."

"In what city?"

She started fearfully backing away from me, "Los Angeles."

"Oh thank the gods," I owed who ever was looking out for me—big time! Sympathetic magic could have sent me anywhere in the world a stash of Gingerbread vitamins were. Instead, it sent me almost exactly where in needed to be.

Before she could take off in fear, I took my boots off and dangled them in front of her, and held out my hand imperiously,

"Your phone, please."

She snatched the boots out of my hands and tossed me her Droid. Nice—she might not treat herself when it came to shoes, but her phone I approved of. I called Morganna, identified myself and before she could say a word said, "I'm in LA with no phone, no money, and no nothing."

"We need you here," It sounded like she was yelling over a wind machine or something, "Prof's plane was diverted to Mexico."

I didn't bother to ask. The power of a Fable is far reaching. "You've got to get someone to bring me in." I looked down at myself. "And tell the driver to look for a barefoot woman who looks like she survived a visit to a war zone."

After giving Morganna my address, I tossed the phone to the woman with an

insincere, "Thanks. Enjoy the boots." When a limo arrived to pick me up, she started ranting again.

After a ride involving more traffic violations than I'd care to recount, I ran to the prop house. As I ran I couldn't help but notice that the hustle and bustle of the set was missing; that the place was empty.

Bev ran up next to me. "We didn't want anyone to know what was going on so Jeff got one of our guys to cause a water main break half a mile up the road. The lot is closed for at least the rest of the day while LADWP is fixing it."

I didn't want to know. Instead, as I ran through the door, and smack into the Morganna and the remaining dwarves. "Did you do it?" "Is Ivory going to be okay?" "What about Kevin" Even Morganna chimed in with "Winsome?"

"Winsome's dead," I said soberly. "I think he is anyway."

The witch nicknamed The Ice Woman sagged back on her heels relief showing plainly on her face, "Thank the Gods," she said.

I shuddered, "Yeah."

Jeff said cheerfully, "So you," he made a motion I assumed was supposed to me magical, "and Ivory and Kevin are all better, right?"

I could feel the curse flickering on the edge of the containment circle, "No." I've done some things I hated, but this was the worst. "I kill Ivory, Kevin, and Georgette with the circle intact. Then we torch the bodies, the prop house and maybe the freaking set. Then we pray that a mutated form of the plague hasn't been set loose to kill millions."

Morganna nodded grimly, but Bev clutched my arm with tears in her eyes. "You can't kill them. That's murder."

"They are already dead," I said savagely. "I freaking failed."

The three agents I didn't know were pale, sweaty and clearly exhausted by holding the containment circle against the curse. I held my hands out, ready to merge what was left of my energy with theirs and enter the circle when I heard, "Screw this." Something hit me like a ton of brinks, knocking me down. I rolled, ready to kick, when I realized that Nina was lying across me. I had to keep myself from throwing her across the room.

"What the…"

Nina was sobbing too hard to answer. Kara squatted down next to us and put her arm around Nina, "You can't kill them, you can't." Kara was crying too.

I pulled myself up out of the dirt. "Winsome cursed them. Killing him didn't break the curse." And added a totally inadequate, "If the plague gets out, most of LA will be infected. Millions will die. Three deaths to save a million."

"You have magic powers. Do something else," sobbed Nina. "Anything else. Just don't kill them."

"I'm sorry. I tried. There isn't anything else to do."

"No," Nina lashed out at my shin with the toe of her shoe. Damn—I'd have more damage from Nina than Winsome if this kept up.

Meanwhile, Michael was clearly thinking, "But you thought

that killing Winsome would break the spell."

It wasn't a question, but I answered anyway, "Yes. It was my best guess."

"Then guess again. You said this was a fairy tale and Ivory is Snow White. Doesn't she need Prince Charming or someone to kiss her and wake her up?" said Michael.

"That can work except we have no idea who the prince is and anyone trying to kiss her is risking painful death via plague," I said.

"Ivory has more than a couple of creepy fans who'd be willing to risk it," said Kara.

"I don't think any are royalty," said Jeff.

"The royal part doesn't matter as much as someone who loves her or is fated to be with her," I said.

"The really weird fan who sends her those pictures of himself dressed up like a gladiator swears he loves her. I'd be willing to sacrifice him," said Kara.

"No, her true love is Kevin," said Nina. "She just doesn't realize it yet."

I hit myself in the head. "Kevin's not a dwarf. He's the prince."

"Who's the seventh dwarf?" Michael asked.

"Morganna maybe. Doesn't matter. Kevin can't kiss her. He's unconscious."

"Take your spell off him," said Kara. "He loves her. Put them next to each other, slap him awake, tell him he needs to kiss Ivory to save her. He'll do it."

"This is the plague, not a sleeping pill," I said.

"It'll work," said Jeff.

"I don't know," I said.

"It's true love. Isn't that what always leads to a happily ever after in a fairy tale?" said Nina.

"It's not that simple," I argued.

"You told me I had good instincts with the asbestos. Everything inside me tells me this is right. It'll work," Bev chimed in.

"How do you know?

"Because it has to," said Nina.

"I have no way to save Kevin. He'll die," I said.

"He'd say do it to save Ivory. And maybe it'll break the spell and save him too," said Michael. Everyone else agreed.

"And if it works, Ivory would have to be cured of the plague right?" said Nina.

Morganna and I looked at each other. "In theory," I said.

"Do it," said Nina. "You can always kill and burn them after if it doesn't work. Of course, it'll be over my dead body, but we can worry about that later."

I looked again to Morganna. She had more time as an agent and witch, but preferred support work to being on the front lines. "You're the agent in charge. Your call."

After my weakness caused five deaths, I made myself hard so if faced with the choice of a cold blooded killing or stopping a Fable, that I'd make the prudent choice. Not the morally right choice, but the one that would save the most people. I was talking a tough fight but when it came down to it, I still wasn't sure I could do it. Scarily, I was mostly sure I could. What that would do to my mind in the long run I was pretty sure wouldn't be pretty.

"Let's try it," I said. "I need those asbestos gloves."

Nina nodded and ran to get them.

I pulled Morganna aside. "I'm going in. If it fails and I fall, burn all of us to a crisp and get Prof in here for containment."

"Understood," Morganna said, without a word of argument. She was suddenly an ice woman again. No wonder she was Prof's favorite.

We went into the prop house. I thought about trying to keep my fellow dwarves out, but realized it wasn't going to happen. Morganna called in the three other agents to guard the perimeter.

Nina arrived with the gloves and I put them on, then unwrapped the asbestos curtain and pulled Kevin next to Ivory but both of them away from her evil mother. I had the dispel magic potion in my hand. My suspended animation spell was the surface spell, so the potion would go after it before the plague magic. It was also far more fragile. A single drop was all I needed to break it. Kevin gasped in air as if he had just been pulled onto dry land after almost drowning.

It was now or never. "Kevin, Ivory is dying," His eyelids fluttered. "You need to wake up or she'll die."

Against all odds and most types of logic, his eyes opened. "No!"

"You're her prince. Your kiss will save her," I said.

Barely conscious, his face still got one of the most amazing grins I'd ever seen and his lips actually puckered.

I rolled him over toward his ladylove so his face touched hers. His lips reached out until they found hers. Yes, I know lips don't usually reach, but that's still what they did. It was incredibly sweet. And then Ivory's lips reached back and responded passionately. I watched as the Fable that had been riding her changed to the look of a sunset. I expected it to fade back to the Neverafter. Instead, it flew through the ceiling, as intangible as a bad dream.

Ivory sat up. "What just happened?"

Nina and Kara tackled her in tag team hug before I could suggest that they let me check to make sure the plague was contained.

"You're alive!"

"But what's wrong with Kevin and my mom?" she said, looking at the unconscious man and woman next to her.

We gave her the short version. "Jillian, you have to save them."

I looked down. Kevin was out, yet had the hugest smile. Georgette was still safely contained in suspended animation for a couple of hours, but Kevin was still carrying the plague.

"Everyone out. We need to contain this," said Morganna.

"Contain?" said Ivory.

"She means kill them," said Kara.

"No." I heard it before I realized it was me, not Ivory who said it.

"Jillian, you know the protocol. You know…" I raised my hand to cut off Morganna.

I pulled two Gingerbread vitamins out of my pocket. Not an easy task with asbestos gloves on, let me tell you. "I can get him back to EVE labs. There might be more antidote." Mr. Hippy and Mr. Clean Cut may have had a chance to make more. It was a slim chance. "If not, I'll take care of him."

"Wait a second, you are not…" Ivory had started on a full-scale rant.

"I'm going to try to save him." I took off a glove and took Morganna's phone from her. "Ivory, I'm going to EVE labs. In two weeks, you own it. You need to stop Project Appleseed. It's germ warfare on a huge scale. I need a video of you ordering whoever I meet there to give me full cooperation."

I hit record. "Do whatever Jillian Anderson tells you to or in two weeks your ass is fired," she said. "Good enough?"

"Perfect," I said.

"I can get you a plane to get you there…"

"I have a quicker way." I put the phone in my pocket, the glove on my hand and wrapped Kevin in the curtain. "Watch there's nothing up my sleeve." I put one vitamin in my mouth and bit down as I crushed the other into his mouth. A moment later the world went black and we ended up again among a crate of Gingerbread vitamins. Luckily it was the one at EVE.

I wasn't strong enough to carry Kevin through the labs and I had no chicory to go the invisible route. Instead, I ran out into the hall. It was empty. So was every lab and office I came to. I stopped by a window and noticed the parking lot was filled with police cars with flashing lights, crowds of people and reporters with video cameras.

Just great. I forgot I told the lab coat boys to call in a terrorist attack. Looks like they listened.

I quickly backed away from the window. The last thing I

needed was to be seen. My video of Ivory wouldn't mean squat to a SWAT team.

I made my way to the lab. The doors were all open and the power was cut, so I navigated by the emergency lights over the exit signs. My luck held and the lab door was open. Actually, it was half off the hinges and singed from a hit by a lightning bolt.

I made my way through the lab, my heart sinking further with each passing moment. This time I didn't have to worry about trying to pick out which might be the antidote because all the glassware was smashed into little pieces.

I opened all the refrigerators. Empty.

"Damn it."

"My thoughts exactly," said a voice behind me.

I spun and was face to face with Winsome.

"Stupid witch. You just keep trying to blow me up. I have to say I don't like it. You need to stop it. IT HURTS!" screamed Winsome, his cool manner shattered for a moment. He was holding a test tube in his hand. He watched my eyes go straight to it. "Ah, yes. You came here for the antidote. This is the last test sample. It'll take days for another batch to be brewed. More than enough time for my plague to spread over most of California."

"Why?"

"Simple. Those using Gingerbread products will be spared, These very rich survivors will soon realize they will need to keep buying or die. In short order, I will own most of the wealth in California. I will control movies, television, radio. I will be rich and be able to have people see what I want them to see. Soon I'll have them believing what I want them to believe. I'll create new Fables that will bend the world to my will. I'll be the most powerful man in the world. And anytime someone tries to cross me, I'll sic a Fable on them."

"You're insane."

"You have a knack for stating the obvious, don't you? I'm surprised you didn't shout 'You're alive' as soon as you saw me. Besides I think it was Poe who wrote the only difference between a genius and a madman is the genius knows he's a madman."

"That's nice, but you think I came here without backup? There's a dozen T-M agents here," I bluffed.

"That's good because the half dozen you sent after me last time were so effective. It just gives me twice as many to slaughter," said Winsome.

"Did I mention Prof was one of them?"

"Your fearless leader? Hardly. I would have sensed him. You're here all by your lonesome. I'm fine with that. Gives us time to play. I owe you. I think I'll start by burning your skin off but using my magic to make sure you do not die or pass out. That way you can appreciate all that I'm doing to you."

I was so scared I peed my designer clothes, but forced myself to yawn as if I couldn't be more bored.

"Your Fable is ended. T-M is here in force. You're done. Now if you hand me that tube, maybe we'll go easy on you," I bluffed.

Winsome tuned to look at the test tube, then back at me. "You want this still? Maybe your happily ever after wasn't so happy after all. I suppose I should chip in to help. Here you go," Winsome said, holding out the tube to me.

I didn't buy it for a second, but I held my hand out. Winsome smiled and made like he was tossing it. And he did, with the force of a quarterback. It would have smashed into the wall if I hadn't leapt up and made a once in a lifetime catch. I shoved the vial into my pocket praying this time it wouldn't break

"Bitch." His hands started to glow and a lightning bolt shot out, but it turns out Mr. Hippy was right. Without the building's power to draw on, it was a static spark on steroids. It stung but that's about it. All I had was my bracelet and a pocketful of vitamins. I could escape but that left Kevin still dying. And at the moment Winsome didn't know he was here.

"Maybe I can still continue the Fable," Winsome said. "Wouldn't that be just nifty?"

"How are you going to summon it back from the Neverafter?" I said.

"Back?" Winsome's brow's furrowed, holding up his hand. It had enough magic in it that it glowed. "I never let it leave."

Within the glow, there was an energy cage and trapped inside was the Snow White Fable, something that should be impossible. The amount of power alone...

"Merciful Gods," I exclaimed.

"I've never found them to be." Winsome took a step toward me while opening his hand. "Get her," he ordered the Fable like it was an ordinary attack dog. And like a pit bull, it obeyed.

I turned and ran for all I was worth. The Fable followed. It seemed to be in no rush and I wasn't about to question why.

Fables are not supposed to be able to attack directly. By their nature, they require a host to work through, usually—but not always—a human. Winsome had somehow managed to change the very rules of existence.

I thought about running outside to the waiting cops and feds. Problem is, unless there was a magic practitioner in the crowd, none of them would see the Fable. Instead, I'd be arrested and the Fable could pick me off at its leisure. Or worse, ride the entire crowd to reenact the entire story at a sped up rate. Normally, that would be against the rules that bound them, but now I wouldn't be surprised if it was possible.

Instead, I headed back to the room where I had left Kevin. Maybe saving the prince would break Winsome's spell and send the Fable back to Neverland. Maybe.

I locked the door behind me and turned toward Kevin. Before I could reach him the Fable flowed right through the wall like it was constructed from mist

I turned to face it. None of my charms were up to this. I bit my tongue to get blood. If I was going to die, I'd cast a spell using up my life force in some hope of at least hurting it.

As I tried to come up with a spell that would double as my last words, the Fable stopped. It was in the form of Snow herself and she was staring at me.

"Why are you stopping?" I asked, never dreaming I'd get an

answer.

I DO NOT WISH TO DESTROY YOU.

It was actually taking to me. "Why not? That's what Fables do."

NO. WE CREATE. WE INTERACT. SOME DIE BUT THERE ARE ALWAYS MORE TO TAKE THE PARTS.

"So why don't you want to hurt me?" I doubted it was because of my amazing fashion sense.

BECAUSE TO DO SO IS OUTSIDE OF THE CONVANTS. BECAUSE TO DO SO WILL WEAKEN ME. TO CONTINUE TO IGNORE THAT WHICH BINDS US ALL WILL DESTROY ME.

So killing me would help forever destroy a Fable? If I was going to die regardless, it was good to hear I'd at least take it down with me.

"So why break the rules?" I asked.

THE PROTANGONIST HAS BEEN STEALING POWER FROM EACH FABLE HE HAS HAD A PART IN. BEFORE HE COULD ONLY SUMMON US. AFTER PLAYING HIS PART FOR ME, HE HAS ENOUGH POWER TO CONTROL US.

Damn.

"So you're fighting Winsome?"

YES.

"What part did he play?" I had my suspicions.

THE MIRROR.

I was right. "So how do we stop him?"

I DO NOT KNOW.

"How are you still here if we reached The End?" I asked.

HE HAS BOUND ME.

Winsome had reached the room and was banging on the door in an attempt to get in.

"So technically you aren't over yet."

YES.

I had an idea. "We need to work together to beat Winsome."

BUT YOU AND YOURS ARE DEDICATED TO STOP-

PING MY KIND. ALLOWING THIS WOULD DESTROY ME.

True. I could hear Prof's voice yelling that in my ear. "But it would leave Winsome with the power to control the other Fables and break the rules. Nobody would know the rules had changed. We'd be slaughtered and he would rule the world. His body count would surpass even yours."

SO THE DEAD WOULD BE HARDER TO REPLACE?

"No, we don't want there to be any dead."

BUT YOU HUMANS WILL DIE ANYWAY. ISN'T IT BETTER TO DIE IN THE SERVICE OF A STORY?

"No."

I FIND THAT ODD. There was an awkward pause. WHAT WOULD YOU WANT TO AID ME?

Actually I was thinking I was the one asking for its help, not the other way around, but Gran Anderson didn't raise any dummies.

"A boon that I may call in at any time that must be given, regardless of what it is that I ask."

The Fable hung in the air contemplating.

"Do you want to die?"

WE DO NOT DIE. I WOULD CEISE TO BE AND UNLIKE YOU HUMANS, NO MORE WOULD RISE TO TAKE MY PLACE.

The door finally smashed in and Winsome stepped inside.

"I told you to kill her. Why is she not a corpse?"

The Fable turned to me.

VERY WELL. PROVIDED YOU DO NOT ASK ME TO BAN MYSELF FROM THE MORTAL REALM, WE HAVE A DEAL.

"Deal? There are no deals to be made. I won't allow it," said Winsome.

"Wrong, Winnie. You are going down," I said.

WHAT WOULD YOU HAVE ME DO?

I smiled. "Transform him physically into his part. Modern version."

IT IS NOT WITHIN THE NORMAL STORYLINE, BUT IS WITHIN THE BOUNDS OF THE COVENANTS. IT SHALL COST ME POWER, BUT WILL BE DONE.

The Fable suddenly had a tendril which reached out for Winsome. He screamed as his flesh transformed into wood, metal brackets and glass that held a reflection of his face. I grabbed a board that had broken off a wooden pallet and ran forward, smashing it into the silver glass. It cracked, but didn't shatter. At least I had specified modern. The original magic mirror had been metal.

I let loose another swing, but the mirror actually moved. Worse, Winsome had managed to transform himself into the toad creature he'd been down in Tennessee. Half his face was bloody where I had smashed the mirror. The Fable sent out another tendril and it was back to damaged mirror. I hit it again and this time pieces of glass flew off.

This time Winsome transformed into a giant wolf with half his face missing. Winsome the wolf leapt at me, jaws slobbering. I managed to swing the board and catch him in the jaws. The Fable transformed him back to his mirror form and as he was in a crouched position, Winsome-the-looking-glass fell glass first on the floor. I jumped on top and smashed my foot down into his frame. I heard a satisfying crunch, but a second later I was headed toward the ceiling as a result of his next transformation, barely managing to jump down before the giant smashed me into the ceiling. Winsome the giant was still on all fours, but had smashed through the floor above and the ceiling above that. With a single hand, he swatted me like a fly and I flew over to crash into the curtains that surrounded Kevin. I landed on my left side and felt the vial crunch, glass cutting into me and liquid dripping onto me and onto Kevin where my landing had dislodged the asbestos. The antidote better be topical or I was dead from having touched Kevin and more importantly, the prince would die. Without the prince the Fable would never come to a conclusion and, even with our alliance, the fable would take

Snow White to a dark ending.

The giant turned toward me. Half his face was blood, teeth, and bone. His other arm was broken at what I hoped was a painful angle.

"Witch, you might have at least enjoyed the imagination behind the tortures I had planned for you, but now I'm just going to eat you," boomed Winsome the giant, reaching out for me with the hand that had swatted me.

The Fable moved in again to transform him. It got the tendril to touch the giant, but Winsome reached out with his good giant hand and somehow managed to grab hold of the Fable. When his hand opened, the Fable was back in the cage. And a second later, he again was in mirror form. My best guess is Winsome was using his power to transform into the parts he had played in various Fables. It was probably too much to hope that he had exhausted his reserve.

I AM TRAPPED. I WILL BE ABLE TO HELP YOU NO LONGER.

"Thanks, I've got it from here," I said, hoping the plan forming in my mind was more than bravado.

I yanked the asbestos curtain out from around Kevin. Plague was the least of my worries. I wrapped it around the mirror, twisting the frame so it broke at the base.

The mirror screamed then laughed maniacally. A mystic bolt flew out through an opening in the curtain and hit Kevin. A second later, he rose to his feet looking more dead than alive.

"The green plague is my magic to control, so the prince is mine to command," said the mirror.

Kevin grabbed me from behind in a headlock and pulled me off the mirror.

"Kevin, let me go," I said. Not only did he look a lot like a zombie, he was acting like one. I hoped he wasn't thinking my brains would make a good snack. I pulled his pinky back until it broke and manage to get free.

I sprinted toward Winsome but he was already transforming. The curtain had only slowed him down and Kevin was coming up behind me. I couldn't see what the latest form was as I tried to pin Winsome with the curtain around him.

"Fable, a little help here."

HOW? I AM TRAPPED.

"Kevin's your prince. He's a part of your essence and the story. Because of that connection, you don't have to physically touch him to cure the plague and give us a happy ending,"

BUT THAT WOULD END MY HOLD ON THIS WORLD AND THIS TALE.

"You'd rather stay here than return to the Neverafter?"

I WOULD STILL BE TRAPPED.

"Maybe or maybe the jolt of power the story ending again will be enough to break you out of your prison," I said, smashing my fist into what I hoped was the head of whatever Winsome had transformed into this time. At least it was smaller than a giant.

IT MIGHT AT THAT.

I couldn't spare the effort to look but I heard Kevin say, "What's going on? What happened to my finger?" His broken pinky was bent at what had to be a painful angle.

Scratch one plague, at least on this end of things.

I kept hitting and Winsome kept changing. I put everything I could into causing as much damage as possible. Winsome started to grow and I was lifted off the ground. I held on with my hands and started kicking. Winsome convulsed and threw me aside, then managed to shake himself free of the curtain.

He had been a beast before in spirit and now he was one in body, although it was not in good shape. Half his face was still destroyed, a leg dragged uselessly behind him, one arm hung without moving and his back looked like that on a hunchback. All that and he still managed to stand.

"My first Fable. How fitting," said Winsome. "Pity there is no beauty to play with."

"Hey, I'm hotter than you've ever gotten," I said.

"Hardly witch," he said and limped toward me.

"Kamikaze." Every charm on my bracelet save the shields went active and bore down on Winsome the beast. Lightning, arrow, paralysis, water, wind, fire and more. When the smoke cleared there was a crater in the floor and Winsome was in the center of it. He was on his knees, but was barely battered.

"That all you got, witch?" he said.

"Just the warm up act," I lied.

Winsome leap more than ten feet through the air to land on me. I barely got my shield charm up in time, but he was clawing with his good hand and sending raw, uncontrolled magic at my shield. It wasn't going to hold. I barely got my last shield up before it failed. I reached for the necklace around my neck and tore it off.

The shield flickered and died. Winsome smiled and wrapped his good hand and claws around my throat.

"Any last words, witch?"

"Nope. Don't need them," I said and pulled the trigger on my Swiss mini-gun. I aimed at his missing eye and the bullet went straight into his brainpan. I changed the angle and fired again. Winsome the beast went limp and fell to the side.

I crawled away and got to my feet. He still wasn't moving. I kicked him in the groin. Twice. I figured any male would at least twitch from that. Kevin did and he was just watching. Winsome lay still.

"What the hell just happened?" he asked.

"Long story," I said.

"Is Ivory okay?"

"Yes," I said, which is when I noticed the Fable floating toward me.

I MUST RETURN TO THE NEVERAFTER, BUT YOU HAVE EARNED MY GRATITUDE. I SHALL HONOR OUR COVANANT.

I nodded, not willing to risk speaking.

FAREWELL.

The Fable vanished in a flash of magic light.

"What was that?" asked Kevin. I turned to look at him realizing that the Fable's curing him had left him with the ability to sense the Fable.

"All a part of that long story. Right now however, we are inside a building that is locked down by the FBI because of a suspected terrorist attack. We need to get out without being noticed first," I said, starting to rummage through the crates of Gingerbread Industries products in the storage area with us. I figured at the very least the cops and agents outside heard Winsome's giant form breaking through the ceilings so it wouldn't be long before they sent someone in to investigate. Most likely a team of heavily armed someones.

"How are we going to manage that?" Kevin asked.

I opened the last box to find six containers of chicory baby powder. "You'll see, but they won't."

I made Kevin carry Winsome's corpse, even with his broken finger. I wasn't about to risk something happening that would somehow bring him back to life.

Prof and I incinerated Winsome's body together, mixed his ashes with concrete, made bricks and had all but one dumped over five oceans. The last is in a Templar-Mason vault under constant video and mystic surveillance.

Ivory and Kevin did indeed get their happily ever after or at least the start of it. They are engaged to be married. The tabloids are having a field day with her marrying her bodyguard.

Georgette and Antone's bodies had to be destroyed; the risk of spreading the plague was too great. Morganna took care of that unpleasant task. Ivory and the sensational six all knew the truth, but the tabloids ran with a story that the two had run off together to a deserted island love nest.

Ivory put a stop to EVE's darker projects, even having me

supervise the dismantling. The insurance covered the damage to the building my battle with Winsome caused.

Prof was happy I had eliminated Winsome, but when I told him I did it by making an alliance with the Snow White Fable, things got weird. I didn't hear from him the entire time I was working to clean up EVE.

When that job was done, he texted me to met him at a place that was far out of my budget range, but at which any of the Wades or Ivory would have been perfectly comfortable with. I arrived early, expecting that we'd have to wait. Prof was already waiting for me at a table.

"Hi, boss."

"Jillian." Prof's tone was cool, his face stone. Not a good sign.

"How's things?"

"Can't complain."

"That's something anyway," I said. It got a smile out of Prof.

"We have certain matters to discuss." Prof reached under the table and handed me a box. "First, a little matter of my debt to you."

It was both pairs of Kate Spade boots he had promised me.

"Thank you," I said, taking out a black and a red one, putting them on and taking a short walk around the table. Gorgeous and fit like they were molded for my feet. Heaven.

"Happy?" he asked.

"Very," I answered.

"Good. Hopefully what I have to tell you next won't ruin that," he said.

I froze in my seat. What was happening? Prof had never taken me to a restaurant anywhere as expensive as this one before. This had happened to me once before with an old boyfriend.

"Oh Gods," I said. "You're dumping me."

"Excuse me?" said Prof.

"Dumping, firing. Same thing. You just took me here so I wouldn't make a scene," I screamed.

"And that's working so well so far," said Prof with a smirk.

"You are so not going to invoke the separation clause." T-M spends much time, energy and magic training its agents. We can quit, but it's costly in more ways than just money. If we're fired, there's a penalty added to it. "No freaking way. I did good. No, I did great. So what if I had to make a deal with a Fable? I stopped a greater threat. And it owes me. I should be rewarded, not fired."

"I agree."

"And I won't go quietly. I'll fight this. I'll… Wait, you agree?"

Prof nodded. "I do. You did an exemplary job. And because of that, you are being promoted."

"Supervising agent?" Each promotion level at Templar-Mason Investigations came with a sizable increase in salary. I'd be able to upgrade who I was wearing.

"Worse. Regional Director."

"What? You're Regional Director of North America. I'm getting your job?"

Prof laughed. "Hardly. We are simply dividing up things a little differently. You will be in charge of operations in the Western third of North America out of LA."

"Since when do we have an LA office?"

"Since now."

"And I'll be running it?"

"And then some," Prof said. "If for no other to reason to make sure no good deed goes unpunished."

"Unpunished? And why is a bigger promotion worse?" I asked. The money alone took me through the next two tax brackets.

There was a glint of mischief mixed with pity in Prof's eyes. "Talk to me in three months. If you don't know the answer to that by then, I may have to demote you."

"So you'll still be my boss?"

"Yes, but I'll expect you to run things. I'll be available for advice, but you will be in charge of the day to day. The Board and I have come to the conclusion that the rich and famous are the new royalty and you are the best equipped of all our operatives to understand the Hollywood and fashion types. This way we are positioned to stop the next Fable and the hundred after that. We're even starting a Bollywood office."

"Makes sense," I agreed.

"With your new connections, especially with Ivory, we expect you to be a rainmaker and bring in a lot of new clients."

Ivory had told me I was permanently part of her magnificent seven. I'm even a bridesmaid, but I already had her locked in as a client. "How am I supposed to bring in new clients?" It was actually something I hadn't been trained for.

"That's why we're eating here. We can't have you goo-goo eyed just because you're eating in a exclusive 5-star when you are trying to hook a client. You'll have an expense account. We expect you to attend the in parties, the gala openings, walk the red carpets, be at the fashion shows. You need to become one of the beautiful people and then make Templar-Mason the premier security firm for them, bar none."

I jumped out of my seat, grabbed hold of the side's of Prof's face and kissed him full on the lips.

"Do I need to file a sexual harassment claim here, Jillian?" Prof said, but he was smiling.

"As long as I get to do all that, you can do what you want," I said. "To fit in, you realize I will have the wear the current and top fashion designers?"

"Sadly, yes. You actually have a clothes allowance." He told me how much and my jaw dropped.

"That much every year?" I said.

"Every quarter."

I kissed him again.

"Can I take Morganna with me?"

"Dream on."

"This is perfect. Nothing could ruin this day," I said, fully believing it.

"Want to bet?" Prof said.

It took me a minute. "You're not really going to collect on

that month of knock offs bet, are you? Not after everything I've done."

"You better believe I am. We better hurry up and order because you have an appointment at two at the Shoearama."

"You don't need an appointment to shop at the Shoearama."

"I know, but I made you one anyway. And that's just the start of our day shopping."

As Prof described something out of my worst nightmares, I breathed in deeply and looked down to focus on my new boots.

It didn't make everything better, but at least it kept me from screaming.

PARTNERS IN CRIME

a
MYSTIC INVESTIGATORS
book

PATRICK THOMAS & DIANE RAETZ

PADWOLF
PUBLISHING

FOR ERIN & COLIN, TWO YOUNG PEOPLE I ADORED
FROM THE MOMENT I MET THEM.
-DR

DITTO.
-PT

IF AT FAUST
YOU DON'T SUCCEED

A Tale from the histories of Fable Investigations

*T*he seal on the package my brother had sent me was undisturbed, as least as far as I could tell from the light of the single candle I allowed myself. Still, better safe than sorry.

"Rivelare," I muttered under my breath. The seal glowed gold in the dim room for a moment and then faded. Good, it's not been tampered with. Quickly I unbound the linen and rope, and was left holding a thin letter and a small book. A quick glance showed that he'd sent me a grimoire. I carefully put it aside to study in depth later and opened the letter.

He wrote in English: we all did since it was ignored by the church and nobles. It was, as her Highness was wont to say, "The language of the peasant, not the civilized woman." This time he'd used a Caesar code with a shift of three letters; meaning A=C, B=D. As soon as I found the word Caesar, actually Ecguct, in the letter I knew what to look for. An hour later, I had the letter translated. It read:

My dearest sister in faith and birth
Greetings
I trust that you and your royal charge are, by our Lord's good graces, in fine health and well being. And I hope that Your Lady's confinement will take place without hindrance. Yet it is for this very reason that I reach out and contact you. I have heard from the Argel Poblogi that your charge has had dealings with one she should not know. I pray you; seek out what the Lady in question

may be involved with, lest some disaster strike. I believe the Knight's Hidden Grand Master placed you in this position foreseeing this event.

As for me, My Lord Henry VIII grows despondent at his lack of a royal heir. There are rumblings that he has petitioned the Pope with a request for a divorce from Queen Katherine. Heaven knows how the Spanish will react to that!

The rest of the letter dealt with doings of the royal court of England. I skimmed through it quickly to ensure there was nothing I'd missed and then stared at my small flame wondering what Her Royal Highness Princess Margaret Tudor of England, Queen Consort to the Late James IV had gotten herself into. I didn't have to wait long to find out.

I should have known better. But the Princess Margaret was asleep and the rest of the court was on a fox hunt. I'd thought I had some time to myself so I'd hid myself away with the book my brother had sent me. I was intrigued by a spell that would, if done right, reveal creatures hidden to mortal eyes when I heard my name called.

"Anne!" The princess came walking into my room as quickly as eight and a half months of pregnancy allowed, her eyes swollen with tears, her headdress askew. "You have to help me. I've made a terrible mistake."

It was a death sentence if anyone saw the book I was studying so I slammed it closed and hid it in my heavy skirts, hoping Margaret wouldn't notice it was there. I looked up at her, striving to appear innocent.

"Yes, Highness?" I asked. I thought the most likely cause of My Lady's unhappiness was her second husband. My Lord Douglas was famous for his wandering eye and groping hands. Just that previous morning I'd attracted his attention and he'd had no problems letting me see his interest. He also offered to let me feel it, with any part of my body I chose. I'd refused out of loyalty to the princess, but I must confess that his strong body and beautiful eyes had tempted me. As far as I could tell, I was the only one who'd told him no. Sooner or later Margaret was likely to find out about his womanizing. And as she had the Tudor strength and temper, heaven help the one she blamed.

Tears were pouring from her eyes as she cried, "It's my child."

I sighed in relief, assuming that she hadn't discovered Angus' latest indiscretion. Instead, she was focused on the custody battle she'd been fighting with My Lord the Duke of Albany over James V, King of Scotland; her three-year-old son. "Yes, yes," I agreed soothingly, like I had a hundred times before. "James is your son. You should of course, have guardianship of him."

"No, no, not that," she replied impatiently. Consciously or not, her hand went over the child in her womb. "It's this child."

"Milady?" I couldn't understand what her unborn child had to do with anything.

Tears filled her eyes again, "I, no I can't, it's too awful."

"There, there, princess," I stroked the bright red head that had somehow come to rest on my lap. "You know I'll help you. Just tell me what you did." Margaret and I were almost exactly the same age, but there were days when I felt twice our twenty-three years. There were weeks I thought she behaved as if she were half that.

"I made a deal with the devil," she whispered into my lap. My body stiffened, but I made sure to keep my hand moving soothingly across her head. Satanic magic is as evil as it comes, and almost impossible to break. The Lord of Lies had a tendency to make airtight bargains.

"Tell me more," I cajoled her. "What do you mean by the devil?"

"It was Doctor Faust," she said in a rush. "He told me he could get me nearly unlimited gold. But the price would be that

I had to give him the child that lived in my body the very hour it was born."

"For the devil?" I asked carefully.

She shook her head against my legs. "I don't know," she cried. "But surely his power comes from Satan."

I could feel myself relaxing. Margaret would have no means of knowing it, but there were those of us who were born with power. I believed it did not come from Satan but was simply born within; a gift from God. And even if Faust had made a deal with the devil, she hadn't. A human opponent was far easier to defeat than the Horned One. "Don't take the gold he offered you," I suggested. That would be the easiest way of getting her out of trouble.

She sat up, gulping back tears in the process. "Too late," she said despairingly. "He said I made my bargain, now I have to live by it."

I sighed. "Tell me what happened."

"Remember when Henry sent me the…" She spat out the next word. "…missive ignoring my request for money?"

"Yes." There was no need for her to elaborate. My Lord Albany had bribed far too many nobles for Margaret to make much headway without a significant loan from her brother. His terse one line, "Marry in haste and repent in leisure," was a death knell for Margaret's case. Personally, I thought Albany could at least let Margaret see young Jimmy, if only for the boy's sake. A three-year old was much too young to foster out. Most noble sons weren't sent off to be pages in other households until seven years of age. And Margaret would be much calmer if she had visitation rights. But no one listened to me.

"Well, I was fuming to myself." I choked back a comment and the princess found a watery smile for me. "Not too quietly I admit," she said in response to the noise I'd made. "When Faust came upon me in the garden."

"What was he doing there?" I wondered.

"Probably waiting for me," she suggested acerbically. "Half

the court hopes to find me in the garden to beg me for favors. The rest, the most influential, cater to Albany."

"But Doctor Faust?" I asked trying to get her back to the point. Faust was, I suspected the "One" my brother had warned me about.

"After the usual pleasantries, he said to me, 'Well my queen, what course shall you take now?' I should have known he was being too helpful when he called me queen," she added sadly.

"And you said?" I prompted her.

"I admitted that I knew not what to do next. And then he made me the most astonishing offer. He said if I got him a basement filled with wool, he would spin it into gold, but the cost would be unthinkably high. That as the gold he offered me would win me back my son, so he would lay claim to my unborn child."

"And you said yes?" I asked amazed that after fighting so hard for James, she would willingly offer up the child within her.

Margaret's eyes became stern. "Do not judge me," she warned.

"Of course not, your highness," I said backpedaling madly. Margaret was a dangerous woman when she chose to be. "I meant no harm. I was only shocked by the nerve the man had in making you such an impossible offer. How could any man ask you to choose between two children?"

She sighed heavily. "And how could any woman actually make that choice? Is that the question you are too tactful to ask?"

There was no good way to answer that question. I said nothing more and Margaret sighed as she admitted, "I didn't think he could do it. Why would I? Do you know the reward my brother, His Right Royal Stinginess has offered for an alchemist that could change lead into gold?"

"The immediate elevation to Lord Chancellor, with the lands and titles to go with the position," I replied promptly. It would make Faust one of the ten most powerful men in England. I'd been surprised by Henry's proclamation, since the Pope forbade studies into alchemy. But I guess Henry's perpetual quest for money was more important to him than far off Rome.

"Was he able to produce a basement full of gold?" That was the most pressing question.

Margaret nodded her head and whispered tearfully, "Yes."

"How did he manage that one?" I asked aloud. I was unable to imagine the amount of power he'd have needed. I couldn't have done a simple transmutation if my life depended on it. My brother had once, just once, changed a single flower into a feather, and he'd been so exhausted afterwards that he'd slept for nearly a day.

"I told you," she said sounding annoyed. "He made a deal with the devil."

"Maybe he did," I agreed. I was wondering if he'd offered Satan the child's soul when I said, "What do you think he wants with your child?"

Margaret's eyes opened wide. "Lady Anne, are you daft? What would any man want with the fostering of a royal child? Power of course." She stroked the bump the baby made unconsciously, "This child can lay claim to the throne of England."

I nodded, although odds were Faust was more interested in the child for mystical purposes. Otherwise, he would have taken the Lord Chancellor's position and used it to run England himself. Henry was shrewd, but he was no match for a wizard of that power.

While I was lost in thought, Margaret's hand found the book I'd all but forgotten about in our discussion. She opened it idly and then gasped, "A spell book!"

I sat there, and the only thought that went through my mind was not for my no-doubt-bloody forthcoming death. Instead, it was, 'When did the princess learn to read English?"

She backed up, still holding the grimoire in one hand. In the other, she held a cross up in front of her for protection. "Get behind me Satanic One," she ordered.

I was going to die. I threw myself to the floor and begged desperately, "It isn't what you think. I use herbs and natural ability. It is a gift from God. I don't call upon the devil."

"Witchcraft," she spat out. "Thou shalt not suffer a witch to live."

That didn't stop Solomon from seeking one out after issuing that edict, but as I could already feel the flames kissing my toes, I didn't think a biblical debate was going to help me any. The book she held in her hands was evidence enough to damn me in a church court. My great uncle's death as an alleged follower of the demon Baphomet during the dismantling of the Knights Templar would only convince the courts further. The royal princess' testimony would more than finish the job. If I was going out, I wasn't going to do in on my knees. I stood up and went on the offensive.

"It wasn't me that bartered my child for gold with a known alchemist."

Princess Margaret actually looked surprised at my attack. "Anne, I told you, I thought he was just bluffing."

Her momentary fear of me seemed to have faded. The Princess was back to the way she'd pretty much always treated me. I should have wondered why. Instead, I pointed out, "Well, he wasn't. And now your royal child will most likely be sacrificed to the devil."

She smiled at me. It wasn't the friendly smile I was used to from her. Instead, it was cold and extremely calculating, the kind she used on her enemies in the court. "Not necessarily."

"And you'll save her how?" I asked.

"I'm not going to," she said smugly. "You are." Her hand stroked over her swollen belly. "His life for yours. You find a way of keeping Faust away from him, and you get to keep your life. If not..." She smiled evilly, "Women in childbirth say such awful things."

I bit my tongue and tried to ignore the flush in my cheeks. Her behavior shouldn't have hurt me, but it did. After spending ten years in Margaret's service, I'd made the mistake of liking her. We are warned of this before being sent out into the world, but somewhere along the way I mistakenly decided that rule didn't apply to me. I'd seen her ruthless streak, but it had never been targeted at me before. Something of what I was feeling must have shown because she said impatiently, "Oh come on. I've been more than fair and you know it. I'm giving you a chance. By all rights, I should report you now, and you could be burnt by Saturday." Margaret grew cruel, "Or they could decide to question you. I saw a witch questioned once. They racked her, and I guess they went too far, because she couldn't use her arms or legs after they were done."

"Yes, it is horrible. Far worse than labor, I'd imagine," I said and watched her eyes grow colder still as she realized I had learned a thing or two from watching court politics for the last decade. "And women do say such horrible things in childbirth. Can you imagine what they would say under torture?" Now I smiled and imitated answering unheard questions. "But the Princess ordered me to read that book. Of course, she was the one who taught me to read English. How else could a lowly lady in waiting have learned it? She's the one who took me to the Black Sabbath and made me dance naked before her and the rest of her coven. Why yes, she was the leader of us all."

"You would not dare!" she spat.

"At that point, I would have nothing to lose, would I?" I said.

Margaret's mouth almost smiled. "No, you wouldn't. But now you have much to lose, don't you? True, I would be burned, but not before you."

I stayed silent but met the Princess' eyes unflinchingly.

She changed tactics or maybe just let down her guard, because her voice turned cajoling, "Please Anne. It's my child."

She was right about one thing. At least this way I had a slim chance of survival. "I'll do it," I said. Margaret's smile faded as I raised my hand, "But you have to make me some promises."

"I hardly think you're in a position to barter," Margaret replied, every bit the princess.

I shrugged elaborately. "Then take me away now," I said, feigning unconcern. Unlike the attitude I'd adopted, the next words I spoke were total truth. "You expect me to go up against a known power. One more skilled and talented than I am; who you yourself suspect has ties with the devil. Who's to say that he won't sacrifice my soul to the Lord of Lies. At least if the church gets me, my soul will be safe. Without your promises, I'd rather not take the risk."

Margaret must have believed me because, without any more argument she sighed, "Tell me your terms."

"If I succeed, I am free to leave your service with no threat of you reporting me to the church or authorities." After this confrontation, I couldn't stay even if my cover hadn't been entirely blown.

She nodded her head once, "You have my word."

"I want no retribution, regardless of whether I succeed or fail, against my family."

Margaret looked troubled. "Where witchcraft is suspected in a person, the church will often suspect the family as well."

"Then call the priest in now," I suggested. "Make your case against me to him. With luck, a witch judge can be brought here in a day or so." I thought of my elder brother Christopher and his family. Chris, the Earl of Summerset, born without any of the ability that flowed through our family's blood. Who just wanted to be left alone to run his land the way he thought fit. He didn't need to be dragged into this disaster. "And I will make my case in turn."

The princess was pacing the room. "Anne, I can't make that promise. The church is not under my control." She sounded rueful as she said, "My influence isn't that great even within the court. What if I promise to use all of my power to protect your family? Is that a fair bargain?"

This time I nodded. "Good enough. I assume I have your permission to do whatever is necessary to save your child?"

Margaret took my hands in hers. Once again, her mood had

changed, this time to something that resembled caring, "Anne, you've been my friend for a long time; at times my only friend. Do whatever you can, except please, nothing with demons or the devil. I don't want you putting your soul at risk."

I almost laughed. In one conversation she'd threatened my life, all but promised to have me tortured, blackmailed me, convinced me to fight an alchemist, and was concerned with the shape of my soul. And the funniest part is she'd done all of that to get me to do the job I'd been placed in her court to do anyway. "I swear not to call upon any demons or the devil," I agreed freely. "But I will have to fight whatever Faust has called upon."

She nodded her head, looking scared. "I understand." She leaned over and kissed me on my cheek. "Be careful," she whispered before fleeing the room.

I sat down and thought hard. I was a member of the Knights Templar. Well, technically a member of the Ladies of the Temple; the sister order. For over two hundred years, we—the Knights and Ladies—were responsible for, among other things, the regulating of magic in Europe. For the past one hundred years we'd been doing it in secret, since our order had been violently disbanded.

I needed to figure out what kind of magical power abuse I was dealing with. One kind dealt with common misuse of power, such as the witch who called a curse down on her neighbor or gave a love spell to a married man. The other dealt with fables. Some magical stories seemed to repeat themselves over and over, each time with a special twist. Otherwise, they'd be easy to solve. The fables were beings unto themselves, constantly inserting themselves into human affairs. There were also the hidden ones, the fey and the like. And of course, there were always the blackest arts and deals with the devil. Of course, there was nothing preventing all of them from working together. I wished I knew what I was dealing with.

My Uncle Patrick, also a member of the Knights, had been involved with the fabled Rapunselle. Only what was different about the story this time was the girl in question's hair had been enchanted into pure gold. The witch kept her for the money. The so-called prince that rescued her had kept her as a prisoner as well, so he could use her as his own private gold mine. By the time my uncle had found the poor girl, she was traumatized and completely unable to function in the world.

It took Patrick a year of constant experimentation to discover that the only way to break the curse was to cast a spell on her completely shaven head. Unfortunately, that meant no hair would grow in at all. After waiting six months to make sure she remained bald, Rapunselle joined a convent and prayed for the destruction of all magic users—Uncle Pat exempted. But at least my uncle had known what he was dealing with. I didn't have a clue. I couldn't think of one fable that dealt with children being offered up to Satan or basements filled with gold. It was even possible I was dealing with a new fable. It was rare and I didn't relish the thought.

From the letter my brother had sent me, he had a lead on my case. So, late that night, when the castle was still, I contacted Michael praying all the while he was alone. While I'd known the magic mirror spell for years, we never used it to contact one another. If anyone saw we'd be branded as witches. I took a silvered mirror and placed a hops and mandrake in a specific pattern around it. Then I said, "*cyfareddol drych*" and called his true name.

Michael appeared in the mirror at once. "Anna Christina, what happened?"

"Are you alone?" I asked worried that I'd exposed him.

"Yes." He sounded like he had a thin hold on his temper. "What's wrong?"

I summarized quickly everything that had happened in the last twenty-four hours. Then I added my very strong recommendation that he leave Henry's service immediately and go to one of the Templar sanctuaries.

"I'll be gone in the morning when everyone wakes," he promised. "But let's concentrate on your crisis. A member of the royal family of England and Scotland pledged her unborn child to a known alchemist in exchange for gold? You've got a hell of a problem there."

"Yes," I agreed. "Your letter indicated you'd heard Margaret was involved with someone she shouldn't be. Was it Dr. Faust?"

"The hidden ones just said someone she shouldn't be," Michael admitted. "And God knows Faust, the alchemist, would fall under that category. He's already been chased out of England, France, and Germany under suspicion of black magic. Allegedly he's been practicing for nearly twenty-four years."

"Princess Margaret seemed to think Faust had made a deal with the devil," I told Michael. "Do you think she knows something I don't know?"

"The Dominicans were going to arrest," his voice was full of sarcasm, "the good doctor on charges of having sold his soul to Satan." Michael couldn't hide the pain in his voice as he added, "And we know how well they do their research, now don't we." The Dominicans had been appointed by the church to hunt out and destroy all magic users. And we, the remains of the Knights and Ladies, were their common target.

"Their research is a little too good for my taste," I admitted. I wanted to pace, but needed to stay within the mirror's view, so I was held to something more like shifting backwards and forwards. "So, let's say they are right. Faust flees London for the courts here in Scotland several steps ahead of his accusers. Since the Dominicans don't have an order here, he figures it will take them several months to be able to arrest him. Instead of going into hiding, he makes a play for a royal child. Why?"

"What if his deal with the devil is almost up? And he doesn't want to pay?" Michael suggested.

"So he thinks that the Dark One would accept the soul of an innocent child in place of his own?" We seemed to be making a lot of assumptions, but it did all fit together.

"Not just any innocent child. We are talking about one who could easily take the royal throne. Henry's only child, Mary, isn't exactly well loved here. If it was a boy…"

"Margaret's carrying a girl," I said automatically. It was one of my gifts. I always knew the sex of an unborn.

"But Faust doesn't know that. And even so, if she was married off to someone in the right family—say York's Plantagenet son—the claim to the throne would be very strong. God knows half of England thought of Henry VII as a usurper. Within twenty years, with Margaret's baby on the throne, we could all be worshiping at the Light of the Eternal First Fallen."

We both sat silently, letting what Michael had said sink in.

"Faust could go to the Horned One with that offer," I agreed finally. "And the child's soul would be rightfully his, since it was pledged while still in the princess' body. Dear God," I prayed, "What do I do?"

"Whatever you have to," Michael replied bluntly. "Including, if necessary, killing the girl at birth and telling everyone it was stillborn. I'll leave London in the morning. With luck, I can be with you within the week."

"Wait…"

The first smile of the night crossed Michael's face. "You don't think I'm going to leave you to have all the fun, now do you?" Before I could reply, he'd severed the connection. I hated to admit it, but I was glad Michael was on his way. My brother was far more powerful than me. Still, I knew I couldn't wait for him. Margaret was far enough along in her pregnancy the baby could be delivered before Michael arrived. And I didn't think I had it in me to kill an innocent child.

The next day I faked an illness and locked myself up with my books. As I'd expected, the princess made sure everyone left me alone. I don't know what she told them, but I wasn't even disturbed with the offer of a meal.

By the end of the day, I'd confirmed there was nothing in any of my spell books which would help me fight a man of Doctor Faust's power. My best magics were what tend to be thought of as women's magic. Love spells, healing spells, ones to make a delivery easier. My personal theory was that it wasn't so much the gender, but what society viewed as a man or woman's place that limited the scope of the magics.

Regardless, was there any point in trying to get Faust to love me? I doubted it. For starters, rumor claimed Faust's interest was in men, not women. Secondly, self preservation was stronger than any spell I knew how to cast. But still, I thought to myself, if he did show any interest, I'd enhance it with magic.

I was so hungry from my day's unexpected fast I couldn't think straight by about ten that evening. And I was even more depressed by the fact I had literally no idea how to stop the bad doctor. I wanted something sweet: marzipan or even honeyed fruit would do. So a sneak trip into the kitchen was absolutely required.

A couple young men had beaten me to the food. I stood, hiding in shadows, as I watched the young pages, not more than twelve or so, digging into left over roast. It smelt like deer. There's little I like in the world better than a venison roast except Spain's new addition to cuisine, chocolate. There was nothing better in the world than chocolate. That was, so far, the greatest discovery the New World colonies had brought to Europe. I'd even accept assignment to Spain if chocolate went with it.

I stood in the shadows, hoping the young men would leave soon, so I could accomplish my raid in peace. As I stood listening, I smiled at their conversation. One of the boys was speaking, trying to sound like a philosopher. "Yes, but would changing the name make a difference? If you renamed your horse 'Racer' would he run faster?"

"Would a rose, by any other name, smell as sweet?" the other one asked, much more poetically.

"It would depend on whether you called it by its true name," I muttered to myself, recalling Uncle Pat's words when Michael, Christopher, and I had had a similar debate some fifteen years earlier. He'd told us, "True names have power, impossible to ignore. If you knew the true name of the rose, you could make it smell sweeter. Or more importantly, call upon its properties in a magical spell." Then he'd promptly taught us the true name of the rose. Well, taught Michael and me. Christopher had never been able to pronounce *plantago rosa aucuparia.*

'By God, that's it!' I whispered. If I had Faust's true name, I could steal the right to the baby back from him; probably. At any rate, it was a plan. Who knew a midnight kitchen raid could be so useful. I still hadn't gotten any food, so I stumbled into the room coughing and acting very ill. The boys looked horrified.

"Mind if I help myself?" I said, inserting coughs between words.

"Here, take mine," said the philosopher, handing me the meat he had cut on a wooden plate.

"I couldn't take this from you," I said, pretending to hold onto the wall for balance.

"I insist Milady," he said.

Thanking him, I went back up to my room and climbed into bed. While I snacked, I tried to hit upon a plan to steal Faust's name.

The next day, miraculously healed, I rejoined the court activities with a vengeance. I hunted, feasted, and danced, all with one purpose, to keep an eye on the alchemist. And through the day, I learned a lot. He was a small man; shorter than my own five foot two inches and an ascetic. He ate little, rode well and danced not at all. He dressed all in black, had a mysterious scar across one cheek and spoke with a distinct German accent. Half the women of the court had tried to attract him, with no luck.

I had Princess Margaret arrange for Faust to be my dinner partner, and he spoke of his travels, falcon hunting and Plato. He *did not* speak about magic and I couldn't figure out a good way of bringing up the topic. And damn it all to hell, the rumors about his sexual orientation seemed to be half right. He certainly wasn't interested in women. The virtually unobstructed view I gave him of my breasts didn't even bring a spark of interest to his eyes. Faust didn't seem interested in men either. Actually, he didn't seem to be interested in sex at all. He also didn't drink enough for me to try to trick anything out of him.

My first plan now failed, I settled on my second, more dangerous one. Three nights after the princess had first trapped me was the night of the new moon. If Faust was going to work witchcraft, it would be that night. And it had better work, because I was out of time. Margaret had warned me just an hour earlier that she was feeling the early pangs of labor. Within twenty-four hours the latest Tudor princess would likely be born.

Faust could not risk performing any rituals in the castle. The risk of discovery was too great, so I reasoned he'd have to leave the grounds. The darker magics work better at night. Faust didn't seem the type to over exert himself when horses were available, so I hid in the barn. I was dressed in a pair of black breeches that I'd "borrowed" from the laundry and my own black shirt. I could imagine the scandal I'd cause if anyone saw me. Then again, scandal was the least of my concerns.

I'd found a piece of bracken fern and muttered its true name *pteridium auilinum* while shaking its spores on me and my favorite horse, Holly. I'd named her after a plant well known for its protective abilities and I prayed Holly would carry them with her as well. Bracken fern didn't grant invisibility like I would have liked—invisibility, inaudibility, and a lack of footprints would be even better—but it did make the bearer less likely to be noticed. Houndstongue on Holly's hooves and under my boots made us as silent as possible. I carried a small hawthorn branch for protection in my left hand.

As I'd expected, Faust slipped into the barn an hour or so before midnight, saddled a horse without fuss and rode out quickly. I noticed he headed east and waited until he was likely to be far enough ahead that he wouldn't hear me and close enough that I'd be able to follow. I took lavender scented water and rubbed it on Holly's head to keep her calm and quiet. Then, praying feverishly, I rode out.

Luck was with me. There was a light fog and a heaviness

to the air that seemed to muffle the noise we made. I blessed my brother Chris for treating me more like a little brother than a little sister and teaching me to track deer. Compared to those elusive animals, Faust was easy to follow.

He pulled up, with me behind him, at the edge of a marsh. I tethered Holly about two hundred yards back, far enough I hoped that if she whinnied he'd hear it in the distance and not realize I was following him. I slunk forward praying that Faust wouldn't notice me. When I got close, I saw he was using rope to form a pentacle– a circle with a pentagram inside of it.

I stood silently, barely breathing, as he drew symbols I couldn't see into the ground. Then he chanted something I couldn't understand. The words fell around me, incomprehensible syllables, but with an underlying evil that I could feel.

A creature formed inside the pentacle, made out of smoke and flesh. It smelt of brimstone, its seven eyes glittered malevolently a sickly greenish yellow. Its three hands lunged at Faust and were forced back by the power of the pentacle. If there had been even one small gap in the circle, the demon would have been free to roam the country at will, wrecking devastation and causing plague along the way. I hoped with everything inside me that Faust's spell would hold.

My hand went to the cross I wore around my neck; for protection, maybe comfort. I wasn't sure which. With the stick, I drew a simple magic circle around me in the dirt. It wouldn't hold back the demon, but it might help me hide.

"Rumplestiltskin," the demon said, "Your time grows short. In two weeks our bargain comes to an end, and your time serving our master begins." Its laughter was a sound that stole the strength from my body and I nearly fell to the ground. "Unless you wish to begin your unending servitude early," it suggested. "Our master would like that."

"Mesthoploles," Faust said evenly, "I have another bargain for the devil. Tell him I offer another soul; a royal and untouched innocent in place of mine. Surely it is of more value to your master than my own."

"Why would my master wish for any soul except yours?" the demon snarled.

Faust paced impatiently around the circle. "Don't be a fool," he commanded. "My torn and tattered soul is barely of any use compared to what I offer. The child, not yet born, has a valid claim to the thrones of England, Scotland and Wales. With the right marriage, the child could rule France as well. With one of Lucifer's own—say you at its side—the child could rule all the Christian world and in a generation or two eliminate the Catholic Church entirely. How many more years would need to pass before you walked the earth freely?"

It was good, I supposed, that Michael and I had guessed properly. But at that moment I wished, with all my might that we'd guessed wrong. Because if I failed, the world as I knew it was gone.

The demon smiled hideously. Its teeth glowed red and orange, as though a flame lived inside his mouth. "Our master might accept that bargain. To walk the earth freely? I like the idea myself. But be warned, there is one who works behind the scenes to make sure your plans fail."

Oh God! I thought to myself. I was dead and worse. Demons could do worse than just kill. An eternity spent in hell was, was… I was so scared I couldn't think.

"He hides himself from me," the demon said. I perked up a little. My protection worked better than I thought, especially if the demon thought I was male.

"Rivelare," Faust commanded. I could feel his magic searching me out. With one hand I held onto the cross around my neck. With the other, I grasped the hawthorn branch meant to protect me from magic. I made sure I was still inside the circle. I was so still I wasn't even breathing. The magic slipped around me, searching, but my protection held.

"Not here. At least not within listening distance," Faust declared. "When I'm back at the castle I'll find him. Contact me through the usual means once you have His answer. Now go."

I estimated Faust still had a few minutes of magical cleansing to do, so I snuck back to my horse. Once on her, I rode as though the demon I'd seen minutes earlier was upon me. I pulled up in front of the stable to see it milling with people.

"Lady Anne," Elizabeth, a minor baron's wife, called out to me. "Her Highness is calling for you."

"Her labor?" I asked quickly, jumping off the horse. The woman stared at my clothing. I could feel the scandal brewing already. "I thought she might enter her confinement tonight," I said impatiently, "so I went to gather herbs to make her evening easier." Lemon balm and lavender had been used in birthing rooms forever and no churchman had the courage to call their use magic.

I almost ran to Margaret's room, the woman following behind me. I fell to my knees in front of the pacing princess and took her hands. They clenched mine. "Well?" she demanded quietly.

"I have it. Or a plan anyway," I promised her, speaking so that only she could hear. "But I need your help, and I need the room empty." Quickly I filled her in on my idea.

"Lady Anne," the princess said smiling, "You smell like a horse and look like a boy. Kindly change your garb into something more suitable."

"Of course, your highness," I curtsied awkwardly—breeches are meant for bowing, not curtseying—and ran to my room. As I left, I heard her ordering the women about.

I threw on clothing and after grabbing several sacks of 'medicinal' herbs I ran back into the room. As Margaret had promised, the room was empty except for her.

"Move fast," the princess ordered as she bit back a scream. "I don't know how much longer…"

"You've asked your women to get Doctor Faust for you?" I confirmed while casting ninety percent of a circle with sage and myrrh. I left the door open so Faust could enter.

"Of course," Margaret said impatiently while climbing into her bed, "The women think it's normal to want a doctor to attend me, and Faust will be expecting my summons."

I scattered lemon balm and lavender around the bed and gave the princess a ruby for luck to hold in one hand and a sapphire for health for the other. In my hand, I had sage and myrrh to complete the circle, in the other a cross. I took a deep breath. This would work, or it wouldn't. Only time, and not a lot of it, would tell. She screamed in pain as a contraction hit, and Faust came running into the room. I closed the door behind him.

"My baby?" he demanded desperately.

I ignored him and finished the sage and myrrh circle. He didn't seem to notice what I was doing. Then I turned looked at him. "Your baby," I asked archly. "Funny. I thought of you as a magical eunuch when you didn't seem to notice my interest. But perhaps, Satan's spawn, your master allows you to *enjoy* yourself with royalty?"

"You!" he spat at me, realizing, I guess, I was the one he was warned against.

"Me," I agreed striving for a calmness I didn't feel. My back was against the door, and someone pounded on it, trying to get in.

Faust muttered a word I couldn't understand, and for a moment fire danced in his hands. But as he drew his hand back to throw it at me, I screamed, "Extinga!" and the ball disappeared. Good. As long as he was in my circle, my magic would hold. If I'd been in a circle of his making, I'd have died almost instantly.

He surprised me by abandoning magic and lunging at me then drawing his hands tight around my neck. It was time to see if the name would hold him. "Stand still, Rumplestiltskin," I choked out.

He stood as if his feet were planted in the earth, but he fought the compulsion, his hands tightening around me. The world grew black around me as I struggled to hold him. "Rumplestiltskin. Rumplestiltskin. Rumplestiltskin," I croaked out through my restricted breathing. The threefold calling of his name seemed to take the fight out of him. I hoped. "Release me." His hands dropped away and I took a deep breath.

"The child is not for you." I held up a cross. "In the name of Jesus, I claim Margaret Mary Anne Tudor Stuart Douglass and her daughter Mary Douglass as children of Christ."

My words seemed to echo in the room and I knew the baby had been claimed by God. Faust could not have her. Margaret screamed out in pain again, and I could see, from where I stood, the beginning of a baby's head crest. "Anne," Margaret cried. "She's coming."

Faust's eyes met my own, tears streaming out of his. "You've condemned me," he declared.

"You condemned yourself," I told him.

"I will name you witch," he threatened me as I had threatened the princess. Margaret screamed again, "I might be tortured by the church, but you'll be right along with me. As will the princess. Let me go and we might all get out of this."

I smiled grimly. "I think not, Rumplestiltskin." I emphasized his name reminding him of the power I held over him. "I command you to silence, Rumplestiltskin. Speak not, until I tell you otherwise." When I was sure that he was now locked in quiet and added an inability to write as well I sighed. It was over.

I could hear more than one voice yelling for us on the other side of the wall. I released the circle and opened the door. The ladies came barreling into the room, to help the princess. I stood meekly and accepted the scolding that Dame Elizabeth gave me. Minutes later a baby girl wailed and an exhausted Margaret smiled.

"Mary Douglass sounds angry to meet the world," she whispered.

"A world she's free to explore on her own," I agreed. Then, I heard a voice that made me happier to hear than any other. "God's teeth! She's my sister. I demand to see her." I opened the door again, prodded Faust out in front of me and announced to the nobles waiting, "It's a healthy girl," I announced and moved out of the way as the crowd descended.

Michael hugged me. "And you, little sister?"

"Well," I replied. "You made good time."

"I was worried," he admitted. "I owe Ruby thanks for a good ride." His voice dropped, "And the little princess?"

"Safe." I smiled. "You haven't had a chance to meet Faust yet. I'm afraid he can't greet you, as he's been commanded to silence."

Michael raised an eyebrow. "You did that?"

"You expected less from your own sister?"

"No, of course not," Michael stammered. "But how?"

"I found out his true name," I said. No more need to be said, but I could see my sibling was impressed.

I slipped back into the princess' room. "My brother has come from England to tell me we are needed at home," I told Margaret.

She looked at me sadly. "Must you?"

I shrugged, "Yes Highness."

"I'll miss you, you know," she said. It was the closest to an apology she knew how to offer.

"We'll meet again. Next time you're in England perhaps?"

"Count on it." We smiled and at each other and then I slipped away. Michael already had Holly saddled for me. Faust was thrown up on a horse between us, and with him as a prisoner we rode away to our Motherhouse.

Faust rode in silence and was put in Templar custody. Two weeks later, the shadows in his cell came to life and attacked the alchemist, dragging his soul off to Hell.

As disturbing as that was, moments later his smiling corpse rose up off the stone floor holding a piece of straw between thumb and index fingers. The other hand brushed against the straw, then blew the guards a kiss. The corpse fell to the floor, again lifeless. Instead of straw, a strand of gold lay between the fingers.

There was a new fable to wreck havoc in the world. Since I was the first to discover and defeat it, the Knights Templar offered to name it after me. Not wanting my name to be associated with something so evil and destructive, I declined. So Faust got his own taste of immortality by having the fable named Rumplestiltskin after him and I write this in the hopes that someday it may help another beat the fable again.

TANGLED LIVES

A Kiki Adventure

Kiki flipped idly through her favorite manga. It was worn to death, but she still scoured every frame looking to see if there was something she'd missed. Rhoze, The Rouge Hunter, wasn't sold in the United States and she had to wait for family in Japan to send her the latest edition. Usually, her cousin liked to gather two or three issues before sending them onto her. So she was perpetually behind in trying to follow Rhoze's adventures. She wished that Mori Mozardi would create an e-zene, but the man was an old school artist and wanted nothing to do with digital technology. Gazing at the details in the scene where Rhoze captured the killer android, Kiki could understand his point. His manga was spectacular because he kept to his standards.

Kiki glanced down at herself. Blue plaid miniskirt – check. White starched oxford – check. Shiny blue wig – check. Bobby socks and Mary Janes – check and mate. From her hair to her toes she looked just like Rhoze – and about as unsexy as the teenage cartoon superhero. And at 4'10" tall and a whopping ninety pounds, she probably looked just like a teenager too.

She thought longingly of the Cat Lady costume she had hidden in her office; that's what she would have liked to wear to the Imari Halloween Dance instead of a superhero schoolgirl costume. But if Grandfather got just one hint of the five-inch heeled, thigh high leather boots or the skin tight bustier she'd be grounded for life. And it was inevitable that Grandfather would find out when it seemed like half of the Imari staff was from the same small town in Japan that Grandfather was born in.

Twenty-three years old, the owner of her own very small

massage therapy practice and afraid to move out into her own place – God, she was pathetic. But the scene that Grandfather would throw if she even thought about getting her own place made Kiki feel weak at the knees. Even Sami – Kiki's much loved half sister – didn't move out until she was twenty-nine and had been made a partner at her law firm. And at that, he'd only allowed Sami to get her own home after deeming her "unmarriageable."

The alarm on Kiki's phone went off. Oh, Thank God! It was time to lock up. She swore that she'd never do Karen, the owner of Elements Holistic Center and the woman who owned the 10x15 space Kiki rented as her massage studio, a "little favor" again. Manning the front desk on a Friday night that just happened to be Halloween wasn't a little favor. It was pure torture!

It was just as Kiki was walking to lock the front door than a man came staggering into the store.

"Oh My God!" she shrieked, "Are you hurt?"

"No," the man gasped out. He was sweating, very pale and seriously out of breath.

Kiki sniffed delicately; she didn't smell alcohol but even in boring old Albany that didn't mean the man wasn't on drugs and approached carefully. "You don't look okay."

"I'm not." The man was panting and seemed to be on the verge of collapse. "Can I…"

Kiki already had a slid one tiny shoulder under his and wrapped an arm around his warm, slim waist.

"This way," she half led, half dragged the man over to a round papason chair a few feet away. She felt a surprising reluctance to let go of the stranger. "I'll get you a glass of water," she offered and slipped away.

David looked after the girl-woman with appreciation. The wig was silly, but the face was breathtaking, with oval eyes, an upturned nose and a perfect complexion that seemed to have almost a pearly glow to it.

"Stupid," he yelled at himself. "She's much too young for you."

But then again, a dying man could dream, couldn't he?

Kiki bit her lip, wishing she wasn't wearing the schoolgirl uniform. Some girls could make the Lolita look sexy as hell. Kiki wasn't one of them. She was convinced that any man looking at her was more likely to think about school books then beds. And she didn't want the stranger to think of her as a child because even staggering around and out of breath that combination of pale skin, black hair, and blue eyes was Hot! With a capital HOT!

Kiki hurried out of the back room to find that her guest hunched over. She ran towards him, the glass of water sloshing backwards and forth. "What happened?"

He raised his pain dulled sky-blue eyes to her, blood dripping out of one ear. "I'm…"

Kiki grabbed the phone. "I'm calling 9-1-1."

"No!" he said with surprising force, "You can't. No hospital. No ambulance."

"But you need help."

"No. I can't. Please, promise me," he pleaded frantically.

Somehow her hand was in his. "I won't. I promise."

He slumped back into the chair, still clutching her hand, "Thanks."

Kiki stared at him. "You still need help," she repeated. Something needed to be done.

"No."

Kiki wasn't a doctor, but she'd had some basic medical training while getting her license. This guy wasn't in good shape. In fact, she kind of suspected he might be dying. Bleeding out of the ear was so not a good sign. It could be something as simple as cut but given the pale skin, sweating, exhaustion and… she put her hand on his forehead and was shocked by the heat. It was probably something much more serious. "Damn it – you're burning up. I've got to get you help."

"No. I just need to rest and then I'll get up and out of your way."

David shivered in the chair and prayed to gods he wasn't sure he believed in, that the girl would leave him in peace. For the past two weeks, he'd known that he was dying. Poison was working its way through his body. There was one known cure and he'd sworn the price was too high – now even that temptation was out of his grasp. He was too weak to steal. Too weak to do anything. But oh, he didn't want to die. He'd tried to squeeze every last second out of the short time he had left. That time was apparently up.

Kiki worried her lip as she decided what to do. She had the funny feeling that if she called 9-1-1, or even picked up the phone, the man currently slumped over in her chair would somehow or another find the strength to leave the store – even if he had to crawl. On the other hand, if she did nothing, he was probably going to die.

She couldn't let that happen. Something in her revolted at the idea. Her thoughts were so tangled. He called to her in a way she couldn't explain and didn't have time to explore. She just knew that there was only one real choice; she was going to have to help him. She had a secret ability that no one knew about. It wasn't a really good power like super speed or strength – but it was hers, and in this case, it might just help. She was able to psychically manipulate energy. She'd sworn to never let anyone know about her Talent – but this was a special situation.

She got down on one knee next to the man, held his hand, concentrated on grounding herself and pulled power from her solar plexus, pretended that she was giving a massage back in her studio and tried to push a tiny bit into his body. The energy tumbled into the man quicker than she expected – but then again she'd never tried anything like this with a person that ill.

Normally she only tried an energy exchange with a patient who had a bad back or hurt knee – apparently, illness absorbed energy faster.

Maybe rest helped a tiny bit. Maybe he wasn't as sick as he thought he was. Maybe the gods were listening. All David knew was that his body seemed to be shaking a little less, he was a little warmer and maybe – just maybe – he wasn't going to die in a center dedicated to a healthy life style. Maybe fate wasn't as ironic as he thought.

In for a penny – in for a pound. The energy transfer seemed to have worked – now she was going to try to see what was going on with the stranger. Aura reading wasn't easy – she'd accidentally discovered her ability during a class on chakras in college. Unfortunately, neither the teacher nor her classmates had been able to see auras – or believed her when she'd claimed to see a series of colors – so Kiki had had to teach herself. The unkind laughter in the classroom had also taught her to keep her mouth closed about anything to do with auras.

She crossed her eyes, dug deep down into her belly and "Whoa!"

David cracked one eye open. "What?"

"That's just not right. It can't be!"

David didn't bother to answer. The girl seemed nice – very nice actually. He liked how her hand kept finding his. He liked holding her hand – it was both soft and strong. He liked her. While it really sucked that he was going to die right there in her store, part of him hoped she'd keep holding his hand the whole time. It made him feel cared for. Less alone. Less afraid.

"Your aura's all wrong. I mean all kinds of wrong."

David cringed. "What are you talking about," he croaked out.

"You – you've only got four layers to your aura. There should be seven." Kiki couldn't stop her voice from shaking.

Maybe he should claim that auras didn't exist? Nah – he admitted to himself, she spoke with enough certainty that she probably had seen his aura. He needed to give her an answer she'd understand. "I'm dying," he didn't look the girl in the eye as he said it. "My auras diminished because of that."

"Your aura is black, grey, brown and faded as all hell," the girl agreed, sounding both sympathetic and confident. "but that doesn't account for the lack of layers. Dogs and cats have only a couple of layers to their auras – not humans. Every human I've ever *looked at* had seven layers."

He didn't have the energy for this, but couldn't let her think something was different about him, "How many dying people have you *looked at?*"

"Only a couple," Kiki admitted. "I did an internship in a nursing home when I was studying and a few people were really sick. Their auras had faded but they weren't missing layers, you know?" Of course, none of them were hours away from death, she thought to herself. Maybe being that close to dying made a difference.

"Oh damn," David muttered. Now he didn't know what to do. No matter how sick he was, she was a loose end he couldn't leave behind – for her sake. He put both hands on the chair and tried to raise himself up. And collapsed back into the chair.

"Please don't," Kiki found herself holding his hand again. "You don't have the strength. Rest a little longer."

"To sleep perchance to dream…" David found himself feeling whimsical. Maybe he was suffering from a touch of delirium? "Pretty soon I'll be sleeping an endless sleep."

She couldn't let him die! She didn't want anyone to die, and certainly not in front of her, but she really didn't want this man to die. She looked down at where their hands were entangled and admitted to herself that she felt a connection to him. Maybe the connection was caused by how close he was to death but she didn't want the reaper to have him. "Tell me what's wrong," she begged. "Maybe I can help."

Defeat made his voice crack. "No one can help me."

"Maybe not, but I'd like to try."

"You can't."

Sometimes actions spoke louder than words. Kiki summoned as much personal energy as she could. "Feel this," she said and carefully fed him the energy.

Tingles ran through his body, his hair stood on end; the current running between them was warm, soothing, and oddly erotic. He felt good. Better than that – he felt whole.

She dropped her hand and sank down to the floor next to where the man was sitting.

"Tell me why you have only four layers," she demanded.

As soon as the contact was broken, pain fought with health. Still-even as the poison began to overwhelm him, strength remained. Strength he hadn't felt in days. "It's dangerous. If anyone found out…"

"I don't care," she said stubbornly. "I want to know."

David should probably take the strength she'd given him and leave. It would be safer for her, but oh, the hope that she offered was sweet. Almost as sweet as she was. So, breaking the training of a lifetime, he said, "I'm not human. I'm a vampire."

Kiki jumped to her feet. That was the craziest thing she'd ever heard. Vampires were scary, sexy, fiendish, sexy, dangerous and sexy. They weren't real. And most of all-they were dead. "You aren't dead," Kiki said, sounding a little hesitant. It seemed rude to say at least not yet. He did have the sexy down though.

"Your legends and Hollywood movies have gotten it all wrong. We are not undead. What a ridicules term that is. We are living creatures, born of living parents. A race apart. We cannot make anyone else a vampire. We have souls; the Divine has not abandoned us. We live what to you is an abnormally long life and healthy we are stronger than humans but in order to live we feed off of those around us. We need the blood of a human to provide certain – let us say – nutritional and energy deficiencies."

It seemed impossible that a man of another race – much less a vampire – sat in front of her. Still, his aura was all wrong and there was truth in his voice.

"Show me your teeth," she demanded.

"Are you sure?"

"Yes." If he had teeth that could pierce human skin maybe she'd believe him. But he wasn't biting her. Not if she had anything to say about it at least.

David held her eyes with his. He smiled broadly – showing teeth that looked perfectly normal.

Kiki slumped. "Oh." She couldn't believe how disappointed she sounded. Apparently, part of her wanted the man to be a real live vampire.

"Watch," David willed the change to come on, and could feel his teeth changing – becoming sharper and thinner – more like a weapon and less like an ordinary set of teeth.

"Whoa!" The man's mouth seemed to be filled with shark's teeth.

He slumped down into the chair. "Yeah, whoa." There was no need to ask if she believed him. She was ashen faced and shaking.

"Do you kill people?" she asked, her voice shaking.

He shook his head. "We only need a couple of pints of blood once a month or so." It was the truth, but not the whole truth. There were a few circumstances that vampires killed in. But the beauty in front of him seemed scared enough as it was. He didn't want to feed that fear.

"If I cure you, will you hurt anyone?" Kiki's voice shook. She wasn't sure it was possible to heal him – but she did have an idea that she wanted to try. Maybe. Probably.

Of course, she had to have asked that question he thought to himself. The answer was going to frighten her again. "No!" He was quite forceful in this. "There is one known cure for my problem and I rejected that possibility. The known cure is to drink the blood of a donor dry and that I refuse to do. It is not acceptable that I should kill to live."

The flatness in his voice was more convincing then any ranting and raving would have been. David had made his choice

– otherwise, apparently he'd be healthy and Albany would have had one less homeless person. An ethical vampire sounded weird, but then again since he'd stumbled through the door nothing had been normal. She would trust him. "I have an idea that might help you – but first I need to know why you're sick."

Kiki thought that he looked embarrassed.

"Food poisoning."

"You're kidding me!"

"I wish."

Given all the legends associated with vampires, it wasn't hard to guess. "Garlic?"

"Or sage, pennyroyal or MSG. All of them will kill us. I don't know why though."

"I do," Kiki said, enlightenment dawning. "Each one of things you listed, except for MSG is used as an energy blocker. I bet MSG would do the same, but all the new age people I know are into nature and stuff. They'd never think to put MSG in a candle or tea or anything like that."

"Great. So now I know why I am dying." He sighed. "However, since there is no allowable cure, perhaps I should leave now." David didn't really want to go anywhere, but it was dangerous to Kiki for him to stay. She knew too much as it was. He didn't want to leave her unprotected with his brethren. He put his hands on the arm of the chair and tried to stand. His legs collapsed and he fell panting back onto the chair.

Her small fingers clasped his. "I have an idea."

Unbidden, unallowed hope rose. He tried to hide from her how much he wanted another option. "Yes?"

"Do you understand what a chakra is?" she asked.

"I've heard of them, but I really know very little about them."

"We learned about them in class. Simply put, chakras are energy points in the body, which govern various systems in the body. They act sort of like very complicated filters and are supposed to allow "good energy" to progress through the body and remove "bad energy."

"If one or more chakras are damaged in any way then energy fails to flow and those systems wither. I think what happened to you is similar in effect to a person who receives alcohol poisoning. With a human who has had too much alcohol hospitals put them in detox and clean their systems."

David excitedly interrupted, "And since vampires gain energy through human blood-draining a person to death would act as an intensifier – adding power to the filtration system."

"Exactly," Kiki smiled satisfied that David understood her.

David looked disconsolate. "But how does this help me? I'm still not willing to kill another to live."

"I can manipulate energy," Kiki announced, attempting to sound more confident then she was. "I'm going to see which chakras are damaged and try to heal them." She didn't tell him that she'd never done a chakra healing before. Why plant doubts in his brain?

"I have a couple of questions before I begin," she stated as confidently as she could.

The hope on David's face made Kiki scared. If she failed how much worse would it be for him? "Yes?"

"I'll be opening myself to your aura completely and will have to drop all my shields. Is there any risk that you could feed on me while I'm in a trance?" She hastily corrected herself. "I don't mean that you'd deliberately suck my blood. I mean could you feed on my energy?"

"I don't know. I will try not to," he said.

"Fine. While I think that there is a chance that you could accidentally drain me, I will trust you to control yourself to the best of your ability."

"I don't want to hurt you. It would be better if we forgot about this experiment." Although he seemed emphatic about this, the look on his face was too hopeful. "I will protect myself," Kiki said firmly. She thought aloud, "I want to augment my natural abilities. Since you have a sensitivity to herbs, I'm going to see what kind of crystals and candles are out back. Do you have any problems with gem stones or candles?"

"None to crystals. Generally, unscented candles are better than scented ones."

"No problem." She grinned. "I'm pretty sure that's all we have anyway."

It wasn't easy dragging David into the massage studio. He was heavy and Kiki shied away from admitting to herself that he was all but dead weight in her arms. Still – there were reasons for him to be in the studio. For starters, she arranged him so that he was laying down; which was a lot easier to work with then him huddled into a round chair. For another reason – the studio was *her* space, and she felt more comfortable. Safer. She could open her shields more easily in the massage room than in a public space. The last reason was the most important; and the one she was hiding from David. Once he was settled into a chair, she ran a quick search on energy healing. She downloaded the instructions into her cell and smiled. In case she got confused, electronic guidance was only a screen away.

"I need to touch you in order to see your chakras," she said a little self consciously. Maybe he'd think she wasn't that talented if she couldn't just cross her eyes and see his chakra. It was stupid – but she wanted him to think well of her.

He nodded, apparently not seeing anything unusual in her request.

"You have seven chakras, starting from your spine to the crown of your head, including your sexual organs. I promise not to hurt you, but I must lay my hands on each one in order to get a reading. You shouldn't feel anything strange while I am doing this." Touching David's penis was difficult. It seemed wrong to want to linger, yet part of Kiki was entranced by his body – and not in a healing way.

She was sweating lightly when she was done with the

scan. Manipulating energy around the vampire was harder than around a human. It crackled under her hands in a way she didn't expect. Still, she was pretty proud of herself to have gotten that far.

"You appear to have taken the most damage to your Solar Plexus and Heart Chakras. The Solar Plexus Chakra is where your strength and energy come from and the Heart is where the physical healing is controlled as well as blood and circulatory system maintenance." She was shamefully disappointed that it wasn't his sacral – or reproductive – chakra that was damaged. She'd been distracted enough during the scan. Losing her focus during a healing ritual could be deadly.

"So what do we do?" There was a look of complete faith in his eyes that Kiki could cure him, a look that made Kiki feel ten feet tall – and terrified. "For the moment, while I get ready, pray," she suggested.

Kiki decided to treat this healing as though David was a normal human being, mostly because she had no idea how else to proceed. Heck, some part of her didn't believe he wasn't human – even as she was working on him. Plus, there was no research book entitled, "Healing the Non-Human" in the store or online – at least nothing she was able to Google on the phone. Thus, for tonight, David was human.

The article Kiki had read on Chakra healing mentioned a containment circle. So she took a piece of packing string and created a circle on the floor around the massage table, making sure to overlap the edges. The article had been very clear that no outside energy was allowed into circle. On the circle she placed seven rainbow candles-the colors are very important-that are meant specifically for chakra work. Kiki marveled that the small metaphysical collection had the rainbow candles. It was almost as if she was supposed to do this work.

According to her training chakra work is always done in the same way; it is started at the base chakra, located at the spine and always works towards the crown chakra at the head.

This was crystal and candle work and the crystals needed to touch the skin directly. Kiki frantically used pieces of scotch tape, while wondering what a real psychic would use. Somehow tape and string didn't seem particularly mystical.

At the spine she placed a garnet, as the color of the base chakra is red. Following that, at the genital organs, she put orange citrine, feel completely unnerved as her hand lingered without her permission for just a moment longer than she should have. As weak as David was, she could feel that he wasn't unaffected either. Yellow Jasper was placed at the solar plexis and an extremely poor quality ruby was on the heart. At the throat chakra, she placed a Turquoise and between his eyes, at the Third Eye a piece of Lapis Lazuli. Finally, at the Crown she placed a piece of Amethyst.

Once all of the crystals were in place, Kiki stepped back and lit the candles surrounding them. Then the more dangerous work started. She sat down dropping naturally into the locus position and put herself in a light trance, dropped her shields and probed outwards towards David.

She tried to keep the instructions clearly in mind as she began the healing, trying to trigger each one, starting at the base. As she added energy to the base chakra she imagined it working like a flow of water that she needed to direct from hip deep inside the stream. As the base chakra triggered Kiki followed/floated with the energy lines up to the Sexual Chakra. She felt warmly pleased to note that it was not in bad shape at all.

Then she tried to direct the energy to the Solar Plexus. It was as if her little river of power hit the ocean – right where it looked like a whirlpool of a cyclone of energy was forming. All of the energy in David's system had accumulated there over the weeks unable to move. It didn't dissipate as the article had said it would. It just sat growing – building into a stronger and stronger force.

"Oh Shit," Kiki screamed to herself. "This could kill me." She struggled, trying to fight the vortex, but eventually was forced to give up. She was too weak, too unskilled. They say that in your last moments your life flashes before your eyes. That didn't happen. Instead, as she said goodbye in her heart to those she loved a sense of peace came over Kiki. It hadn't been a long life, but she'd tried to do the right thing, and that counted for more than she'd ever believed. She could leave this world in peace with herself.

Giving up, she got swept under the vortex in what seemed like a rip tide. There, as she was drowning in David's energy she could psychically "see" the blockage – something that looked like nothing so much as a large boulder.

Having nothing better to do – as she was dying anyway – she thought it would be a wonderful thing if David could live. She tried to swim her way to the obstruction. When she got there, it seemed huge. She dove down even further fighting with the last of her strength to get beneath it and pushed. Once. Twice but nothing gave. The third time – just as she expected her heart to stop beating-the boulder moved. Just a little bit but it was enough. The force of the accumulated energy got underneath it and literally pulverized the blockage out of existence. She got caught in a current that was swirling upwards and surfaced helplessly – with no more control than an average swimmer in the ocean during a hurricane.

All the built-up energy went boiling up towards the heart chakra and she was tossed about as it pounded the blockage located there out of existence. Fortunately, there was only one way for the energy to flow – upwards. So she tried to stay with the energy wave which was sort of like surfing if you've never surfed before without a surfboard. Not precisely easy but she went through the other three chakras and out of his body.

Kiki came back to herself panting, bruised and as utterly exhausted as she had ever been in her life. David lay collapsed inside the circle and all the candles were out.

Kiki crawled over to David and reached for his wrist. Good, there was a strong pulse there. His breathing was easier. She was so drained that Kiki couldn't have read his aura if her life depended on it. She'd done what she could. Unable to move, even an inch, she collapsed partly on David's stomach and partly on the floor.

She woke up some time later. She hurt. Everywhere.

She rolled to look at the man beneath and beside her. "David are you all right." Kiki hoped so. She hated the idea of him dying and of having gone through all of that for nothing.

David stirred then looked at his body and moved his arms ttentively, then his legs. Next, he stood up.

"You did it!" were the first words out of his mouth. "I'm better. I owe you endless gratitude. Is there anything I can do for you?"

"Help me up?"

He did, holding her hand a quite a bit longer than necessary and even at the point of awkwardness still seemed reluctant to let go.

"It seems well awkward to put money on tonight's work, but can I pay you for your help?"

"No, not for this. Besides, what does a healing go for?"

"Everything." David paused awkwardly. "I would ask a favor of you?"

"Yes?"

"I must tell my family what happened. How you healed me. Some of the older members may not react well. They may be upset that someone outside of the family has discovered their secret. For the time being…just the next day or so, could I ask you not to tell anyone what happened? To keep the information to yourself?"

Kiki smiled. "Who'd believe me?"

"And if any of my family or their friends have the same problem, can I send them to you?"

Kiki took a step back. "I don't know. It almost killed me."

"What? I am so sorry. Nevermind. I will not ask you to risk your beautiful life again."

"You think I'm beautiful?"

"Of course. Even before you healed me."

Maybe it was the adrenaline of having lived or being dressed like a manga character, but Kiki was feeling strangely confident.

"Then why haven't you asked me to dinner?"

David was caught off guard but smiled. "Would you say yes?"

"You'll just have to ask and find out."

"Will you go to dinner with me?"

Kiki thought about it then and wrapped her hands around his elbow. "Sure."

OPEN MOUTH, RESCUE BIGFOOT

a Blood & Bylines story

"No mom, I really can't come to your Fourth of July barbecue," I held the phone away from my ear, as predictably my mother's voice blasted out of the receiver. I was more than grateful that the office was—pardon the pun—dead to the world.

"I have to work," I lied smoothly. I wasn't sure how to tell my mom that her twenty-three year old daughter had slept with the wrong man and woken up dead. Three weeks was barely enough time for me to get used to fangs and craving blood. My mother will take much longer, especially since I never plan on telling her. She'd probably start off by calling me a soulless monster. Sadly, it wouldn't be the first time. The first time I was a kid and had put on her dress and high heels. I tripped and skinned my elbow; I'd also torn the hem. How was I supposed to know it was a designer original? I was eight.

Add to her normal judgmental nature, that she is a devout Presbyterian who thought that my job as a paranormal reporter was putting my soul at risk and you get a really bad situation. Besides, my mom thought I was still a virgin and I didn't want to disillusion her. I don't deal well with guilt.

I tuned back into the conversation to hear my mother belittling my job. I interrupted the tirade. "Mom, I have the greatest job in the entire world." I exaggerated a bit. I love my job, but the greatest job… that would be a nationally syndicated columnist or a bestselling author. I hadn't decided which was better yet. I planned to be both, but I wasn't either…yet. For the umpteenth time I swore to myself I'd get myself there.

This time I couldn't tune out her response. "You work for a tabloid rag that glorifies ungodly things," she said judgmentally. We'd had this argument a dozen times before and I could predict word for word how it was going to go.

"World Beyond News doesn't glorify ungodly things," I protested, but our view of all things godly differ greatly. I couldn't argue the tabloid status, but I've never understood what's wrong with a tabloid. Can all those millions who buy them at the checkout counter in the grocery aisle be wrong?

"Stacy LaMonica's daughter graduated from the same school as you and she's a cub reporter for the New York Times."

If there was one thing I hated more than any other, it was being compared to the always saintly Lori LaMonica. The girl never gained weight, still lived at home which allowed her to take a job that paid peanuts and was engaged to her high school boyfriend, Aaron Kruger. He had been the captain of the football team and was now an investment banker. Worse, Lori attended church every Sunday with her parents. I don't even know if I can still set foot inside one without bursting into flames.

"Mom, Lori types up the obituaries. They don't even let her write them. And she makes about a third of what I make." The money was only one of the many reasons why I'd turned down New York's most prestigious newspaper. Unlike Lori, I was guaranteed a minimum of one story a week but usually wound up with three or four, could work whatever hours I wanted and was paid a princely 48K a year. The Great and Exalted alternative wanted to pay me a measly 16K. Get real. My current salary wasn't enough to fulfill my dream of living in the Village, but Hoboken wasn't so bad.

My Mom ranted some more. I flipped through some story notes. I realized she was done when she said, "You have no place to go." That's the advantage to re-having the same conversation over and over. I know when to start paying attention again.

"There is plenty of room for advancement. World Beyond

does a lot of celebrity stories." Pretty cheesy celeb stories, I admitted to myself, usually involving their involvement with aliens or Elvis. Regardless stars sell, so every week there was one on the cover. "Lots of magazines look for that kind of experience. Plus, since I started working here I sold *two* short stories."

Mom went off on another rant, this time about the premarital paranormal sex in my stories, but I'd had enough. It wasn't my fault that she didn't like paranormal romance stories, and I didn't want to hear about how I was in danger of going to Hell. It was too confusing, especially given my new status as the undead. I wondered—did I even have a soul anymore? Even for a semi-lapsed Presbyterian girl, it was too depressing to think about. "Could we talk about the barbecue," I asked in desperation. "How late do you expect it to run?"

She shifted gears as swiftly as I did, now that she had a chance of winning and getting me out to her house. "It'll start around four o'clock, and we'll be serving dinner at six thirty..." her voice trailed off.

I quickly googled sunset on the internet—8:27 PM. My mind raced, making plans as I spoke. "I'll try to get out to Long Island by nine o'clock." It could work if I got my massively cool roommate Janey to drive. She had tinted her car windows about two and a half weeks ago to make life easier for me. We'd leave Hoboken about eight when the sun was low and I'd hide under a blanket. I hadn't been warm since my undeadly conversion, so even in July, the blanket wouldn't be uncomfortable. Besides, if I knew Janey she'd want to blast the air conditioning. Maybe I'd wear a coat as well.

"I'd like you to be there earlier," my mother was saying. Thank God the phone on my desk started ringing.

"Mom, I've got to go. Work." Before she could ask me why I was working on a Tuesday night at ten o'clock I added, "Janey and I will be at the barbecue around nine. See ya then." I knew she'd complain about my bringing my roommate—my mom had this weird aversion to blue highlights in a natural blond—so I hung my cell up before she could say anything and grabbed my work line. "Angela speaking."

"There's a Bigfoot at the Rathskeller," a person I'd later quote as an unnamed source told me in a shaky voice. "Come quickly." She hung up and I was left with a million questions.

The phone rang again. "There's a Bigfoot at the Rathskeller." This caller was a man whose voice made my knees go weak."

"That's what I hear," I said.

"Really? Then can I assume you'll be coming to cover the story?"

I could swear this guy was flirting with me. "I'm thinking about it."

"Good," he said and hung up.

Three weeks and three days ago, I would have assumed that the person in question would be an unshaved college student on a bender and the source one of the hundreds of New Yorkers who liked to wear tinfoil for a hat. I still thought that the odds were high that I'd find my drunk, but now I wasn't able to scoff at the idea that there was such a thing as a Bigfoot. After all, some would consider me a figment of someone's imagination too.

The Rathskeller, named after the hundreds of rathskeller basement beer bars located all over New York, is right off of Astor Place in The Village. A glance at their web page told me that Apollo's Arrows, a retro punk band that had been garnering excellent reviews, was playing. I decided to head down there and meet my sasquatch. And if he didn't pan out I'd write a review of the band. The paper had a "Get Out NY" section. Granted, the boss preferred an esoteric twist, but with a band called Apollo's Arrows I could always make something up.

A quick call to my roommate and some major cajoling later, Janey agreed to meet me at the club. The entire time I was on the phone I was composing my band story's lead sentence. I'd never seen them perform but I kind of liked something like, "With a godlike body and the voice of an angel lead singer Helios is a worthy heir to the god that blessed his band." It'd go over well with the boss. Assuming that most of our readership knew that Helios was another name for the sun god Apollo and the singer wasn't a total geek.

Twenty-minutes and one subway ride later, I got my first inkling that the evening was not going to be a normal one. Not even for the intrepid paranormal reporter I considered myself to be. There was the usual crowd of people waiting outside the velvet rope. I'd put it at five hundred, which was a sizable number. The music that burst out onto the street was loud, raucous and in its own primal way unbelievably good. I was more in touch with primal these days. None of that was odd, not even the three cop cars parked in front of the building. A little excessive, but there *was* an all-night donut shop on the corner. What attracted my attention was the large black town car. Its windows were tinted to the point of looking like onyx and it had federal government plates.

"What's going on?" I asked a cute Goth guy in line ahead of me. He would have been a 9 at least on the Hunk O' Meter if he hadn't had quite so many piercings or makeup. I'm okay with an ear or tongue ring, but multiple heavy steel rings in tongue, lip, eyebrows, and nose was just too much. And call me old fashioned, but when the guy wears more mascara than I do, it's a turn off. Even with all the negatives, he registered a solid 7.5-pushing an 8. I tampered down the part of me that screamed to use my vamp sexual powers to seduce him with a look and focused on the matter at hand. Then he smiled and went up by another .5. Maybe I wouldn't even have to resort to vamping him. Goths are supposed to be into vampires, aren't they?

The tongue ring made him lisp and he lost the extra rating. "Some totally hairy guy got trashed and totally flipped out. I saw him go in. Walked to the front of the line and he was so big, nobody stopped him. Hairy was totally minding his own business when some babeage like hit on him. They talked in some foreign language for like a minute. Then he majorly freaked out and threw a table across the room. Then the lady started yelling he's a sasquatch. The dude was hairy as hell and had some huge fur boots on and was a little crazy, but Bigfoot? Get real. ”

A Goth who spoke Valley. It was a weird blend of two distant decades. For a moment I wondered if he was a vampire trying to pass but was too out of touch with modern lingo. It was a depressing thought that I didn't want to pursue; not that I knew how. I mean there wasn't some secret vampire handshake. At least not one that I'd been taught. Not that'd I'd been taught anything.

Meeting the Goth made me question myself. In twenty years would I be standing around wearing platform stilettos with a mini and trying to pass as twenty-two? No way. At that moment I made a vow to myself. Classic styles only. Lost in thought, I paused at least a second too long before responding. "Sounds like a normal Friday night." Of course, it was actually Tuesday. My neck shot to the side as the door to the government car opened.

Valley Goth guy joked. "Looks like the Men In Black came with the police." But he was actually right.

Ca-ching! The boss would flip out over this story. I casually snapped a couple of photos with my phone. That's usually why a lot of tabloid photos are so blurry. If these guys saw a real camera, first amendment or no, they'd take it. Other things would react more violently if they knew they were being photographed. "So why did you call the big guy crazy?"

"Everyone knows to get out of Dodge when the fuzz show up, right?"

"True," I agreed, although I can't remember the last time I'd heard police called the fuzz.

"The hairy dude stayed and resisted arrest after the coppers show. Tossed around the cops and broke a lot of furniture. Probably ate the worm out the tequila bottle if you know what I mean. Most of us came outside until it was done."

That didn't sound right. "But the music's live."

Valley Goth guy shrugged. "The band totally refused to stop playing. Cops tried to move them out, but the lead singer totally Obi Waned them. Did this, 'We are here to play our music' thing and the cops agreed. I'm waiting to see the rest of their set."

Two stories in one night! The boss was totally going to love me. Damn, Valley speak is catching.

The cops probably wouldn't let me in the club, but intrepid paranormal reporters don't always listen to the police. At least not if they want to get their story.

As a vampire, I was supposed to have a whole bunch of nifty new powers, at least according to the research I'd been doing, both online and using the mostly hardcopy resources of World Beyond. Life would have been easier if the rat bastard who'd turned me into a vampire had bothered to instruct me in anything. It's why we're currently somewhere between a feud and a war. I'm winning, the pen being mightier than the fang and all that.

I'd been practicing, but mesmerizing large groups of people, or even my boss, was not something I had mastered yet. Hiding in darkness was another matter. That I rocked at. And the Rathskeller had plenty of shadows.

I thanked the maybe vampire Goth guy and slipped away from the crowd. Out of the streetlight in the shadow of the alley, I drew a cloak of darkness around myself and skulked into the club.

Some New Yorkers claim that a person could walk naked down Fifth Avenue and no one would notice. I find that hard to believe. Fashion watching is a spectator sport for some people. The Bigfoot obviously wasn't one of them. The police were trying to wrestle him to the floor and had his fur practically dosed in pepper spray. There was a pup tent sized overcoat on the floor that looked like it had been torn off his back.

He was big, at least seven-foot-tall and completely covered in hair. So covered, in fact, that he didn't seem to be wearing any clothing; just fur. From the look and the smell, it was obviously real. In fact, one clubber with a black PETA t-shirt was screaming at him that fur was murder and was spraying him with red paint whenever he got away from the cops.

It was obvious to me this guy wasn't human, but nobody else seemed to think so.

"Damn sci-fi geeks. Bad enough they're running around the village dressed as vamps. Now they gotta try Wookies," said one of the cops.

"Drinking in this heat in that get up. No wonder he's going crazy," said another.

The pair pinned him to the ground. "Get the mask off. We don't want him choking on his own vomit."

The other one pulled on the sasquatch's head which got him a growl. "Boy, this guy likes to stay in character. And he must have glued this thing to his head, cause it ain't coming off."

"Big feller aren't you?" said the first cop.

"Drunk as a skunk," said the other as he pulled the Bigfoot's hands behind his back and snapped cuffs on them. I got a picture with my phone, but I knew the cloak of darkness would make it cloudy at best. I could see the headline now. "FLATFOOTS MANHANDLE BIGFOOT".

"From the smell, he's been on this bender a while." He took a deep breath and choked a little. "A long while." The cop searched the hairy hide up and down then back again. "Damn it! I can't find the seams on this damn costume."

"Don't worry, Hal. We'll cut it off him when we book him at Midtown. He'll smell better in a nice clean orange jumpsuit."

"Yeah, well, you don't have to ride to the lock up with him, Dan. I do."

"Sit up front and keep the AC on."

"Maybe I'll just use one of our gasmasks."

Hal the cop searched through the torn overcoat but didn't find a wallet or ID. "Hey jerkoff, what's your name?" The Bigfoot didn't answer. Hal shook him more than a little. "Look, Buddy, so far we've got you for public drunkenness, disturbing the peace and resisting arrest. Don't make it harder on yourself. Tell us who the hell you are."

Nobody was the least bit intimidated by the non-human creature on the floor. A couple cops were pissed off that they had to work to take him down, but that's not the same thing. The feds in the black suits were watching and looked like they were scheming. My reporter's instinct said they were the greater threat to the sasquatch. If they got their hands on him, I doubt he'd end up in a drunk tank or even Riker's. Maybe the government would use him to prove that humans weren't the only people on the planet. Or worse, the feds already knew and were really covering it up as part of some huge conspiracy theory. I'd bet Bigfoot wasn't a citizen. He might even end up imprisoned at some super-secret meta-normal Guantanamo Bay.

The sasquatch on the floor grunted and sniffed at the air. How he could smell anything over his own stench was a mystery to me, but his head twisted towards mine. I don't know if he saw or just sensed me, but he knew I was there. He had the saddest eyes of any person I'd ever seen. Those big monster browns held a look of utter desperation. In that moment I went from gleeful reporter to an involved and concerned citizen.

I realize the guy wasn't human, but he was still a person. I'm embarrassed to admit that the look he gave me reminded me of Peaches. Not the fruit. I wasn't that far gone. Peaches was my childhood dog. She gave me a similar look the day some idiot ran her over with a car right in front of me and kept driving. I ran to her. Peaches was in agony, whimpering, but she looked to me to make it all better. I put my hand on her head and she licked my fingers. We took her to the vet, but they couldn't do anything to help her. The only thing they could do was end her pain before it ended her. I held her and sang to her, told her everything was going to be all right as the vet gave her the shot that ended her life.

I still have nightmares about that day.

I couldn't save Peaches, but maybe I could save the Bigfoot. However, if he tried to lick my fingers, all bets were off.

The question was how? I hadn't managed to get my cloak

of darkness around another person. Janey and I had tried a few times to get into clubs without waiting in line or paying the cover, but it didn't work so far. This guy was twice Janey's size.

I hadn't tested a lot of my research on vampiric powers. The whole mind control thing wasn't about to magically start working for me. Supposedly we can turn into animals like bats and wolves, but I'd been too afraid to try. What would happen if I couldn't change back? And a little bat wasn't going to be able to do squat against six of New York's finest. A wolf would only get captured by animal control or shot. Neither thrilled me.

The mind control wasn't just limited to people. Supposedly we can make like Dr. Doolittle and command vermin. It might be cool, but who needs a pet wolf in Hoboken? Especially with the pooper scooper laws.

I was super-strong, but I wasn't going to get into a fight with a bunch of cops who were just doing their jobs. A friend of mine from high school was on the job. Looking at these guys, I saw him. If I hurt them, I'd never forgive myself. I could grab Bigfoot and run like a bat out of Hell or Hoboken, but I'm sure I'd get us both shot in the process. I might be able to take a few non-silver rounds, but I doubted big, hairy, and drunk could.

The lead singer was still belting out his songs. His last lyrics started going on about a rock and a hard place and it got my attention. I looked up at him and he winked at me. Great. Why was I bothering with the whole cloak of darkness thing? Was it even still working? I waved at the nearest cop and he ignored me. That was something at least.

I gave Helios a look of desperation that probably paled beside the one the Bigfoot had given me. Valley Goth guy said the police did as he told them. Maybe I could get him to tell them to go away.

"We're going to take a break," Helios announced to the mostly empty room. "We'll be back in fifteen minutes to start another set. Remember to tip your waitresses and hug a cop."

The PETA chick actually obeyed. Hal the cop just got

annoyed and took her can of spray paint.

Helios walked off the stage like he owned the place. He was easily off the hunk-o-meter scale in every category. He veered so he passed right by me.

"Help me," I begged as quietly as I could. The cops didn't move.

He stopped and touched my cheek. My face felt warm, like it was alive again. It was amazing. You never even notice little things like having body heat until are missing them. He leaned and whispered in my ear. "The power you seek is within you."

"That's not exactly the type of help I was hoping for," I whispered.

"You can't always get want you want, but you already have what you need." And with that bit of wisdom lifted from the Stones, he walked off. Then he stopped and turned back. "Glad you decided to come, Angela."

Well, now I had a good idea who the male caller had been. That was freaky. Maybe it made me shallow, but if he had been less hot I would have thought it down right disturbing. Like stalker disturbing. Instead, the idea that he knew who I was made me tingle. I'd deal with him later-when I had time.

My stomach felt as if a hundred bats were trying to break out. I was never going to pull this off. The cops were lifting the Bigfoot to his size gazillion feet. Next would be the police car and the ride to Midtown South, the biggest and scariest police station in the entire world.

Maybe I could try to bail the guy out of jail. Bad idea. I doubt I have enough money and I don't even know his name. If he got to booking, the game's over.

Or he might not make it to Midtown South if the Feds take custody. They could really be Men In Black. My guess is the cops would willingly turn him over. They weren't going to get promotions from arresting a drunk and disorderly.

I started to pray, hoping that God still listened to prayers from vampires when I got an idea. A rat ran across the floor in front of Dan the cop as they were dragging their furry perp out. The cop jumped a good foot in the air, landing to catcalls from his fellow cops.

"Shut up! I hate rats."

Maybe one or two rats wouldn't scare away New York's finest, but I wondered what a thousand of them would do? New York City rats are legendary for not only being the size of cats, or occasionally dogs, but are also said to carry diseases. If I saw a bunch of rats rushing toward people, I know I'd be thinking rabies. It should be enough to at least distract them from Bigfoot. If the rat thing worked, I'd be running once I freed Hairy. Rats, belch.

How was I supposed to do it? The only way I knew how to call animals was to stand in the middle of the street and yell, "Here Kitty." That probably wouldn't work. However, I'd done a story on a Manhattan witch circle. They'd spent a lot of time droning on about the Will and the Word and the importance of visualization in spells. I hadn't tried to learn any of their magic. It seemed wrong to the good Presbyterian girl I was raised to be but fell far short of. Problem is, she's in the back of my mind giving unwanted commentary. Worse, sometimes she sounds like my mother.

I'm a vampire, which meant I shouldn't need a spell. Visualization made as much sense as anything else.

I sat down cross legged in the shadows, leaning back against one wall of the bar. I mimed for Bigfoot to keep struggling. I worried it looked like I was having a seizure, but the sasquatch seemed to catch on. I tried to open my mind up to the rats, but the whole concept had a shiver running down my spine. Ick!

Lots and lots of rats. Squirmy icky rats. I was grossing myself out, which lead my mind to want to change the subject, and what I saw instead was Peaches. I tried to get back to the rats but instead, I saw more dogs. The poor strays at the animal shelter I used to volunteer at before my untimely demise. I hadn't been back since and I missed it. I could envision every dog that had been in the place, from Walter the mournful Basset Hound to a pair of overactive Dalmatians siblings named Spot and Fritz. My brain took off and I found myself thinking about a toy poodle I'd seen walking her owner earlier this evening. She'd been very prim and proper with a pink coat, ribbons in her hair and the absolute knowledge that she was the most important being in all of Manhattan. From how her owner behaved I knew he agreed.

Focus Angela, I scolded myself. Thinking about Golden Retrievers and toy Poodles wasn't going to help. Rats would help. Big, scary, disease ridden rats. That's what I needed.

The cop called Hal opened the door in preparation for moving the Bigfoot out. He was standing on the first step out of the Rathskeller when I heard a dog's deep bark. Followed by another. Then three more different barks.

I was horrified. I hadn't just… But I had. Hal was knocked to the ground by a huge Bernese Mountain Dog. The thing must have weighed close to two hundred pounds and it whined as it headed right for me looking for some petting. Moments later he was followed by three Labs, a handful of mutts, four Dalmatians, a sleek Wolfhound and the toy poodle from earlier who looked very proud of herself. All of them had leashes attached, but the four hungry and slightly tattered looking mutts that followed did not.

Great, just great. I'd accidentally summoned possibly the friendliest animals on Earth. Maybe they could lick the cops to distraction.

I took a deep breath to help me focus and almost choked myself since vampires don't have to breathe except to talk. When I could see straight again, I ordered the dogs to knock down and sit on the nice police and Men In Black. They obeyed with varying degrees of success as more and more dogs—some with owners still attached—came running, jumping and galloping into the club. I spared one moment to smile as I saw the poodle pawing imperiously at the nose of Dan the cop. The big Mountain Dog sat on his chest, but apparently, the poodle princess thought that the "kill" was hers.

It was time to play super-vamp. Using my super-strength and speed I grabbed the sasquatch. Putting him over my shoulder, I headed out the door. The guy probably weighted nearly three fifty but felt more like ten. The cops started yelling orders, but the dogs were still listening to me. Nobody reached for a gun, afraid of hitting the dog owners. Not to mention the PETA chick was threatening what she'd do if anyone harmed a hair on a single dog's head.

I paused at street level and saw Janey who, along with a huge crowd, was watching the Rathskeller dog show. I said hi and she stared at what I had over my shoulder. Before anyone else could get a good look, I put her under my other arm. I was rewarded by the occasional "Ouch" or "That hurt" as I headed for the subway.

There was no time for using my Metrocard. The dogs may have stopped listening the moment I left, which meant the cops might be right behind me. I threw Tall Dark and Hairy over the turnstiles and took a flying leap over them myself, Janey still in tow. She screamed something about my parentage when her knee hit. I had similar questions, so I didn't give her grief. I pulled at the cuffs and broke the chain. The bracelets were stuck on for the moment.

"Thank you," he said, speaking in front of me for the first time.

"You're welcome," I replied. "Better stick with us for the time being."

Large and hairy was back to being strong and silent. He answered with a nod.

An uptown 6 train pulled in and we all got on. It was late, so it wasn't crowded. We acted natural. People stared but by and large let us be.

I briefed Janey and she started barking out the best route to throw anyone off our trail. She insisted we transfer subways three times before we were allowed to catch the Path home. As had become normal since I became the undead, I was sick the entire time we were under the Hudson River and the Bigfoot's odor didn't help. At least there was a tunnel to Jersey, I consoled myself. I was quite literally unable to cross the river over a bridge without help.

Once we were safely ensconced in our apartment, Janey turned to the Bigfoot. "Okay buddy, start talking. Who are you? What were you doing in a bar in Manhattan?"

There's nothing my roommate loves more than subtlety. Hairy's hide was still covered with pepper spray and red paint. I didn't want any of that on the furniture, so I threw an old blanket over the couch and invited the sasquatch to sit. "Would you like anything to drink? Beer, wine, coffee, tea, diet soda?"

He grunted, then said, "Beer."

I didn't even bother asking Janey. I grabbed two microbrews out of the fridge along with a cup of frozen pig's blood for me. I'd been experimenting. Since I couldn't keep anything down but blood and red wine I was trying to come up with new things to do with blood. The frozen cup o'blood was my attempt at an Italian Ice. For the record, it was a raging failure, but it did get those little frozen crystals on the bottom like regular Italian ices. It was the only part that was half decent. Maybe next time I'd add sugar and cherry syrup. Or find a diabetic pig. Or both.

"What's your name?" I asked when I was finally settled in my dad's old recliner. I might have laughed at him all the way through my high school years over his maroon monstrosity, but the man was right. There was no chair on earth more comfortable to watch a football game in. I snapped it right up when he upgraded to a more modern natural leather one. Three times he'd tried to get me to switch back with him. He even offered to throw in a leather sofa to sweeten the deal, but I'm no fool. That chair was perfect.

"They call me Cocheta" he replied with an odd accent. It was part French Canadian, part Native American and part Bronx.

"Let's shorten that to Chet. Where you from?" I asked. He

had a cool voice. It was deep and sounded like a refined grunt.

"I guess you won't believe Jersey?"

I shook my head. "Toxic waste isn't that bad yet."

"My people live in what humans call Upstate New York near the Canadian border."

"You're a Bigfoot, right?"

"We prefer sasquatch, drinkers of blood." The growl was deeper as though I'd managed to offend him somehow.

Janey cut in. "She's the vampire around here. I'm just a plain old human." There was a warning in her voice that any male, human or non would recognize.

Chet tried to undue his offense. Half standing out of his seat, he bowed, "I apologize, Lady." Sitting, he was as tall as Janey. Standing, his head practically brushed our ceiling. His action gained a smile and, astonishingly enough, a blush from Janey.

"So what are you doing here?"

If it was possible for a walking rug to look sheepish he pulled it off. "I was bored."

I lost it. The terror I'd felt watching the cops trying to arrest Chet, the mad dash for the subway, the fear that the police or, even worse, the Men In Black would know I was involved and for what? Boredom! I was slightly pissed. "Are you out of your ever-loving mind? Are you an idiot?" My voice hit an octave that made both Janey and Chet cringe.

Chet slumped deep into the sofa and whined, "You don't understand."

"You're damn straight I don't understand, mister. You've got some explaining to do." A second later what I said hit me. Oh, my God. That didn't come out of my mouth.

"Turning into were-mom now?" Janey asked coolly, confirming that my verbal diarrhea had indeed actually occurred.

I didn't know that I still had enough blood in my system to blush, but I managed it. "Sorry."

Janey threw me a glare that told me my coolness factor was definitely on thin ice, at least for the moment. Sounding like my mom was a near unforgivable offense. Janey decided to ignore me and turn her attention toward the sasquatch in our apartment. She gave him a warm smile. He smiled back, which was a little disturbing. His incisors were almost as pointy as mine. "So how did you wind up in the Rathskeller?"

I muttered, "Bad luck." It earned me another glare from my roomie.

"My people..." He hesitated and started again. "My tribe hides from humans in the forests following the ways that have been old before this country even existed. We migrate with the deer and we live in camouflaged tents and caves. We do much to keep from being seen." I had an image of a tribe of Sasquatch hiding out in a state forest. The reporter in me wanted to know how the heck the Park Rangers hadn't found them.

"You sound like you came from a Native American tribe from a couple of hundreds years ago," Janey offered.

He squirmed in his seat. "Men of my tribe did kidnap and mate with Osawa women." Janey's face got dark. She was big into woman's rights. Chet hastened to add, "It was many years ago. Generations."

Janey's expression changed. Her pupils got wider and she got a sly smile. "So your people have mated with humans before?"

"Yes." Chet was smiling back.

"Can we get back to how you ended up in New York City?" I said. Chet looked embarrassed and Janey glared at me.

"One day I found a radio."

"You got here because of litter?" I was incredulous. Even World Beyond's audience was not going to believe this story.

"It had a crank so it never ran out of power. The radio spoke of many things. Amazing things beyond our way of life. I wanted them."

"Why New York?" Janey asked.

"The radio talked about how anything could happen in New York and how anyone could be accepted. I thought it would be a good place for me."

Janey and I shared a glance. "Well," I conceded. "You probably passed longer in New York than you would have in Peoria."

His brown eyes gave me a confused look. "It's a saying of sorts." Then I thought about what he'd have to do to survive in the city. "You have no money. What have you been doing for food?" I didn't even ask about where he'd been staying since I'd bet any amount of money the answer was Central Park.

He seemed genuinely surprised at my question. "There is much small game roaming free through the city. I found missing cats and dogs upset people. Squirrels and pigeons are the tastiest of the rest."

The thought made me gag and I lived on animal blood. "Are you crazy? Do you know how many diseases those things carry?"

Janey raised an eyebrow. "Another were-mother moment?"

I shuddered. Becoming a vampire was still better than becoming my mother. "Call it a reporter moment. Are you hungry?

"Very," said Chet.

I all but ran to grab my phone. I had the local pizza parlor on speed dial from the glorious days before I went on the blood diet. "Can I get a large, double on the sausage, meatball, and pepperoni?" I glanced at the size of the sasquatch. "Better make that two."

"Ever had pizza before?" Janey asked.

"What was left in boxes in dumpsters and on plates in clubs," said Chet.

"You ate off other people's plates?" asked Janey.

"Finished their drinks too. We did it when campers left food behind at home. Here it's just easier to find. It's how I found out I like beer," said Chet, finishing his microbrew. "I really like beer."

"Well, pizza's better when you get your own piece unchewed straight out of the box." I noticed that she punctuated her comments with a stroke of his fur that lasted a moment or two too long to be a causal touch. Janey's love life had been slow of late and she loved to take in strays. She was the one who got me to volunteer at the shelter. I guess Chet offered her the best of both worlds.

I sighed sadly. Not over the interspecies flirting. Over the pizza. One of the many things that I wasn't able to enjoy anymore was pizza. They all seemed to have a trace of garlic in the sauce. Ran through my system like battery acid.

Her hand was resting on Chet's thigh as she was laughing at whatever he said. He seemed to be enjoying it. Problem was he wasn't wearing any pants and if the amount of fur being moved was any indication, it was true what they said about guys with big feet.

"Conference?" I asked Janey.

"Please excuse my friend for her rudeness," Janey said to Chet, then used her body to shield the fact that she was slapping me in the shoulder. "Be back in a minute."

The Sasquatch heaved himself to his feet.

"I go," he volunteered.

"No," we replied in unison. I was thinking about the police and possible federal interest in our visitor. Not to mention a question that had just popped into my brain—who was the woman who'd identified what he was in the first place and called me? Was it the same one that set him off?

Janey had different concerns. "You have no money, no place to stay. We can't ask you to leave." Her hand was on his arm again.

I glanced at the nearly seven-foot-tall guy in my apartment. Janey and I shared a small two bedroom. For a day or two, tall dark and hairy could stay on the couch, but I wasn't hugely enthusiastic about the idea. For starters, he stunk, not badly, but like a wild animal. And that didn't include how big he was. How much space he took up. How much food he'd eat. Janey had had two pieces of pizza. Chet had the rest and there wasn't even a piece of crust left.

I still had to agree with Janey. We couldn't let him loose in the wilds of Hoboken. It was just dead wrong.

I turned on the television and flipped around until I found a baseball game and left Chet playing with the remote.

"I'll explain the rules of the game when we get back," I said.

"No need. Learned all about baseball from my radio. I've already snuck into two Yankee games," he said. "I hope they cream Boston."

We'd wordlessly decided to use the kitchen to talk. I set up the popcorn popper. One of the worst things about being a vampire was the lack of food. I'm a total foody. Still, no reason why I couldn't introduce our guest to real popcorn; not microwave. I'd top it off with real butter, none of that favor crap, and sea salt. Yum. My mouth watered just thinking about it. Smelling it was as close as I'd get to enjoying it.

"Janey, he's got to go back to the woods or something."

"You mean set him free?" asked my roommate.

"Basically."

"He's not a wounded bird. He can decide what he wants for himself," she said.

"He can't stay here. How would we hide him?"

I got the gimlet eye in return. "We aren't kicking him out. You heard him; he doesn't want to return home." Actually, he hadn't said any such thing. But I kind of suspected that he didn't want to leave the city either. It was in his sad eyes.

"And the fact that you've got a mad crush on him doesn't enter into it," I said sarcastically.

Janey pulled a few of the popped kernels out of the bowl and put them in her mouth. She was having trouble looking me in the eye and her face was bright red. I could sense her quickened pulse. You know I've always liked them tall and hairy."

"It'd be hard to beat Chet in either of those categories," I conceded.

"And did you see the size of his…"

I shook my head. "And I don't want to."

"Can you just imagine…"

"Ick and yuck. Too much information," I said, covering my ears. "There's a visual I'm not going to get out of my head for weeks."

My roomie shrugged. "What can I say? I'm a non-traditional kind of girl."

"Janey, keeping him here too long is too dangerous."

Janey's always had a trump card and she finally played it. "Look, I didn't say 'Ew she's a vamp' when you were changed, did I? Nope, I tinted the apartment windows and the ones in my car. I gave up shrimp scampi and garlic bread in the apartment. I called my cousin the butcher and got you a steady supply of blood, regardless of what the tongue wagers in my family are saying about why I need it. Well now we've got old Chet the Bigfoot here and we need to help him too."

I caved because a snowball had a better chance in Hell than I did of winning this. I really didn't want to win the argument anyway. I was just worried about the logistics of keeping him. "Did I tell you that I promised my mom we'd go to her July 4th Barbecue?"

She made a face. "What about staying in NY and watching the fireworks instead."

"No can do. And you have to go. You've got to drive. My stomach won't let me drive under, over or around water. Plus, we can leave for the shindig earlier if you're in control."

"In return for helping Chet?"

"I'd help him anyway," I said.

"I know," she said.

"It's going to be hard keeping tall, dark and hairy from being noticed. I mean eventually, someone's bound to say something about a walking carpet in the hallways."

I got kicked for that one, just hard enough for her to make her point. "That's not nice."

I shrugged. "I know."

"Hairy is a problem." Janey's face lit up, "What if he wasn't hairy?"

"Um… you have seen him, right? Didn't forget your contacts today?"

"Nair," she said, grabbing my shoulders and jumping up and down. "Nair!"

A huge grin broke out across my face. "It could work."

Janey basically told him she wanted to get rid of his hair. He cringed and backed up into a corner of the apartment like we were some sort of monsters. After everything we had done, it was insulting. We weren't monsters. Well, technically I qualified but I hadn't joined the union. I wonder if there really was one. What would they call it—Bloodsuckers 666. What would the dues be? Better not to dwell on it, but I jotted the idea down. Might make an interesting story the next time the city had a major labor strike.

Janey calmed him down and explained the benefits. She also pointed out the bad shape his fur was in from earlier. Chet reluctantly agreed but was feeling self-conscious about what he would look like.

I tried to get out of the dehairing operation but wasn't successful. It was definitely a two-person job.

Before we started I insisted on taking photos. After all, I wanted my story. Janey and Chet enjoyed popcorn—damn them—while I choked down a mug of pig's blood. I melted some mozzarella on the top like French onion soup, which was every bit as gross as it sounds. The little bit I ate made me heave up the rest.

First, we cut his body hair as short as possible. We left his head hair long enough for him to pass as a rocker. I had to take a run to the twenty-four-hour convivence store after we blunted the first two scissors. The second time I cleaned them out of Nair and paid a hundred bucks for hair clippers. It was worth every penny. I planned to expense them.

Janey took Chet into the bathroom with twenty bottles of

Nair. I stayed in the living room watching the game. I was happy to be excluded. It smelt awful, especially to my vampirically sensitive nose. And things had been getting a little too friendly while we were shearing him.

An hour later, she came out with tall, dark and muscular. "Isn't he stunning," she cooed, definitely exhibiting all the signs of being in the crush zone.

Though I didn't say it, I thought better her than me. Chet cleaned up nicely; his skin was a gorgeous mahogany. And his body was, well, at least an eleven on the Hunk O' Meter chart. And that was out of ten. He or Janey had hung a towel around his waist, but from the bulges, I'd say our guesses had sized up. Chet's bod might even be a twelve bare naked.

There went that visual again, but it was less mentally toxic without the fur.

But the face… I guess I'm a xenophob because I found it kind of fugly. He had a huge, overhanging forehead, brown eyes that didn't have nearly enough whites to them, a nose that was way too large for his face and very thin lips. From the way Janey was hanging on his arm, she didn't see the same thing I saw.

"He'll definitely pass for human." Or at least not a sasquatch, I added silently to myself. Then I noticed something. "How'd you get the handcuffs off? They just slide off when you got rid of the hair?"

Janey glared at me. "An old… friend used to… Keys were left behind."

Again, more than I need to know.

Chet was staring at Janey with approval as well. "Thank you, Janey, for all your work on me," he said formally. "And for your rescue as well, Angela." His eyes never left Janey's.

They sat very close to each other on the couch, touching everywhere they could in public. He complimented her blue hair, she his muscles. Even though I was in the room, their conversation was obviously private; the early giggles and closeness of two people who were interested in finding out everything there was about each other.

Fatigue snuck up on me. Dawn wasn't far away, and vampire that I was, my body was winding down with the night. I don't think they even noticed when I left the room to get some shuteye.

I was feeling depressed as I slid into bed. Sure, I was happy for Janey. She'd found someone. Sure, when they met he wasn't exactly the man she wanted, but she changed him. How many women can honestly say that?

It just left me feeling a sense of loneliness. Where was my godlike Mr. Amazing? Then I had a thought that made me grin. What on Earth would my mom make of Chet? He was definitely coming to the bar-b-que.

I wrote everything up and my boss loved it. Ran the story and my pictures on page one—my first front page byline. Of course, I hadn't figured out all the ramifications of signing my name to a story like this had. For one thing, it meant people from the club who realized Chet was a Bigfoot knew I was involved in his vanishing act. The Men In Black and the mystery woman would come after us and, even with the benefit of hindsight, it was hard to say which caused us the most trouble.

PATRICK THOMAS is the author of more than 40 books and over 150 short stories. Among his works is the fantasy humor Murphy's Lore series, which includes *Tales From Bulfinche's Pub, Fools' Day, Through The Drinking Glass, Shadow Of The Wolf, Redemption Road, Bartender Of The Gods, Nightcaps* and *Empty Graves, The Mug LIfe* — as well as the After Hours spin-offs *Startenders, Constellation Prize, Fairy With A Gun, Fairy Rides The Lightning, Dead To Rites, Rites of Passage, By Darkness Cursed, By Invocation Only,* and *Lore & Dysorder.*

His Mystic Investigators paranormal mystery series includes *Bullets & Brimstone, From The Shadows, Once More Upon A Time, Mystic Investigators, Mean Streets,* and *Fear To Tread. Assassin's Ball* is his first traditional mystery, co-written with John French. He co-edited *New Blood, Hear Them Roar, Camelot 13* and was an editor for the magazines *Fantastic Stories of the Imagination* and *Pirate Writings.*

His science fiction works include *Exile & Entrance* and *As The Gears Turn.*

Patrick's humorous advice column Dear Cthulhu has been running since 2005 and includes the collections *Have A Dark Day, Good Advice For Bad People, Cthulhu Knows Best, What Would Cthulhu Do?, Cthulhu Happens, Cthulhu Explains It All.*

His short stories have been featured in over fifty anthologies and more than three dozen print magazines.

A number of his books were part of the props department of the CSI television show and have been spotted on the program. His urban fantasy Fairy With A Gun was optioned for film and TV by Laurence Fishburne's Cinema Gypsy Productions. Top Men Productions has made his Soul For Hire Story, *Act of Contrition*, into a short film.

His writes books for kids as Patrick T. Fibbs including the *Undead Kid Diaries: Over My Dead Body,* the *Babe B. Bear Mysteries: Bad Hair Day,* and the *Ughaboos* picture book *5 Silly Monsters Jumping on the Zed.*

Visit www.pathomas.net to learn more.

DIANE RAETZ is the editor-in-chief of Padwolf Publishing. She co-created The Wildsidhe Chronicles YA series and is the co-author of Once More Upon A Time and Partners in Crime (collected in the Mystic Investigators omnibus Once More In Crime. Diane edited Apocalypse 13 and co-edited the vampire anthology New Blood.

Help is only a Rainbow *Away...*

"Mix Gaiman's American Gods and Robinson's Callahan's Crosstime Saloon on Prachett's Discworld and you get an idea of Thomas' Murphy's Lore." -David Sherman, author of STARFIST and Demontech

"ENTERTAINING, INVENTIVE AND DELIGHTFULLY CREEPY." -JONATHAN MABERRY, New York Times and Bram Stoker Award Winning Author

"SLICK... ENTERTAINING." -Paul Di Filippo, ASIMOV'S

"HUMOR, OUTRAGEOUS ADVENTURES, & SOME CLEVER PLOT TWISTS." -Don D'Ammassa, SCIENCE FICTION CHRONICLE

PATRICK THOMAS

"Thomas certainly brings the goods to the table
when it comes to writing urban fiction...I promise, you will love...
Terrorbelle: Fairy With a Gun. Who doesn't love a well-stacked,
ass-kicking, gun-toting, woman with bullet-proof, razor-sharp win
that investigates all manner of supernatural spookiness? I know
and Thomas's humor shows through in every tale. Jim Butcher an
Laurell K Hamilton have nothing on Thomas." The Raven's Barro

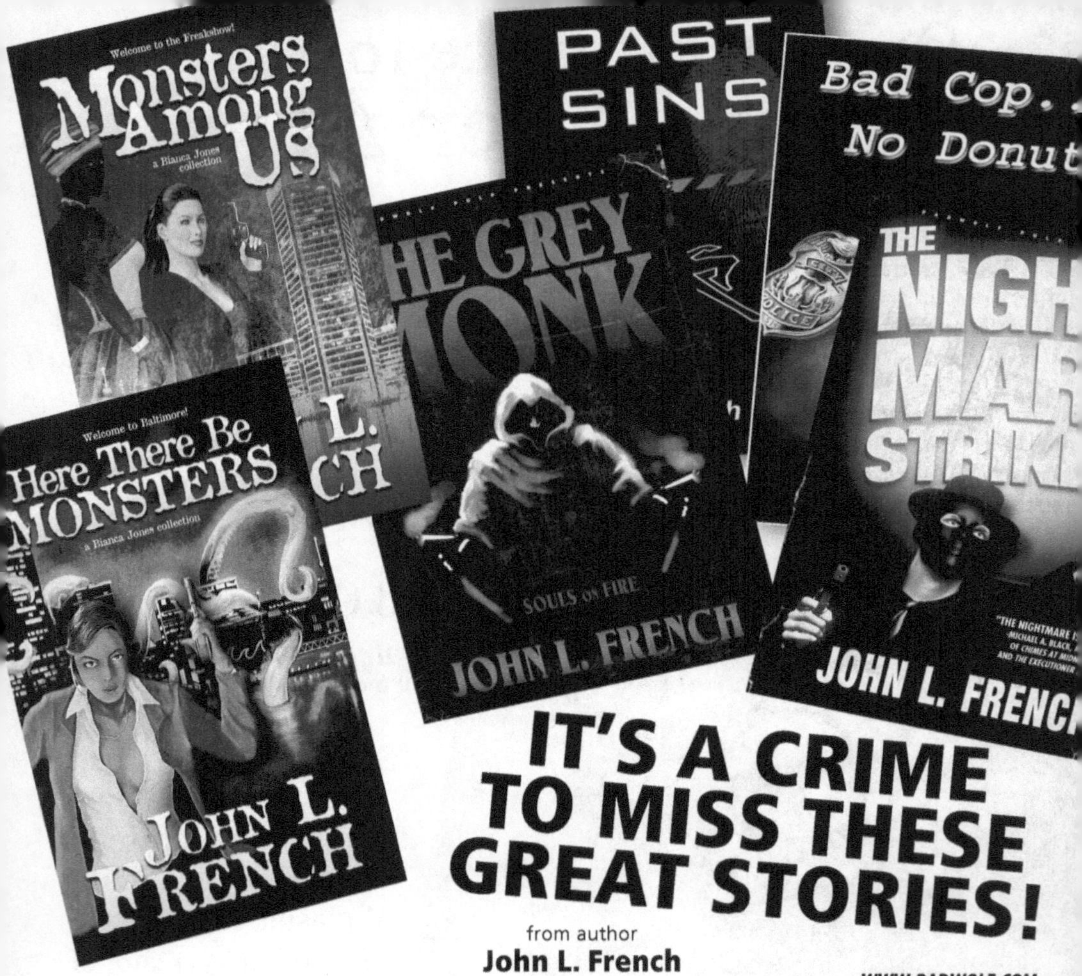

A detective's work is never done.
And don't call him Baby Bear...

15th Aniversary
Omnibus of
Books 1-6

The zombie apocalypse is over...

Now even undead kids have to go to school

5 SILLY MONSTERS JUMPING ON THE ZED

a picture book
for kids

www.talehaven.com